VALENTINE

A LOVE STORY

CHET RAYMO

BRANDON

First published in 2005 by Brandon
an imprint of Mount Eagle Publications
Dingle, Co. Kerry, Ireland

ISBN 0 86322 327 3

2 4 6 8 10 9 7 5 3 1

Mount Eagle Publications receives support from
the Arts Council/An Chomhairle Ealaíon.

Cover painting *Saint Sebastian Tended by Irene* by Hendrik ter Brugghe
© Allen Memorial Art Museum, Overlin College, Ohio. R.T. Millar, Jr. Fund, 1953

Cover design by Anú Design [www.anu-design.ie]
Typesetting by Red Barn Publishing, Skeagh, Skibbereen

For Victoria

Acknowledgements

Thanks to my friend Bartley MacPháidín for introducing me to Valentine and Julia; he will be surprised to find that I have turned the story on its ear. John Lanci and Erika Schluntz generously shared their expert knowledge of the time and place. I thank all the scholars of classical antiquity and early Christianity, too numerous to mention by name, whose hard work and talent contributed to my story. Jerome Carcopino's *Daily Life in Ancient Rome* and Lionel Casson's *Everyday Life in Ancient Rome* were particularly helpful. Robin Lane Fox's *Pagans and Christians* is a useful work of exceptional merit. Robert Wilken's *The Christians as the Romans Saw Them* is a book that can be read with profit by anyone interested in questions of reason and faith.

As for Saint Valentine, patron of lovers, we know almost nothing of his life, or even if he existed at all. Several Valentines have a shadowy existence in the ancient records. The tale of Valentine and blind Julia is just one of the stories associated with the saint. My characters are fictitious, as are the events that encompass their lives. I trust that the story itself, however, limns a greater truth.

My thanks to Terry Fitzgerald and Steve MacDonogh at Brandon, for treating my story with care and making Val a book.

I

Valentine runs through the streets of Alexandria. He is sixteen years old, of average height, with the gangliness of youth. His skin is dark. He has dark, almost black eyes, full lips, the hint of a beard and a mop of curly black hair. Already one can see the good looks and thoughtful countenance that will later attract the matrons of Rome. He scampers through the crowded streets, dodging vendors, hawkers of charms, tradesmen and tourists, leaps a sleeping dog, threads a line of a laden camels. He arrives at last at the house of his master, the physician Theophrastus, and pounds on the door. Admitted by a household slave, he runs to the peristyle, where Theophrastus sits reading, taking the morning sun.

The physician looks up from his scroll. He is forty-seven years old but appears much older. His hair is thin and white. During the course of a long medical career, he has seen his share of suffering and death, pestilence and violence, and has now reached an age when he prefers silence and solitude. Valentine's interruption is not welcome, but Theophrastus shows no anger. He queries the panting boy.

"The midwife bids you come," the boy gasps. "The baby refuses to be born."

Theophrastus rubs his eyes. His near vision is failing. He asks, "Did the midwife administer the oral concoction I prescribed?"

"Yes, sir."

"And did she apply the balm of linseed and mallow?"

"Yes, sir."

"Did she inject the vagina with marrow and sweet olive oil?"

"Yes, sir."

Theophrastus sighs wearily. "She is using the birthing stool?"

"Yes, sir. The midwife says to tell you that the mother will die soon. She says to tell you that only cutting . . ."

Theophrastus raises his hand and Valentine falls silent. The pregnant woman is the young wife of Julius Favus, Roman official, jailer and supplier of gladiators for the Alexandrian games. At the first signs of labour, Julius had sent for the man who is reputed to be the finest physician in Alexandria, trained at Pergamum by disciples of the great Galenus. Theophrastus demurred from the summoning; it was not his habit to go rushing off to do a midwife's job. He sent instead his young assistant, Valentine, with a potion and a balm to relax the mouth of the womb and hurry the infant on its way. But now he knows that he must rise up and go to the home of Julius Favus, who is, after all, an acquaintance of sorts and, as an appointee of the emperor, a man of modest influence. Theophrastus rolls up the scroll and places it aside. He asks Valentine to fetch his surgical kit: the blades, scoops, traction hooks, clamps. He goes to his pharmaceutical cabinet and gathers the necessary drugs and herbals.

"Hurry," says Valentine. "Hurry."

II

I am Julius Marius Favus, and it was my daughter who was forcibly torn into the world on that twenty-third day of Maia in the year of Valerian's ascension to the throne. I make no apology for having called Theophrastus to the birthing room of my wife Fortuna. I could afford his services, the midwife was at a loss, and my wife suffered terribly. It was clear that if I did nothing Fortuna would die, and the infant, too. And so I availed myself of the person who was reputed throughout Alexandria to be a magician of medicine. But I also sent servants with silver coins to buy prayers and sacrifices at the temples of Juno Lucina and the Carmentes. Another servant I sent to an astrologer, to see what advice the stars might have for easing Fortuna's labour. And so we waited, myself and the frantic midwife—who did not inspire confidence with her flushed cheeks and laboured breath—for the gods, for the stars and for Theophrastus. Fortuna screamed, bit her knuckles until they bled, twisted her hands in the sweaty bed clothes and looked at me imploringly through eyes as red and wide as beets. And still the infant battered its tiny head against the unopened door of her womb.

Theophrastus came with his boy. The physician's calm demeanor immediately restored confidence to the birthing chamber. His toga was immaculately white and fashionably Roman in its cut. Beard combed and trimmed. Sandals soft and silent against the tiles. The midwife shrank into a corner of the room and ceased her shuddering. Even Fortuna seemed to sense that an ordering principle had arrived to ease her torment. Theophrastus calmly apprised her anguish. Then he ordered the boy to sweep the room clear of the midwife's charms—the snake sloughs, sticks and vulture feathers. He pushed aside her foolish potions of goose semen and sow's milk. He held Fortuna's sopping cheeks between his palms and looked deeply into her eyes. He felt her pulse. He placed his hands on her belly and felt for the disposition of the infant within. He examined the mouth of her womb. All of this without a word, as the boy, the midwife and I watched with interest and anxiety. Fortuna ceased her wailing and latched on to Theophrastus's kindly face through eyes puddled with tears.

The physician beckoned for me and the boy to step outside the room.

He said, calmly, "Julius Favus, I can forcibly extract the child; the child will die, but your wife will likely survive. Or I can cut into the mouth of the womb and bring the child to safety, but the risk to your wife is considerable."

That is all he said. He uttered these terrible words as if he were giving his cook a choice of menus for dinner, then waited for my decision.

I stammered, "'Cut the mouth of the womb? I have never heard of such a thing."

"You must trust me."

From the birthing chamber, Fortuna resumed her wailing. I asked, "*Likely. Considerable.* What do these words mean?"

"You are asking me for a calculus?" Theophrastus was impatient.

"I am a practical man."

"Very well. If I kill the child, the odds that your wife will live are three in five. If I cut into the portal, the child will almost certainly be saved, but your wife's chances diminish to one in five."

I watched the boy Valentine's eyes gape wide. I saw that he understood the magnitude of the decision I was being asked to make. It was not a decision that any human soul should willingly embrace; these matters of life and death properly belong to the gods or to the Fates. I thought briefly of waiting until my servant returned with word from the astrologer. Perhaps the stars might signal the course of my action.

Theophrastus read my mind; he, too, was a practical man. "We have only moments to decide," he said, "or all is lost."

Fortuna was young, this child her first. We had been married in Rome on the eve of my posting to Alexandria. For the year and a half since we sailed from Ostia, she had been my boon companion, my heart's desire. At first glance, then, the decision seemed simple: save Fortuna at all costs. But, as I said, I am a practical man. Who am I to measure the value of a life or place my own happiness or unhappiness in the scales of fate? Let us assume that the gods weigh equally the souls of Fortuna and the child. Then by Theophrastus's arithmetic, the joint probabilities for life were three in ten if he killed the child and six in ten if he employed the knife. I considered what Fortuna would choose if presented with the same choice. *Cut,* she would unhesitantly say, *save the child.* But still I dithered, paralysed by the unpalatable consequences of either decision.

"You must choose," urged Theophrastus, and indeed Fortuna's terrible cries from the chamber within would have wrung tears from the gods.

I am a man whose career required daily decisions concerning life and death. Let us say that ten men are required for combat in the arena. One hundred prisoners are in my custody. Who do I send to almost certain death? I peruse the roster of potential gladiators. I consider each man's vigour, his probable fighting skills, the magnitudes of his crimes. A tick by this name, and another, and another. Ten men sent to fight and die in the sand with no more anguish on my part than if I were sending them off on a pleasure trip to Rome.

"Hurry."

I knew that the consequences of whatever decision I made would be with me all of my life. "Cut," I said.

I did not re-enter the birthing room. I went instead to the shrine of the household gods and prayed. Meanwhile, Theophrastus placed a clean white cloth on a table by the birthing stool. He arranged his instruments one by one in a gleaming row. He asked for fresh olive oil, warm water, clean sea sponges and freshly laundered cloths. He administered a powerful concoction of mandrake in wine to Fortuna, forcing it between her lips. He lashed her legs more firmly to the posts of the birthing stool. Then he asked the boy and the midwife to hold his patient down.

And so it was that Valentine saw my darling daughter swim into the world on a tide of blood, her face auspiciously covered with her caul; his life and hers, it seems, were fated from her birth to intertwine. The child delivered, Fortuna lapsed into a faint, exhausted. Theophrastus removed the caul from the baby's face , tied the cord with white woollen yarn and cut it cleanly. He placed the infant into Valentine's unsteady hands. The boy held the child gingerly, astonished at its miniature perfection, the miracle of birth. Never before had he been present at the birth of a child; he felt somehow an immense gratitude, though the child was not his. Then, suddenly, he was unaccountably frightened. He passed the curiously silent infant to the midwife, who placed it on a pillow and sponged it clean. The baby's eyes were bathed with drops of olive oil to wash the residue of birth from the lenses. Limbs, digits and body cavities were examined. What the midwife did not discern in her inspection was that the infant's eyes were blind; those little windows of the soul were open wide but utterly opaque. It would not be until several days after the birth that the child's nurse would begin to suspect that something was amiss, weeks more before we knew with certainty.

Fortuna survived but three days after the birth. For most of that time she was delirious, racked with fever. I did not blame Theophrastus for her death. I saw that he had employed his skill as best he could. He had given me the odds. I blamed the gods. I blamed the stars. But most of all I blamed myself, for having made the fateful decision. For the rest of my life Fortuna's death would rest upon my conscience. But how could I regret that my darling daughter had been saved, my blessed Julia, who would bring such joy to her father's heart, who in her sweet darkness would reach out with her tiny hands for mine, who would smother me with kisses, pamper me with love? My slaves and colleagues sometimes questioned why, when Julia's blindness was confirmed, she was not exposed to die. Every day babies with lesser infirmities, especially baby girls, were placed alive beyond the city walls and left to die. Such a thought never entered my mind. The pretty child was all that remained of my adored Fortuna; she was the receptacle of her mother's beauty and virtue. I clasped little Julia to my heart and prayed that the gods would lead her unharmed through a lightless world.

The boy, Valentine, never forgot the drama of that terrible birthing, the first he experienced in the service of his master Theophrastus. As he held the silent baby briefly in his hands, he marvelled at the skill that had guided Theophrastus's hand, at the gleam of the keen edge cutting flesh, the balms and potions. He thought, too, what a wonderful thing it is to save a human life. He passed the child to the midwife, then stood staring at the blood on his hands until ordered by Theophrastus to assist at closing Fortuna's wound. During that brief moment of enraptured contemplation, Valentine decided to become a doctor. At that moment his soul was taken from the gods and given to philosophy.

III

Valentine would not see Julia again for fourteen years. Their lives crossed briefly as she entered adolescence, then, a few years later, he became her friend and lover. It was I who brought them together on that second occasion, while he was a prisoner in my care at the Tiberian Prison in Rome. She was a headstrong girl of seventeen years, curious, stubborn, searching for wisdom, unwisely attracted to the agape of the Christians. She was not yet baptised into that faith, but she was preparing for that fateful step, and I considered that Valentine, with his firm philosophical mind, might dissuade her from her course. When love ignited between them, it was I who unwittingly facilitated their ill-starred assignations. Then, only days later, it became my duty to release Valentine into the custody of the soldiers who took him to his awful fate.

On the night of the festival of Lupercalia, in the second year of the reign of Claudius Gothicus, in the 1022nd year since the founding of the city, at the order of Quintus Mimmius, procurator of games, Valentine was lashed to a post outside the Flaminian Gate of the city and shot dead with arrows. And so was extinguished one of the great spirits of the empire. He was thirty-two years old at the time of his death, physically robust and at the height of his intellectual powers, a physician trained in the tradition of Galenus of Pergamum. He was medical attendant to the elite of Rome, called even—with unforeseen consequences—into the service of Quintus Mimmius.

The order of his execution contained the standard charge of heresy—refusal to acknowledge the gods of city and empire, and of loyalty to the cult of the Galilean upstart—but the truth is considerably more complicated. Valentine died for love, yes, but not for love of Christ. He died for my darling Julia. And for philosophy. Like Lucretius, he had sought to *undeceive* his own thought, to scrape through the encrustations of myth that had accumulated between mind and world, to honour the five senses as arbiters of truth and to heal the sick as best he could by his Galenic art and craft. The charges on the warrant of his arrest and on the order that sent him to the arena—and ultimately to the place of his execution—were counterfeit, trumped-up lies contrived by Quintus Mimmius to accomplish the procurator's unholy revenge. As I shall later recount, in the darkest hour of the morning after Lupercalia, the Christians took Valentine's body from the bloody post outside the Flaminian Gate and buried in it a hidden catacomb beyond the city walls. Soon, they claimed him as one of their own, a martyr to their faith. This was the ultimate indignity for those of us who knew Valentine and admired his keen rationality—that his bones should be jumbled up with those of fanatics. But the fate of his mortal body was of no consequence to Valentine himself; he knew with confidence that death is the porch of oblivion and that the gods of Romans and Christians alike are hollow idols contrived by men as props against their own weakness. For Valentine, as for Lucretius, the soul's unhappy mortality was simply "the way things are".

To me then comes the task of recording the truth of his life, now as my own life nears its close. It has been forty-two years since Valentine's death. A dozen emperors have come and gone, most of them murdered by their successors. Christians have been alternately tolerated and subjected to persecution. Now, Constantine, who some suspect of being a secret Christian, has ascended the throne of the Caesars. Who could have predicted it? The world turned upside down. The city of Romulus and Remus gone begging to miracle mongers from eastern deserts. The empire is awash in religious dementia: mystery faiths from Syria and the land of the Indus, the worship of dreadful gods from the north, mystical claptrap from African wastes. People jettison the gods of Augustus, Trajan and Marcus Aurelius for the worship of a provincial hawker of cheap tricks, a Galilean magician who claimed to walk on water and make the blind see. The games that entertained our ancestors may be suspended. Sects are tolerated. The stench of superstition is everywhere. Lucretius and Galenus, Valentine's two great teachers, are forgotten, their books unread.

The city is haunted by shadows, memories of lost souls who move among the crumbling monuments. Valentine is dead. Julia is a Christian. The shadows whisper, demanding that Valentine's story be told. I have the letters he exchanged with his friend Antonius, entrusted to my care by Valentine while he was in my custody. I will use these in my narrative at my discretion; they will give a flavour of the ideas that sustained Valentine and gave meaning to his life. I remember the stories of his life that he told me during the long hours we sat alone conversing in his cell in Rome. And, most especially, I hold in my heart Julia's story, which became so intimately and tragically entangled with that of Valentine. Of these I will make his biography.

IV

And so, let us begin in Alexandria, in Egypt, at the mouth of the Nile. At no other place in the empire are the skies so clear as there. The stars press close—piercing in their light, uncountable in their number. It was at Alexandria, in the days before the city had yet come under the sway of Rome, that astronomers and geographers first deduced the true figure of the world, measured its size, counted its degrees. We have heard of Eratosthenes, master of the Alexandrian library, mapper of oceans and continents. And of Aristarchus, who calculated the sizes and distances of the sun and moon. Hipparchus, Archimedes and Euclid. From all over the civilised world they came to the White City on the Nile. They collected books, translated, calculated, measured, numbered. They wasted no time on gossip, politics or doctrinal squabbles. When a stranger appeared at the city gate, they did not ask, "What is your religion?" or "Where is your city?" or "Who is your father?" They asked, "Can you open your eyes and see? Can you use the straight-edge and compass? Can you put aside the dogmas of your ancestors and think afresh?" Before Julius Caesar ever set foot on Egyptian soil, the Greek passion for mathematics and abstraction had taken hold in this outpost of Alexander's far-flung realm.

It was to Alexandria that Valentine came in the sixteenth year of his life, during the reign of the emperor Decius, from Apollonia in Cyrenaica, a province to the west of Alexandria along the African coast. Even then, so many years after the founding of the city and its heyday of astronomical innovation, Alexandria remained a centre for philosophical speculation. To the harbour guarded by the Pharos light came scholars from all the shores of Mare Nostrum, drawn by two unparalleled resources of the White City: the still impressive remnants of its once superb library and its freedom of thought. These were not, however, the qualities that attracted Valentine. He fled eastward from Cyrenaica because on his first outing in the service of Eros he had managed to impregnate the daughter of a wealthy Apollonian merchant, who swore revenge upon the thin, curly-haired boy, who, because of his thoughtful smile and infectious sense of fun, the girls found irresistible. Valentine simply ran, eastward along the coast to Darnis, where he cajoled passage on a coaster to the port of Alexandria. In that city of sensual delights, he soon forgot the pretty Apollonian lass he had left with child.

Where the Nile river meets the sea, the broad stream fans out into a dozen braided channels, creating a rich alluvial plain in the shape of the Greek letter delta. The landward angle of the delta is near the ancient capitals of Heliopolis and Memphis. The eastern vertex of the delta's seaward base is Pelusium, where ends the trade route from the Gulf of Suez. The western vertex is Alexandria. The fine harbour of that city is partly a gift of nature, partly a work of human genius. The offshore island of Pharos has been connected to the mainland at its midpoint by a broad causeway, the Heptastadium, creating embayments to east and west. The eastern embayment has been further enclosed by dressed-stone breakwaters that reach out into the sea like two embracing arms. The city sprawls between the harbour and Lake Mariut. When the breeze is onshore, the inhabitants breathe deeply of fresh sea air. When the wind comes from the land, it carries with it pestilential vapours from the Nile marshes.

Two great avenues run the length of the city parallel to the shore, one of them, the Canopic Way, a glory of the empire. There is a stadium, several theatres, temples dedicated to an eclectic mix of gods. And, of course, the library. The first of the city's many fine landmarks that Valentine saw as his ship entered the harbour were the soaring obelisks that stand near the quay, granite spires quarried in the upper Nile valley and floated to their present locations by ancient engineers. But quickly, as he stepped ashore, his attention was distracted from the monuments to the people—an astonishing mixture of races speaking an indecipherable polyglot, scurrying to and fro, all engaged in some large or small act of commerce in this premier entrepôt of empire. On the docks, a cacophony of bid and barter. The clack and clang of gangplanks and derricks, the thud of boxes, chests and bales hitting stone, the whine of ropes on pulleys. Fruits and vegetables, cottons and silks, piled in heaps or draped from stalls in rainbow colours. Delicious aromas of sandalwood, resins, honey, camphor, spices, frankincense, fish, oil and corn. And the women! White, brown, black. Some with golden tresses falling to their waists, others with shaved heads. Bare arms and feet. Rouged lips, darkened eyes, tattooed shoulders, braided hair, beads and bangles. Women working side by side with men, glistening with sweat, or watching from aside, elite and aristocratic. A giddy place of shining skin.

Valentine walked away from the docks along streets overshadowed by crumbling, red-roofed tenements, marvelling at the chatter of strange tongues and the curious medley of icons and idols. Worshipers of Jupiter, Apollo and Sol Invictus, Jews, Christians, followers of Mithras, Stoics, Epicureans, agnostics and atheists exchanging coins, rubbing arms, taking wine together. How different was this spirited forbearance from the fearful xenophobia of the towns of Cyrenaica, where the edicts of the emperor Decius had greater currency; those who refused orthodoxy were barred from commerce, and Christians—proliferating infidels!—were given to the lions. Valentine was smart enough to see at once that the one true god of Alexandria was lucre and that even the intolerant but distant Decius was willing, in this strategic nexus to the flow of necessary goods, to moderate with practical acumen his obsession for religious unity.

V

When Valentine was remanded to my custody in Rome, sixteen years after his arrival in Alexandria, I had been administrator of the capital city's Tiberian Prison for several years. Into my cells came rogues and scoundrels, murderers and thieves, heretics and traitors, escaped slaves, army deserters, dishonest bureaucrats. Not so many Christians then as in the times of Decius or Valerian; Claudius Gothicus, who was our emperor and far away on the Danube frontiers, had other fish to fry. My "guests" came from every part of empire: from Britannia in the north to Nubia in the south, from Iberia in the west to Syria in the east. Some few had committed crimes of a heinous gravity; others had merely made the mistake of offending a person of influence. This last was Valentine's fate, and although it was soon clear to me that my prisoner had committed no offence other than the practice of his sometimes fallible healing arts, it was not my place to play judge or magistrate. I had risen through the ranks of the penal service by serving my superiors unquestioningly and well.

Valentine was not like others in my care, nor like any other man I had known. At first, it was his equanimity of spirit that drew me to him, his seeming indifference to his fate, his curiosity concerning his surroundings, his quizzical nature. No sooner had I placed him in a cell with a band of Sicilian brigands than he was interrogating them about their homeland, the circumstances of their travel, the people they had met along the way. I saw at once that he was a man of particular intellectual acuity and moved him to a cell of his own, a tiny enclosure, but one with air and light. I justified this transfer on the basis of the magistrate's special interest in Valentine's case, but the plain fact of the matter was that I was drawn to my exceptional prisoner by the bored curiosity that is the inevitable fate of one whose career requires him to spend his time among lowlife.

Even in confinement, Valentine carried himself with the posture of a Roman, his speech was flawlessly urban, his dress of the city. But his eyes gave away his foreignness; they had a focus and transparency that one no longer sees in Rome, in this city where it is more prudent *not to see.*

"You are from Africa?" I asked.

He nodded assent.

"Carthage?"

"Alexandria."

"No one is *native* to Alexandria," I joked.

He laughed. "You are right," he replied. "I was born in Cyrenaica."

He was born Gaius Valentinus Saccus, the second son of a civil servant, a customs agent in the port of Apollonia. As was customary, he received his name on the ninth day after his birth, together with a charm, the bulla, which was hung about his neck, a bronze locket containing a dried sprig of germander, which the father believed might protect the boy from the colic that afflicted so many in his mother's family. The bulla was put away—left at the Temple of Jupiter in Cyrene—when Valentine, at age fifteen, exchanged the dress of youth for the toga virilis of manhood. It was only then that he was told what the bulla contained, and (as he recounted to me) he was deeply struck that the force of a sprig of herb contained inside a bronze locket might affect the body's humours.

His education was not unlike that of my own Julia: reading, writing, grammar, spelling, geometry and numbering. He read Horace in Latin, and a host of proverbs and moral maxims, too. These he studied under the tutelage of his African teacher in the company of his younger sister Helena and his friend Antonius. Because Valentine was thin and somewhat frail, his father saw to it that he was instructed in boxing and swimming. Sports did not interest the boy; what he keenly followed were the activities of the harbour, the coming and going of ships, the exchange of goods, the *foreignness* of sailors. He sat for hours at the snout of the limestone quay, staring at the sea horizon, beyond which lay, he believed, a multitude of worlds that he would never visit. Sometimes it seemed to him that he could detect on the wind the smell of incense burning on the altars of the one hundred temples of Rome.

At about the time that Valentine put off the bulla, his sister underwent a metamorphosis. She grew tall and thin, her breasts swelled beneath her tunic, and suddenly she seemed older and wiser than the boy. His fascination with her transformation was soon transferred to her friends, other girls in the appealing first blush of puberty. One of these was Olivia, the daughter of an oil merchant and friend of Valentine's father. At first the boy and the girl spent long intervals together sitting on the quay or walking on the strand to the east of the harbour. He regaled her with stories of winds and seasons and waves and birds and shells, making up what he did not know, all the while burning with a thrill he did not quite understand. He could not know, because it was all so new, that the inevitable course of their friendship would be determined more by the coaxings of their bodies—a dumb animal amazement—than by the verbal tokens they exchanged between themselves.

Antonius stood by patiently, waiting for his friend to recover from his infatuation.

All of this Valentine told me as we sat together in his cell, exchanging stories of our respective lives. It was during these conversations that we discovered that he had been present at Julia's birth, seventeen years earlier in Alexandria. He was particularly interested in my time as master of a gladiatorial school in the Alban Hills near Rome, after my transfer from Alexandria and before my appointment to the Tiberian Prison in the city, of the training of gladiators, and of Julia's growing up in such an unusual environment. The blood sports of the arena piqued his medical curiosity: was the insatiable Roman appetite for violence a pathology or a catharsis? If a pathology, what was the cure? If a catharsis, what was the unbalance of humours that required so extreme an amelioration? He asked for books, which I brought him, although most of what I brought he had already read. He was younger than me by a decade, but I was slowly drawn into the spell of his learning, most of which I could not fully understand. I invariably left his company with the feeling of waking from a happily drugged dream, unreal, narcotic, momentarily exhilarating but ultimately unsatisfying. I was reminded of the distressing and illegal Christian alliances being cultivated by Julia to achieve the same spurious euphoria in her own unlearned way.

I should describe Valentine's physical appearance. He was taller than the average Roman, although not unusually tall for an African. His hair was dark and thick, worn curled against his head. When he was delivered into my custody he was clean shaven, and his beard, when it came in, was surprisingly light. His skin was darker than a native Roman's, his body fit and supple. His eyes were his most engaging feature; he had the habit of looking deep into the eyes of the persons to whom he spoke, as if he were searching for the truth of their words. Below his left cheek was a thin white scar that ran down his neck into his tunic. Among the stories he recounted to me was the story of the scar and how its acquisition brought him into the employ of the physician Theophrastus.

VI

On his first afternoon in Alexandria, Valentine was dazzled by novelty. The city was much larger than Apollonia, larger even than Cyrene. After three hundred years of Roman rule, it still had an eastern flavour; the architecture was Greek, the atmosphere oriental. Five great trade routes converged on Alexandria: two coastline roads from west and east (dates, olives, corn, oil), the Nile river (stone, papyrus, foodstuffs, dyes), the Red Sea (silk, spices, incense, porphyry) and the Mare Nostrum, Our Sea (amber, glass, timber, wool). Along each of these channels flowed rivers of goods, to pool briefly on the docks and in the warehouses of Alexandria, awaiting trans-shipment. The best and most luxurious of these commercial treasures were loaded on to ships bound for Rome. The rest passed to lesser outposts of empire.

Or into the teeming shops and stalls of the city itself. Valentine wandered the broad avenues, the forum, the agora, the mazelike streets of the Jewish quarter, excited by the energy, thrilled by the city's exotic and erotic charge. He saw things he could not have imagined: Arabians with golden rings in their ears, black Nubians whose cheeks were crosshatched with scars, elephants, prostitutes plying their trade in broad daylight. He had no money to speak of, only a few copper coins in a pouch beneath his tunic. To assuage his hunger he stole a handful of dates from a merchant's unwatched basket and quenched his thirst with water from a public fountain. Then for a long time he sat on the marble step of the fountain and watched the comings and goings of the Alexandrians.

As night fell the city changed. Streets emptied. Carts rattled off through the city gates and the gates were bolted shut. Awnings dropped across the cleared shelves of stalls. Doors of houses were closed and locked. Even the prostitutes disappeared from their places of solicitation. Overhead the famous Alexandrian stars appeared one by one until the black awning of the sky was pricked everywhere with light. But not enough light to dispel the silent solitude of the streets. Now Valentine recognised the precariousness of his situation. He was in a strange city without friend or acquaintance. He had not enough money to purchase food or shelter. No place to sleep, nor any hope that the morrow would offer better.

With the coming of darkness, his excitement collapsed into fear.

That night and the night after, Valentine slept in empty street stalls, pestered by cats and rats, and awakened at dawn by the rough kick of the stall's proprietor, returning to display his wares. During the days he stole scraps of food where he could and made his way from shop to shop looking for any job that might reward a handy lad with a few sesterces. Costermongers, millers, tailors, jewellers, goldsmiths, ropemakers, cobblers, fullers and dyers: he tried them all and was rejected at every turn, sometimes with a rude clout to the back of his head. Once he stooped quickly to snitch a few copper coins from a blind beggar's plate, only to discover that his intended victim wasn't blind at all. The beggar cursed long enough and loud enough to attract the attention of everyone in the street. Valentine fled. By evening of the third day he was homesick and hungry and resolved to look for passage back to Cyreraica and accept whatever retribution would come from the father of Olivia. He woke in the middle of the night and made his way through the dark streets toward the quays so that he might be ready to beg a place when ships cast off at dawn. As he passed through a covered alley in the old quarter of the city, he was surprised in the gloom by a towering dark-skinned man who blocked his way. Valentine had sense enough to say, "I have no money." But it was not money the man was after, and when it dawned on Valentine what was at stake, it was too late to flee. He tried to dart between his assailant and the alley wall but was blocked by a strong black arm. Without thinking, he bit—sank his teeth into his assailant's flesh. There was a voice—someone else had entered the alley—and then a flash of bright metal near his chin. Valentine put his hand to his neck and pulled it away cupped with blood. And all went dark.

VII

iv Kal. Aprilis
Alexandria

Antonius,

I send this letter with instructions that it be delivered into your hand alone. Please do not tell anyone that you have heard from me, not my mother, father or sister. And especially not Olivia. I have so much to tell you, friend, but first I must apologise for leaving Apollonia without embracing you, without a single word of parting. You are my dearest friend, and not a day goes by but that I wish you were here with me in Alexandria. Yes, Antonius, I am in the White City, and I cannot tell you what an extraordinary place it is. Imagine if Apollonia were suddenly made thrice the size of Cyrene and you would have some idea. It is a place of a hundred languages, people of every race. The harbour teems with ships, the marketplaces with caravans of asses and camels. My head spins whenever I walk the streets.

And listen. I am employed by the finest physician of the city, Theophrastus of Nicea, who some here call "the new Aesculapius". He saved my life. I was cut on the neck by a scoundrel who assaulted me in the night. Antonius, this blackguard's dagger ripped my neck from chin to shoulder blade, and the blood poured from the wound as if it were the Nile itself flowing into my hand. It is a miracle that I am alive. My attacker was frightened away by a servant of Theophrastus, who carried me to his master's house. Theophrastus rose from his bed to treat my wound. He stanched the flow of blood and stitched my neck back together with needle and thread. Have you ever heard of such a thing! I am sewn together like a torn garment. If the dagger's blade had been inserted a finger's breadth to the right or left, or if I had been five minutes longer receiving help, I would have died—or so says Theophrastus. All of that was three weeks ago. Now I am well. I thank Fortuna every day for my great good luck.

I cannot tell you what a great man is Theophrastus. He lives in one of the finest houses of the city, made entirely of stone, with marble columns, mosaic floors and colourful murals on every wall. The furniture is of oak and arbor vitae; never have I seen so large a table as that which graces my master's kitchen. And servants! Two slaves to fetch water. Another to remove the night dirt. A dozen others to cook and clean, fetch and carry, mix nostrums, clean the instruments of surgery. My own small task is to take messages to T.'s patients throughout the city and bring their complaints in return. For this I am given a pallet in a shed at the back of the house, food and the privilege of keeping whatever coins are given me by those to whom I carry messages. The other day I had the extraordinary experience of being present at the birth of a child, which T. assisted by cutting the mouth of the mother's womb. The child was saved— I held the bloody little thing in my hands!!—and the mother lives yet, too, although her survival is far from certain. Such is the power of my master, for surely without his intervention both mother and child would have died.

But Antonius, the greatest of my compensations is this. My master allows me access to his library, an extraordinary collection of books, many of them on medicine, but others on astronomy, geography, mathematics, botany, meteorology and other elements of natural philosophy. I have only begun to dip into these riches. It is hard to explain, Antonius; if at home our teacher had asked me to read these books, I would have found any number of reasons to avoid the task—as you will surely remember. But here—I cannot get enough. Every moment that I am not running about the city, I curl up on my bed with a scroll. Aristotle. Eudoxus. Hippocrates. Lucretius. Names we heard from our teacher as if they were gods from far-off India or Ultima Thule. And here in my hands are the very words of these illustrious masters.

Theophrastus is a Galenist. I cannot recall, Antonius, if our teachers ever told us of Galenus of Pergamum. According to my master, he was the greatest of physicians, greater even than Hippocrates. Physician to Marcus Aurelius! And he studied here in Alexandria! My master urges me to pay particular attention to Galenus's insistence upon the faculties of nature. Every effect has a natural cause, says Theophrastus. Yesterday he said of one of his patients, "If Salvius insists upon making offerings to the gods to remediate his symptoms, then let him do so. But it would be better to leave well enough alone and let his body effect its own cure." I can't tell you, Antonius, how much I admire Theophrastus, and how much I aspire to be like him in every way. Alas, the books of Galenus are written in Greek, so I have turned first to Lucretius. I am reading *De Rerum Natura,* and when I have finished I will write you again and tell you what I think.

I cannot close without mentioning Eppia, T.'s wife. She is a fine woman who has taken me under her wing. She presides in the house like a queen and wears the most extraordinary robes and gowns of silk. Her morning toilet requires hours, and she has a slave girl whose only responsibility is to dress her hair and another to attend her gowns. She has asked that I be the one who brings her breakfast—bread dipped in wine, honey, olives, goat cheese, milk— which at first I was loath to do as it seemed an inappropriate task for a man, but I soon changed my mind. Eppia reclines on her couch, attended by her girl. It is the strangest feeling, Antonius. You would laugh, but I find myself dreaming of her at night. But never fear, she is three times my age and adored by Theophrastus.

Tell no one you have heard from me. Please answer.

Your friend,
Valentine

VIII

It is a matter of infinite curiosity how the course of a man's life depends upon so many seeming accidents. If Valentine had not been assaulted in the night, if he had not been discovered by the servant of Theophrastus, if the dagger had slipped to the left or right, if Theophrastus had not been a man of compassion and generosity, then Valentine's life might have been different. If, if, if. A life is like a leaf carried along by the Nile. At Heliopolis the river branches into several channels, these branch again, and again, and again, and so the leaf might debouch into the sea at any one of a hundred places. The leaf in its course is buffeted by wind and eddies. Perhaps an oarsman's stroke deflects it to the right or left. A child throws a stone into the river; it jostles the leaf. A man relieves himself from a quay; the leaf is nudged towards another destiny. What determines the leaf's course? The gods? Chance? Or is it, as Valentine insisted, cause and effect—a myriad jostling of atoms, the faculties of heat, cold, moist and dry acting on particles of water, as predictable (if we had the knowledge of gods) as the felling of a boxer under another's blow. If so, then the ultimate destination of the leaf must be determined far upstream at the time when the leaf falls into the current—the exact place it falls and with what disposition. But *that* is decided by the growth of the tree upon which the leaf resides, and *that* upon the place where a seed was planted, and so on, back in an infinite regress, until any hope of understanding the ultimate destination of the leaf is lost in an abyss of time. Gods? Chance? Determinism? It is all the same, mere words for what we cannot know. And yet, what we *do* know is that all lives are not of equal consequence. All of Rome remembers Julius Caesar, Augustus, Nero and Marcus Aurelius, although centuries have passed since they sat on the throne. But who remembers Balbinus or Pupienus who ruled closer to our time? A thousand years from now, when the Nile has emptied the waters of a continent into the sea, who will remember Valentine? It is my hope that this brief memoir will ensure that he is not forgotten. As long as Valentine's story is told, so too will be told the story of my darling Julia.

One of Valentine's first acts as a servant of Theophrastus was to attend Julia's birth. Valentine and Julia. Two leaves falling together into the stream of history, then separating by a thousand miles before being brought together again. Was their subsequent meeting in Rome inevitable? Was their love affair the sort of which the poets sing, foreordained by Eros or Venus? Indeed, in the apparent accident of Valentine's presence at Julia's birth and in their ultimate coming together, there seemed something so meet and fit as to be the contrivance of a god. Valentine, of course, would deny this. He would say that Julia was his gift of chance—the toss of a coin. That toss, that spin of the coin in the chancy air, was the cause of their meeting and falling in love—and of the circumstances of his own untimely death.

Sweet, delicate Julia. She emerged from her mother's womb as tiny as a newborn rabbit, but still too big to peaceably enter the world. Within weeks of her birth it was clear that something was terribly wrong. Her little eyes stared into space, oblivious of dark and light, rest or motion. The child was otherwise perfectly formed, each tiny toe and finger delicately in place. She grew in grace and comeliness. By the time she was a toddler, people remarked upon her beauty—her hair as fine and dark as Indian silk, her skin like porcelain, each nail marked with a thin white moon. Long lashes framed eyes of sapphire blue, but she moved in darkness—from the natural darkness of the womb into the unnatural darkness of her sightless world. I struggled to imagine her life without light or motion or shape or colour. By the gods, how I loved her! I watched her step gingerly into the world, eyes open but unseeing, and I closed my own eyes to experience the world *as she knew it* through her truncated senses. I placed her in the care of a female slave who tended her constantly, who taught her to use her hands and ears and nose to see. Julia never cried. Not once. Not even when she emerged so violently from the womb, her face wrapped in her auspicious caul.

Long I talked to Valentine in his cell about the cause of Julia's blindness. He responded with theories of vision expounded by the Pythagoreans, Aristotle, Hippocrates and Lucretius. On and on he droned, spinning out theories of whirling atoms, images, effulgent and sombrous air, and heaven knows what else, until my mind reeled with weariness. In the end, I was no more enlightened than before, and Julia was just as blind. Valentine was convinced that somehow the trauma of Julia's birth had stolen from her the source of the radiant particles that stream from the eyes to dispel the darkness. Well, yes. But that is to say nothing at all. All of the theories of the philosophers do not change the fact that Julia never saw a field of grain resplendent in the sun, a gambolling lamb, a sunset. Valentine asked to see Julia, to examine her eyes, perhaps to prescribe some nostrum or ointment. But I was not yet ready for her to meet him; he was, after all, an indicted heretic, a prisoner, an enemy of the state.

When Julia was an infant, I made my way from temple to temple, offering sacrifices, buying prayers, trying to loosen the pity of the gods by rattling coins at their shrines. I consulted with astrologers and soothsayers, oracles and sibyls. I sought out necromancers the better to invoke the intervention of Julia's mother from beyond the grave. Nor did I neglect the physicians, who it seemed to me were no more certain of the cause or cure of Julia's blindness than the priests and diviners. In the end, I became resigned to Julia's fate, imagining, in my most bitter moments, that her blindness was somehow caused by my own sins of the eyes—youthful incidents of lascivious perception that had somehow weakened or polluted my seed.

Whatever the cause of Julia's blindness, we must be grateful for the gifts that nature gives us, a girl perfect in all respects except her sight. To this day, no memory of Julia is more vivid that that of holding her diminutive newborn body in my hands, after she had been cleaned by the midwife—her eyes closed as if she were asleep, a mist of spider-silk hair, fingers curled into tiny fists, the dimpled indentation of her sex and the ashen stump of her umbilical cord tied with white wool in a tight, neat knot.

IX

Dear Valentine,

No, I have not forgiven you. I understand why you fled—Olivia's father still rages whenever he sees me, as if it were I rather than you who got his precious girl with child. But still you might have had the decency to say goodbye. Who knows, perhaps I would have gone away with you. This place is such a stifling nest of backbiting and gossip. Our parents occasionally go to Cyrene for a day at the theatre or arena, but we must stay at home with our noses in Greek texts and our fingers at the counting frame. How I envy you in Alexandria.

Your parents grieve your disappearance. For days they searched high and low in Apollonia and hereabouts, thinking you might have gone to stay with a relative or a friend. Again and again they quizzed me, assuming that I knew where you had gone. I believe your father has now decided that you were pressed into servitude by the crew of some passing ship and prays that one day you will make your way home. Your mother has a little lamp in the shape of a boat which she swears to keep lit until you return. Tapers burn day and night at the shrine of the household gods.

Olivia, your pretty paramour, has vanished, too. No one knows where. Some say she died of a botched abortion, others that she has been sent to live with relatives in Euhesperides until she has birthed your bastard. Valentine, you'd think you'd know enough to keep your pen out of the inkpot. Watch out for the wife of that master of yours, or she will tease it in again, and then you'll be in a sorry stew.

To tell the truth, I have my eye on your sister. In a year or two she's sure to be the prettiest girl in town. Perhaps I'll follow the example of my priapic friend. Just kidding, Val. You know I'll watch out for her as if she were my own sister, and I'll watch for your parents, too. I've told them nothing, although they'd dearly love to know your whereabouts.

Keep well, my friend.

Antonius

X

The whores of Egypt are the prettiest and most willing in the world. Or so I've been told. Whether this is true or not I cannot say, for during my brief tour of duty in Alexandria I was too much in love with my beloved Fortuna to be much interested in the famous pleasures of that city and then, after her death, grieving too deeply for her loss to care. In any case, Valentine soon made the acquaintance of those exotic courtesans, as he confessed to me during our conversations in his cell—at first obliquely, then in more detail as I pressed him further.

His first two years in the employ of Theophrastus consisted, he told me frankly, of three parts: work, study and fornication. He worked. He worked long hours every day at whatever task Theophrastus might assign: errand boy, keeper of the surgery, household servant, scribe. Occasionally he was sent by Theophrastus to search the markets for herbs, leeches or vegetable nostrums. At other times it was his responsibility to hold a patient down while Theophrastus performed a trepanation, amputation of a limb or removal of a stone. These operations were terrifying for the young assistant—unsettling episodes of blood and pain. More often than not the patient did not survive the cure. Then, the operation done, it was Valentine's gruesome task to mop up the gore and scrub and sweep the surgery. He observed everything, absorbing what he could. Theophrastus was sometimes impatient with the boy's questions but generous with his library. What Valentine could not find out directly from his master, he learned from his master's books. At night by lamplight and at every stolen moment during the day, he studied. Books were his constant companions, and when he could not find what he wanted in the library of Theophrastus, he connived his way into the galleries of the Alexandrian Museum, with its tens of thousands of books—the grandest treasury of knowledge ever assembled under one roof. He worked, he read, and whenever he managed to save a spare sesterce he made his way to the streets of the prostitutes.

At first he went from house to house, experimenting with every permutation of young and old, dark and fair, fat and thin, plain and painted. He found that he was able to squeeze more services from his sesterce than the usual customer; the ladies fancied him and once or twice, when his pockets were empty, advanced him credit. Then he found Nibi. A Nubian. Her skin as black as night. Her head shaved; pudenda, too. Her nipples gilded. She was older than he by a dozen years, but he thought her the most beautiful woman he had ever seen and fell dizzily in love. It was a foolish infatuation, of course. She was very much the professional harlot, with a thriving business among the upper classes of the city, and the pretty boy without a sufficient handful of coins was just another hopeless suppliant to be kept waiting in the street. But although her favours did not come cheaply, his money, when he had it, was as good as anyone's, and she seemed to treat him with the same respect as she afforded the high and mighty, teasing him with flirtatious preliminaries and whispering endearments in his ear which he had the good sense not to believe but nevertheless was thrilled to hear. His visits to other ladies of the night were suspended as he patiently saved his coins to pay Nibi's steeper charge. And when he could not afford to visit her apartment in the Street of the Emeralds, he hung about outside, hoping to glimpse the object of his obsession.

By this time the emperor Decius had met his death in a battle with the Gothic king Kniva in the marshes of the Dobrudja on the Danube frontier. His persecution of Christians had already begun to flag as he attended to military matters. With his death and that of his son, another general, Trebonius Gallus, hurried to Rome to claim the emperor's mantle and make good his claim on the empire. After years of harassment by Decius, the Christians of Rome and the provinces were disorganised, dispersed and momentarily discredited, but under Gallus's more benign administration they began to reassert themselves as a political and moral force. The official policy of persecution was not revoked, but Gallus had other things on his mind. Plague had broken out in Carthage and threatened Rome. The Roman ports were carefully monitored and ships from Carthage quarantined, but soon the infection was raging in the capital city, killing alike the followers of Jupiter and Jesus.

The Christians of Alexandria took advantage of the let-up in oppression to flaunt their overweening pride. Out of cellars and desert caves they came like rats to strut about the city, proselytising, preaching and browbeating ordinary citizens with their message of "the one true God of Love". Men and women who only weeks before had been offering sacrifice in the temples of Apollo and Isis now showed their true colours, taking communion with the Christian zealots and pretending they had never lapsed from the fold.

To tell the truth, there were two sorts of Christians in Alexandria at that time. There were those who believed that a man is saved or damned by grace alone and who looked forward to the resurrection of the body. These people courted martyrdom. They trooped to the arena like children to a sweet shop, believing, mindlessly, that at the moment of their death by sword they would be ushered into everlasting bliss; they organised themselves into bishops, presbyters, deacons and acolytes, the better to administer their self-immolation and transmigration to paradise. And there were those who adhered to the doctrines of Origen, of a more philosophical bent, who believed that every man holds the keys to his own salvation. These Origenists needed no priests to administer their god; they were as likely to sit on a desert rock contemplating their navel as kiss the hands of a bishop. But they were no less fanatical, no less ready to disrupt the good order of the city, no less self-assured in their childish mania.

There is no surer badge of the religious extremist than self-righteousness. The Roman who worships Sol Invictus will allow his fellow man some latitude in religious matters, as does the sun itself, who sometimes warms the earth with its benign rays and sometimes hides itself in clouds. No one can live without respite in the blazing light of day; we need a bit of darkness in our lives, an occasional drizzle of uncertainty. But not the zealot. The zealot has a fierce intolerance of sin. He is so certain of the truth of his cause that he cannot understand why everyone else is not standing in line to share his unctuous incorruption. And, of course, no sin is more anathema to the zealot than sex; there is no better way to demonstrate the certainty of his own otherworldly redemption than to deny the urge that anchors our souls so tenaciously to the earth.

And so it was that one day Valentine was waiting outside Nibi's house, hoping for a glimpse of his adored courtesan, when a gang of Christians took it upon themselves to dissuade her from her trade. Nibi emerged from her house with her maid to make her usual afternoon perambulation about the markets. She wore a red silk gown trimmed with silver that left both arms bare, drawn high above her calves by a girdle of brass links. Her shapely head, shorn and oiled, gleamed like polished ebony. Her eyelids were coloured midnight blue, her lips crimson, her posture erect and elegant. No one would mistake her for a merchant's wife, or for a streetside harlot. She turned all heads as she processed along the street. At the entrance to the avenue, her way was blocked by six Christian zealots—four men, two women—hair wild, eyes aflame, intent on turning Nibi from her sin. They shouted accusations of lewdness. They prodded. They tore her gown from her shoulder. They pushed Nibi's maid to the ground. When one of them hurled a stone that hit Nibi near her eye, Valentine, who had been following behind, ran to her defence. He flung himself at her attackers, pummelling with his fists, fearless in his rage. At first the Christians resisted, knocking Valentine from his feet and pounding him with kicks. But quickly a crowd gathered and the Christians, sensing anger among the onlookers, fled. Nibi, too, turned and hurried back to her house, shooing her girl before her.

XI

Antonius,

It has been weeks since I have written to you. Why haven't you answered? Perhaps your answer has gone astray. Please write and tell me of my family, and of yourself.

I must tell you first of all of Nibi. I told you in my last letter how I came to her defence when she was set upon by Christians. When I wrote to you then my bones still ached from the thrashing I received on her account. My pride was bruised, too, from the tongue-lashing I got from Theophrastus, who warned me to keep my mind on my studies if I ever hoped to follow him into the practice of medicine. He told me, too, to stay away from prostitutes, lest I end up as patient rather than physician. And, Antonius, I tried. For weeks I steered clear of Nibi's house, read my books, practised my Greek and was T.'s model servant, always ready at his call. But there wasn't a moment of the day or night when I wasn't bothered by thoughts of her. Her dark limbs entangled mine in dreams; I woke each morning sticky with love. It was a sickness, I'll admit. What T. calls obsessio veneris. I could not shake it off. At last my purse was once again full of coins, and I appeared at Nibi's door. Her girl told me to return later that evening. There was something about her nervousness, the way she glanced over her shoulder towards Nibi's rooms, that made me wonder what trick she had in store. There was no trick. When I returned, the girl took me to her mistress's private apartments, through the rather plain chamber where Nibi had previously entertained me, into her holy of holies, a room hung with silks and damasks, every horizontal surface covered with rugs of the sort that might be found in the tent of a desert prince. Embroidered cushions. Song birds in cages. Incense burning in silver censers. A purring cat of midnight black. A single lamp casting shadows of bronze and gold. Antonius, in your wettest dreams you could not have fantasised a more voluptuous reward than I earned for Nibi's rescue. You will think I am making this up. You will say, "Ah, Valentine is trying to make me jealous." Listen, friend, if I really wanted to make you jealous I would tell you what happened during that long night—that's right, the entire night!— and how I went away at dawn with my purse as full as when I arrived. I dumped my coins into a beggar's plate so grateful was I at my good fortune.

I soon regretted my generosity to the beggar, for there was no further charity from Nibi. Her debt to me had been paid in full. When next I knocked at her door, her maid asked to see the usual fare and sent me packing when I turned my purse inside out. I suppose, if I'm to have another night in Nibi's sanctorum, I will have to let a few more Christians beat me within a finger's breadth of my life. But I am determined to see her. I will sell my books. Or steal. I have no shame.

But where will I find the time for chasing whores? Plague is in the city. Bodies have begun to pile up in the necropolis beyond the walls. Theophrastos is busy with a hundred patients who seek antidotes and panaceas. The temples are crowded with fools who think they can buy the protection of gods. The Christians preach apocalypse. We have heard what happened in Carthage, the terrible mortality there. Anyone in Alexandria who has a place to go and the wherewithal to get there has fled the city.

When the sickness has passed I will write again. Take care of my family.

Valentine

XII

After the death of my beloved Fortuna, I had no more taste for Alexandria. A few letters to old friends in the imperial service and I was soon at sea again, reversing my earlier journey from the capital to the province. By the time the plague came to Rome, I had taken up a post as assistant to the master of a privately owned gladiator school in the Alban Hills. My duties at the school were purely administrative; others, veterans of many contests, had the task of training the candidates for the arena. Mine was a glamourless job, shifting papers, dealing with tradesmen and farmers, maintaining discipline. In return for the exercise of these responsibilities, I was favoured with a pleasant villa at a distance from the tumult and shouts of the training grounds, an olive grove with its attendant income and a modest salary. I lived alone, except for pretty, dark-haired Julia, who now tottered through her sightless world on tiny feet, and the slave woman Desso who tended her. Other personal slaves were assigned to me, but these I kept at the school rather than the villa, preferring the solitude of my quiet retreat. Whenever I was free from my duties, I spent my time with Julia, bringing whatever objects I could into her curious hands, filling her ears with rhymes and song, her nostrils with scents, her tongue with the tastes of a hundred herbs. I could not be her mother, but I could try to be her eyes. When I was not with Julia, Desso had orders not to let my darling daughter out of her sight—to allow her freedom to explore her surroundings, but never let her meet with danger.

Then came the sickness, wafting on the air, an invisible pestilence. Up into our pristine Alban Hills from the Tiber marshes, from the squalid tenements of Rome, from the reeking, rat-infested docks of Portus and Ostia, and from the crowded emporiums beneath the Aventine Hill. For many days, processions of ashen-faced merchants, landlords, officials and bureaucrats, with their trains of family, retainers, free servants and slaves, passed our camp on their way to their country villas or to the estates of friends or relations. They passed in sombre silence, a grim cortège: there were none of the usual shouted greetings, no exchange of pleasantries. Even the footfalls of these exiles seemed muffled against the cobbles of the road. We watched them pass and kept our distance. But the nature of our business made it impossible to avoid all contact with the city. The city prefect had decreed that the games should go on, in a forlorn, self-defeating effort to distract the citizens from the risk that came with every contact with a neighbour. And so Romans crowded into the arena and then went home and died. Our gladiators went down to the city without concern—they faced a more serious threat than a mortal effluvium they could not see—but the trainers and slaves who went with them first put their affairs in order and made lavish offerings at our shrine to the emperor's gods.

For three weeks of that terrible summer our school escaped infection, then our Syrian trainer fell ill, a man so robust, so tall and firm, with limbs like German oaks, that none would have doubted his robust good health. At first fever, chills, backache, headache. Then, a few days later, painful pustules appeared on the Syrian's face, chest, arms and legs. The transformation was terrible to see, like the decay of a whale stranded on the shore. The pustules on his face conjoined to form a gruesome mask. Two days more, he was dead.

Now the others began to fear. The master would have sent the gladiators and trainers away, but he had no choice. He was required to send down every week a dozen parmularii and scutarii, men who fought with small and large shields, for combat in the games. During their trial by plague the Roman people seemed greedier than ever for the spilling of blood in the dusty arena. Cobblers, hairdressers, fishwives, fruitmongers: they jostled into the terraces of the amphitheatre, eyes glazed against reality, noses oblivious to the stench of burning bodies carried by the wind from the crematoria beyond the walls. "Now he's got him! Strike! Slay!" They roared from their feet as if every sacrificial death in the arena might mean one less Roman would die pustulary in his bed.

My work required that I have contact with other persons. So I quarantined my villa and remained at my office at the school, making Julia and Desso virtual prisoners in the house. Goats and chickens in the peristyle, flour and dried fruit in the kitchen. Milk and eggs, bread and sweets. They would be well supplied until the hot weather passed and the plague abated. In the evenings I walked near to the house, and sometimes my daughter's voice or laughter came floating over the garden wall. To be away from her was heartbreaking, but the thought of losing her to the pestilence was more than I could bear. Her whole life was before her.

According to Valentine, the plague came that summer to Alexandria also, apparently with more virulence than at Rome. It is said that a tenth of the population of that city perished. Theophrastus, who had the means to flee, stayed in his home and offered whatever remedies he might provide to rich and poor alike. Prophylactic or placebo: it was all the same; nothing seemed to work. But the illusion of treatment gave comfort and sometimes encouraged the patient to hold on through the crisis. Theophrastus worked mostly from the theory that the disease was made more severe by a disruption of the black bile, and therefore, following Galenus, he kept his patients cold and dry, no small task in the sweaty heat of summer. Valentine worked side by side with Theophrastus, applying cooling poultices, dry towels—more assistant now than servant. Certainly he had already acquired more training in medicine than most professional practitioners of that art. Theophrastus acknowledged as much, trusting Valentine with difficult cures that previously he would only have hoped to effect himself. And he gave Valentine a bed in a private cubicle of his house, where, at the end of a long day, exhausted by the apparent indifference of the gods to the sufferings of men and the racking afflictions of a hundred patients, the boy fell asleep, dead to the disturbance of his former dreams.

XIII

The plague that came to Carthage, Rome and Alexandria in the second year of the reign of Trebonius Gallus, with its pustules and fevers, bore the same symptoms as the disease that had devastated the empire a century earlier during the time of the Antonines. In that previous outbreak it is said that millions died in Rome; the numbers defy credulity. Certainly, the plague that marked Valentine's coming of age as a physician was not nearly so deadly. But it was mortal enough to put the crowded cities of the empire into a fright. In Alexandria, the infection raged from street to street, beginning in the Jewish quarter near the docks and burning itself out four months later near the western stadium. One in five who contracted the disease died of its bale.

So the gods try men's souls. Some men are made stronger; others are destroyed. Some men discover the mettle of their own resources; others whine for the pity of the gods. Theophrastus rose to the challenge of the plague and threw himself into the thick of it. He roamed the city looking for faces that bore the pocks of an earlier encounter with the disease, perhaps in another city or district of the empire. He observed that those who had previously contracted the plague now seemed immune to contagion. He urged the magistrates to engage these pock-faced veterans in works of mercy: tending patients, cleaning the homes of victims, burying the dead. The poor among them did as they were told; the better off exploited the opportunity afforded them by their apparent immunity—there were fortunes to be made buying cheaply the estates of the dead—and pleaded privilege, which the magistrates were quick to grant.

Theophrastus himself contracted a mild case of the disease—a dozen days abed and pustules only on his upper body. When he recovered he threw himself ever more vigourously into his work, now confident of his resistance. He scraped the scabs from his pocks, and these he powdered and fed to his wife and to Valentine, reasoning that some corpuscular change in the bodies of survivors bolstered their defences against recontagion. His daring experiment was only partly successful: Valentine stayed free of the disease; Eppia died. Her death was the end of Theophrastus's ministrations to the sick and dying. He blamed himself and lapsed into morbidity. Valentine was left to fend on his own, the youngest "doctor" in Alexandria.

On the night of Eppia's death, as Theophrastus grieved, Valentine walked across the Heptastadium causeway to the island of Pharos. The lighthouse was dark: no blazing beacon welcomed sailors to the stricken city. A chain blocked the harbour's mouth. On the beach near the lighthouse, he spreadeagled himself on the sand. Red Mars blazed in Pisces in the south-west, where he could also see the glow of fires in the necropolis beyond the city walls. The Great Bear skimmed the northern sea horizon. In the east, towards the channels of the Nile, rose majestic Orion. Sirius, too, was there, presiding over the pestilent dog days of autumn. As Valentine watched, a crescent moon lifted out of the distant marshes like a silver cup of libation to indifferent gods. Soon, he knew, the Morning Star would follow. He whispered to himself the opening lines of the great poem of Lucretius:

Dear Venus, creatress of the world,
Joy of earth and heaven, mother of Romans:
For you that sweet artificer, the earth,
Offers gifts of flowers, and for you
The deep ocean smiles, the peaceful heavens shine
With shoreless light.

The city slept. A deep silence hung upon the sea. The star-pricked heavens arched from east to west, from north to south, godlike in their uninterrupted turning. Theophrastus lives. Eppia dies. Do the gods roll dice? Does fortune choose? Or is it all a chancy thing, as Lucretius says, a jumble of atoms in the void, corpuscular seeds of pestilence on a capricious wind, wafting here and there, alighting randomly on the good and bad alike, rich and poor, Christian, Jew and acolyte of Venus. He closed his eyes. And then, for some reason that he did not understand, he thought of Olivia, the girl of Apollonia whom he had left with child. It was perhaps the first fully adult thought of Valentine's life—a sudden sense of *consequence,* of *responsibility.* It had been two years. What had become of the child who was his seed? Was it aborted as an embryo? Did it die in childbirth? Or was there even now somewhere in the district of Cyrenaica a toddling boy or girl who would never know a father, watched over by sweet Olivia.

   . . . for you
The deep ocean smiles, the peaceful heavens shine . . .

For the first time since he had come to Alexandria, Valentine was homesick.

The moon cradled upwards. And thinking of his single act of love with Olivia—the impetuous spilling of his seed that had entrained such unintended consequences—his thought turned to Nibi, careful Nibi, with her contraceptive balms of honey and resin, her locks of fine white wool soaked in the juice of balsam. Honey. The resin of cedar. Myrtle oil. Incense. The sweetness of her oiled skin. The delicious fragrance of her lamp. He rose from the sand and made his way back across the Heptastadium and through the dark city to the Street of the Emeralds. It was the first time he had been to the house of Nibi since the sickness had come to Alexandria.

Her door was marked with the magistrates' black "X" of pestilence.

The door was not locked. He pushed it open and entered Nibi's house. No lamp burned in the atrium. The hall and dining room were also dark. As his eyes became adjusted to the gloom, he saw Nibi's maid crouched in a corner of the atrium, her knees drawn up under her chin, her thin white arms wrapped around her legs. He stooped to observe her closely—her eyes wild and frightened, her hair limp and wet on her neck.

"Nibi?"

She did not respond.

He was more insistent: "Nibi?"

The girl dipped her head towards the room where Nibi had first entertained him. Beyond—*the holy of holies*. Valentine made his way to the inner chamber and stood at the door. The room was lit by the tiny flame of a single tallow that flickered near extinction. In the dark array of silks and damasks and cushions he saw nothing, then he discerned a man in a pale garment. The man was watching Valentine with eyes that yielded nothing.

"Nibi?" whispered Valentine.

He saw her against the silk coverlets of her bed.

He went to her. Put out his hand to touch her cheek, then drew it back. It was Nibi and it was not Nibi. Her face was a scabrous mass of erupting flesh. Her neck, too. And her arms. Her eyes, to the extent that he could see them, were moist with a kind of weary peace. She saw him, and the corners of her mouth flickered in the faint intimation of a smile.

He whispered, "I will tend you. I will keep you cool and dry. We must get rid of this clutter." He gestured to the draperies, coverlets, rugs and pillows. "It will harbour the pestilence."

"She will die," said the man in the pale garment, matter of factly.

"No," said Valentine. But immediately he knew that what the man said was true. He has seen enough victims of the disease to know that Nibi's contagion was mortal. And he saw that Nibi, too, knew she would die.

"Who are you?" Valentine asked the man.

Then, from behind, a hoarse voice, barely audible: "He is a Christian."

Valentine turned. Nibi's maid was standing at the door.

"She bid me fetch him."

Valentine turned back to the man. "Who are you?" he asked again.

The man was silent for a moment. Then he said, "I have baptised her. She has forsworn her sins. Christ will welcome her into paradise."

Valentine turned from the man and looked again at Nibi. He brought his face close to her breath. He quizzed her, his lips moving without sound.

She answered him with her eyes. She was reconciled. Astonishingly, she was at peace.

And when she died, the Christians claimed Nibi's body. In the yellow morning light, they took it to a Christian cemetery hidden in the desert west of the city. They wrapped her body in unbleached linen cloth. No silks with threads of gold and silver. No blues or crimsons. No bright brocades. Her perfect breasts bound flat and tight with coarse windings, the pustulant flesh pressed into her ribs.

Valentine was shattered. It was not that he *loved* Nibi; he felt more affection for Eppia, the wife of Theophrastus, who had for two years treated him with such kindness. Yet he had not grieved for Eppia; he would not have given Eppia's death a second thought, only for the concern he felt for Theophrastus. But Nibi.

. . . Ah, goddess of the spring
And pleasant days, when warm west winds
Stir the amorous air, and high in the sky
The chorusing birds attend your coming,
The promise of love . . .

It was not Nibi's death that disturbed him so deeply, nor was it the wreck of her beauty. It was the thought of her soul being stolen away by the Christians—that gorgeous soul that filled the space of her holy of holies like a fine perfume. *How many fantasies the priests invent to overturn our logic, to muddle our estates by fear,* wrote Lucretius. Beauty has no defence at all against the priests' threats of everlasting punishment, their baseless promise that death is a door to paradise—or eternal damnation. Nibi. For days after she had taken him into her honeyed sex, his penis had smelled of balsam and cedar. And now she was stacked like cordwood with other victims of the plague in the Christians' dusty catacomb.

XIV

Pr. Non. Augustus
Apollonia

Dear Valentine,

I hesitate to write for fear that I will not have an answer from you. We have heard that plague is raging in Alexandria, and I know that your work with Theophrastus must place you into contact with the sick. I have a friend, a Christian deacon, who is coming to your city with a message from the bishop of Cyrene to the bishop of Alexandria. I will give him this letter and hope that he finds you well. His name is Cornelius.

The sickness is here, too, in Cyrenaica, and especially in Cyrene. But the outbreak has been surprisingly mild, thank God. Your family are all well. My family, too. Everyone keeps to themselves, commerce languishes, few ships come to the harbour, the desert tracks are empty of caravans.

The big news, Val, is this. I have become a Christian. Two months ago I was baptised by Cornelius. I cannot tell you how happy this has made me. I have found a wonderful peace with the Father who made all things, in the person of his Son Jesus Christ. I was drunk and in darkness, dreaming nightmares, ignorant of my origin and destiny. Now I see everything in the light of truth. Our faith is simple: first, salvation by God's grace, then love, then good works. From these comes life. Eternal life in the presence of the Father. I know it sounds a crazy turnabout, Val, after all the fun we used to make of Christians. We were ignorant. We let our ignorance cloud our judgment. Once I opened myself to grace, the ignorance and doubt were flushed away. Before I accepted Christ I was carnal; that's what Cornelius says. A physical shell filled up with false gods. Now I am among those who live by faith and good works. I want to be like Cornelius, one of the illuminated—the pneumatic, he calls them—who have perfect knowledge of the Father and who will be united with the angels. Cornelius has taken me under his wing. He will show me the way, the truth and the light.

I have other news, which you may not want to hear. Olivia has returned. She is married to a Roman. A tax collector. They have with them a child who is almost certainly your son. He looks like you, the same curls, the same dark hair. He is the right age. But Valentine, you would not recognise Olivia. How old is she? Seventeen? She wears the robe and the gown of a matron, and sashays about the town with a troop of slaves as if she were above us all. A Roman's wife! She will not talk to Christians and snubs me in the street. You should come home and insist that your child be baptised. You, too, should come to Christ, my friend. Don't risk hellfire. Don't follow Olivia and her Roman clerk into the temples of idols. If Cornelius doesn't find you in Alexandria, seek him out. Let him instruct you in the faith. Let him open your heart to the grace of the one true God. Become a child again, as fresh and pure as the day you were born.

Valentine, do you remember what we were like when you were here? We had only one thing on our minds. We followed the girls around like sheep, laughing at the hardness of our pricks beneath our tunics. It was not so many months ago that I tricked your father into allowing me to tutor your sister. It wasn't her Latin or her Greek I was interested in; I simply wanted to be with her, to see the sandal dangling from her foot as she worked with the stylus on her tablet, to see her brow wrinkled above her sea-green eyes and the gentle swellings of her breast. (Don't be angry, Val, I never touched her.) But now all that is past. The Satan who lived within my heart has been expelled. I teach her still, but now my only desire is to bring her to Christ. You, too, Valentine. I pray for you, too.

In the peace of our Lord and Saviour Jesus,

Antonius

XV

Dear Antonius,

Spare me your prayers. And spare my sister, too. I cannot believe that you have surrendered to superstition. Surely you can see this Christian foolishness for what it is: one more contagion of miracle-mongering from the east. In Alexandria, the Christians can't even agree upon what they believe. Sometimes it seems there are as many versions of "the One True Faith" as there are believers. Each sect seeks to convert the other, to issue anathemas, to lay charges of heresy. All of them try to convert the rest of us. If verbal harassment or the threat of "hellfire" doesn't succeed, they wait until you are poor or sick and snatch your soul away then.

The plague has abated. It has been three days since I have seen a new victim. It is only now that I have found a minute to answer your letter. I cannot tell you, Antonius, how tired I am. My master Theophrastus abandoned his ministrations to the sick when his wife died—of an experiment he hoped might render her (and me!) immune to contagion. He blames himself and has lost confidence in his practice. He keeps to his room, reading his books—not medical works, as was formerly his habit, but Horace, Cicero and Marcus Aurelius. Meanwhile, I am left on my own, trying to practise what I learned from T. He lets me keep what I earn, and some of his rich patients—now mine—are very generous indeed. I have amassed what seems to me a small fortune! But it is not for money that I go into the houses of the sick. I follow the example of my masters—Theophrastus, Galenus and Hippocrates—who understood that the healing arts are the highest form of philosophy, and that there can be no more noble calling for a rational man. Don't misunderstand me, Antonius. I do not pretend to be noble, or wise, or "holier than thou". I have much more to learn before I might reasonably call myself a doctor. At best, I try to do no harm. But at least I am sure now of what I will do with my life: *bring medicine down to earth.* For too long matters of life and death have been left to the gods, and to the charlatans who tend the temples. While the pestilence raged in Alexandria, the priests of Apollo and Minerva and Isis and Sol Invictis blamed the Christians for angering the gods of Rome. The Christians imagined that the plague was heaven-sent to cleanse the earth of heathen worship. The Jews thought God was punishing *them* and went about beating their chests and wearing sackcloth. The followers of Mani, too, had their cockeyed theories on the baneful influence of the gods.

The gods have nothing to do with it. Or if they do, then they are not gods that I would choose to worship. I have spent the last few months in the company of those who were afflicted by the disease. I have seen little infants so covered with pustular tissue that one might not recognise them as human. I have seen old women and old men writhing in agony on their beds, their faces oozing pus, their fingers crumbling on their hands. Once I was called to the bedside of Sapphira, the priestess of the Temple of Diana, a woman of impeccable reputation and stately bearing, revered by all in Alexandria for her dignity and generosity to the poor. There was nothing I could do to save her; she was in the terminal stages of the disease. As I stood by her pallet, she reached out and took my hands in hers and drew them to her face. Her face was greatly disfigured by the disease, a mask of fear. I was terrified. I wanted to pull my hands away, to scrub them clean, to run from that ruinous place. She asked, "Why?" Just that one word. She must have wondered why, having devoted her life to the service of divine Diana, she was now abandoned by her goddess. What should I have answered her, Antonius? Should I have told her that her god was false? That the god of Antonius is the one true God? And what of Christians? They died, too. The pestilence took more Christians from Alexandria than the persecutions of Decius ever did—and without the consolation of martyrdom.

Why? Why did Diana's priestess die and Valentine escape? Certainly not because of your Christian god or any other deity. I do not know why I escaped contagion, although I have begun to suspect that I had a mild case of the disease early in the spring, before the general outbreak in the city. At that time I thought it just a fever— headache, backache, a rash on the upper arms—nothing to be concerned about; Theophrastus gave me a prophylactic liquor and in two days I was well. That mild illness may have armoured me against recontagion, as T. believed. Was it good luck, then? Did I have the good fortune to encounter the pestilence before it had achieved a deadly virulence? That is the answer I should have given Diana's votary when she interrogated me through lips that were crumbling away: "Bad luck, Sapphira." Of course, it doesn't matter to her now. A new votary dispenses Diana's favours at the temple, tends the lamps, prepares the sacrifices. The smoke still rises to heaven without Sapphira, who now resides in the Roman necropolis.

I met your friend Cornelius. Your letter was delivered to me at T.'s house by a boy, who also carried an invitation to come to a house near the Museum. I went, more to see if I could obtain information about my family than out of any desire to meet Cornelius. When I saw him, I was surprised: I suppose I was expecting a younger man. He might have been handsome were it not for the marks on his face. I cannot say I was impressed. He treated me kindly, but his manner was supercilious. He presumed more familiarity than I thought appropriate. He asked me questions about you: what had been the nature of our relationship, whether you had had girlfriends, that sort of thing. There was something about his curiosity that made me squirm. You will think I am being jealous, that I resent your friendship with another person. Perhaps there is an element of that; no one in my life, Antonius, is so dear a friend as you. But I think it is not only that. Take care when you are with him. He may snatch away more than your soul.

I have no desire to re-enter Olivia's life. Strangely, I can hardly remember what she looks like. Only those few years ago she seemed such a child—a scatterbrained, dreamy girl, half opened from the bud; it is hard to imagine that now she is the wife of an official, mistress of a house, commanding servants, entertaining guests. But I suppose I have changed, too. Whatever innocence I possessed when I gave my virginity to Olivia I have since surrendered in the brothels of Alexandria. I told you of Nibi. She was my teacher in the school of the flesh. To see her reflection in a mirror—her mere glance in the cold glass, without taste or smell or sound or touch— was enough to make my body clamorous with desire. But she was not a disembodied presence "seen through a glass darkly", like the Christian God I met on the lips of your Cornelius. To Nibi's image in the glass one must add the delicious secretions of her cunt, the taste of honey and cedar. The scents of rose and mango and jasmine and spikenard and cinnamon, distilled in her own sweet sweat. The rustle of silk; the whispered entreaties. The touch of her tongue, darting, tasting; the smoothness of her ebony skin, cool to the touch on her shoulders and the small of her back, burning hot between her legs. What need did I have then, Antonius, for your eastern mysteries, your hocus-pocus miracles—water to wine, multiplication of loaves and fishes, Lazarus raised from the dead? Nibi raised me from the dead a dozen times during the one long night I spent in her sanctuary. Why must we discount *this world,* with its exquisite beauties and pleasures, and go chasing after an illusion of paradise—a disembodied existence that is impossible even to imagine except in terms of *this body?*

You will say that I have answered my own question: "Bad luck, Sapphira." Bad luck about the plague. Bad luck about the wretched scars that would have covered Sapphira's handsome body had she lived. Bad luck about the infants who died like scalding coals in their mothers' arms. Bad luck about the children too weak to cry, their fair skin crusted with scabs. Bad luck about *this* world. And it's true: Nibi lost confidence at the end. The plague came into her holy of holies—her last customer. It disrobed and stood before her, exposed its lizard skin. It pressed its scabrous mouth against her crimson lips and filled her lungs with its miasmatic breath. Did she weep, Antonius, when she saw the first pustules on her perfect breasts? Is that when she called for the Christian priest? Was it something she remembered about the eyes of the fanatics who had assaulted her in the street? The certainty? Is that what she remembered in their eyes, Antonius? *The absolute certainty of faith?*

Nibi should have been laid out with flowers in the Temple of Aphrodite, her body washed with camel's milk and covered with the blossoms of lavender, lilacs and violets, then placed in a sarcophagus of white marble at the blue water's edge with dates and cloves. Instead, she was taken by her soul's new keepers to some dusty catacomb carved out of desert rock. She had been baptised by Venus in the fragrance of a hundred herbs, and now she was sprinkled in her final agony with water from the city's polluted wells—"I baptise thee in the name of the Father and the Son and the Holy Spirit"— then shoved into a rock-carved shelf crowded with—with the mortal frames of women and children. Have you noticed, Antonius, that the ministers of your faith are entirely men—Cornelius with his silver tongue, castrated Origen, cowardly Cyprian—and their congregations are mostly women and children? What sort of place will it be, your Christian heaven? Like the women's bath at Cyrenaica with its lurking male attendants?

No, Antonius. The plague will pass; perhaps it has burned itself out already. Alexandria will come alive again. Citizens and foreigners will brush shoulders in the agora. Shops will spill their produce into the streets. Ships will crowd the harbour. And we will be confident again. Lucretius says:

> . . . *men are afraid because they see things*
> *On earth and in the heavens that they cannot explain,*
> *And so suppose them to be caused*
> *By the will of gods . . .*

And so it is with the plague; we do not understand why we are so sorely afflicted, and so we seek the favour of gods. I have learned many things from Theophrastus, but the thing I value most is his clear-eyed sense that nothing comes from nothing, that everything has a natural cause, and that whatever this world offers, good or bad, is all we are going to get. When Eppia died, T. was devastated, but he did not go whinging to the gods. I admire him for that; he was tested and kept his moral courage—if not his professional diligence. I hope that I, too, will face life as it comes, suck juice from the ripe peach and spit out the spoiled plum, and then, when life is over, accept the dissolution of my self—

    . . . as when jars are broken
    Their water and wine runs in all directions.

As for the boy, Olivia's offspring. The Romans, as we know, can be dissolute and violent, and their gods are so numerous and absurd as to be laughable. But there is also a certain steeliness in the Roman character, a stiff practicality that steadies the world when the winds of anarchy are blowing all about us. I would rather have the boy raised in an honest Roman household than in the hiding holes of Christians. At least the water will be drinkable and the latrines clean.

Your friend,
Valentine

XVI

By the feast of Saturnalia the plague had departed Rome, the last corpses carted from tenements near the Pinciana Gate. In the Alban Hills we had felt safe enough by October, although travellers from the city were still treated with inhospitality and suspicion. The breezes from the west became fresh again; they bore the normal scents of scythed wheat, fermenting grapes and sea salt. We took pleasure again in watching sunsets—those rose and purple conflagrations over the Tyrrhenian Sea—knowing that a tide of human misery no longer lay hidden between oneself and the horizon.

During the course of the disease, we lost as many as one-third of our gladiators, and the normal supply lines of fresh candidates were interrupted. When the games began again in earnest at Saturnalia, we knew we would fall short of combatants for the arena, and for months this was the case. But as always the gods find ways to care for the needs of the Roman people. The emperor Gallus went off to quell a revolt by Aemilian, the governor of the Danube province. He was defeated in Umbria and murdered by Aemilian, who himself survived a mere two months. The new claimant to the throne was Valerian, the former censor of Decius and a man who shared Decius's hatred of Christians. Persecutions resumed, and Romans were again provided with the spectacle of Christians in the arena. None of that, of course, was part of my responsibility. Those hapless victims were a mere sideshow for the games our school was commissioned to provide. Our gladiatorial family were professionals who gave good value for money. A quarrel with the procurators, who wanted our highly trained gladiators to become mere executioners of unarmed Christians—as a sort of warm-up for the actual combats—was resolved temporarily in our favour. Our men were not butchers, and some of them were followers of the Nazarene.

After her long quarantine during the summer and autumn of the plague, then a cruel winter, Julia blossomed with the spring. She was now three years old and a beautiful, normal child in every respect except her blindness. To watch her make her way tentatively about the house and garden was heartbreaking. The words she spoke as she acquired language reflected her stunted sensory experience. She had words for the fig—for its soft down, its sweet juice, the texture of the pulp, the hardness of the seeds between her teeth—but not for the colour of the fig, nor for the orchard white with blossoms, nor the baskets of fruit in carts that rumbled by on their way to the markets of Rome. She knew Rome by its smell, which on certain winds was unmistakable; but she had no word for the silver haze that hung over the city in the early morning hours of a hot summer's day. I did everything a father might do to obviate her affliction. I made the rounds of the temples, and many animals were paid for and sacrificed. I cultivated the physicians, too, that tribe of charlatans. They offered a plethora of foolish concoctions, balms and poultices; I tried them all, even those which burned my darling's eyes. Of course, nothing worked.

I endeavoured to ensure that Julia had as normal a life as possible. I took her with me in the chariot; she held on tightly with her tiny hands as we thundered along the country lanes, exulting in the sensation of speed, the wind streaming against her face and the scents of crushed grass, horse sweat and dust. I took her to the city. She loved the market place, with its cacophony of trade, its cascade of smells, its press of bodies. The temples, too, with their cold, smooth marble and smell of incense, and especially the Temple of Diana, for which she felt a special bond because of the stories I had told her of the goddess.

I poured into her hungry ears every tale I knew, and Desso, too, her minder, spun out sagas of dark forests to the north and strange Germanic gods. Julia's mind was quick; she devoured the world with her four keen senses. She loved vigorous play, and as her body grew stronger she revelled in physical danger: walking the curbstones of the atrium pool, climbing trees, laying flat and still on the back of a horse at pasture. For all of this I held my own fear in check and let her test her limits.

I am not a superstitious person. The older I get the less patience I have with fates and omens. But I do recall that Desso, that mysterious slave woman who was Julia's surrogate mother, promised her tiny charge that one day she would meet a man who would help her see. At that time poor Julia hardly knew what it was that she was missing. Sight is simply unimaginable to someone of her age who is blind. But already there was perhaps an inevitable course to her destiny that would bring her to Valentine—and to a kind of light.

XVII

The plague returned to Alexandria the next year and the following year, but not with the same force. (It would smolder like embers in the various provinces of the empire for a dozen years before it expired altogether.) Valentine inherited the practice of Theophrastus, who remained in retirement, closeted with his books of poetry. The older physician placed part of his household at Valentine's disposal; his medical library, too. He asked for nothing in return but lived off the interest of his investments, which was quite sufficient to maintain the spartan habits of his declining years. Valentine began now to augment the tidy personal fortune he had earned during the plague year. For a man so young, hardly more than a boy, he was well respected throughout the city, as much as protégé of the legendary Theophrastus as a healer in his own right. He applied himself to mastering the works of Galenus and Hippocrates, until both his Greek and his medical arts were second nature. He allied himself with the best herbalists of the commercial quarters of the city. When he encountered an ailment that frustrated his growing skill, he turned to the old man in his study and never failed to find satisfaction.

Valentine knew his life had come to a crossroads. He had fallen willy-nilly into medicine, through the accident of employment with Theophrastus, and although this occupation gave him satisfaction, he felt that he had not sufficiently examined the alternatives, nor seen enough of the world, to settle down into what now promised to be the comfortable life of an affluent physician. He had no lack of women who offered him their favours: prostitutes, of course, but also widows, manumitted slaves, bored upper-class matrons, and the wives of busy businessmen who contrived imaginary ailments to bring the boyishly handsome doctor to their bedsides. He soon became affected by a kind of sexual lassitude that left him dreaming of departed Nibi.

And something else began to trouble him. Valerian had consolidated his position in Rome, and soon orders again went out to the provinces to suppress the upstart faiths. Everyone was required to make sacrifice to the Roman gods, and those who refused were left to a fate to be decided by the magistrates. Alexandria had a long-standing reputation for tolerance; even in the time of Decius, refractory Christians were more likely to be banished from the city than put to the sword. But it happened that the prefect in Alexandria was now a man named Daia, who had himself been involved with a sect of Christians known as the Carpocratians, whose debauched liturgies and penchant for holding wives in common was a source of bemusement to some and of scandal to others. When word came from Rome that Christian practice was not to be tolerated, Daia reverted to worship of the emperor's favourite god and became zealous in his persecutions of Christians. The Carpocratians, in particular, were soon extinguished from the city, as Daia subjected his former co-religionists to agonies of an extreme (and demented) sort. For the first time, executions were carried out in the arena as public entertainment, as was common in other major cities of the empire. This sort of gratuitous violence did not sit well with most Alexandrians, who had never been overly fond of Roman blood sports. Like many of the city, Valentine considered Christians to be naive and superstitious, but he saw no reason why they should be so cruelly treated. He owed at least this much to his Christian friend Antonius—and perhaps, by now, to his sister, too—that he would not by word or deed assist the magistrates in their savagery. But then neither was he inclined to offer sacrifice in the official temples. All religion seemed to him of matter of fractious imbecility. Distressed by what he saw happening around him, he gathered up a few articles of clothing, threw a handful of coins in his purse and left the city. He said goodbye only to Theophrastus, whom he asked to hold his possessions and savings until he returned.

His action was not as rash as it might seem. There was by now a tradition in Egypt of retirement to the desert to escape the tribulations of city or village life. Young Christian men, especially, were drawn to desert solitude; they had taken it into their heads that to be alive to God one must renounce the life of ordinary commerce. They followed Christ's injunction to give all they had to the poor and seek the treasure that could only be accumulated in heaven. In honesty, it must be said that many more of these so-called "desert saints" sought only to escape bad debts or the excessive burden of Roman taxation. Nevertheless, the tradition was established, and something of the notion of renunciation appealed to Valentine's sense of world-weariness and sexual ennui. It was not a heavenly reward that he sought, but peace of mind, a chance to clear his head, to decide what it was that he wanted to do with his life. He had been deeply touched by the ideal of contemplative meditation that he had found in the works of Epicurus and Marcus Aurelius. He vaguely had it in his mind that he would seek out some desert cell and, with the few coins that rattled in his pocket, live for a few months or years away from the hubbub of the city. If nothing else, he wanted a respite from the burdensome responsibilities to the patients who came to him unbidden.

He walked eastward along the sea, through Nicopolis and Canopus, until he reached the western channel of the Nile. His choices there were limited. To continue along the coast would mean repeated crossings of the Nile's many branching channels. He turned south and walked along the western bank of the western channel until he reached the ferry at Nucratis, a two-day's tramp from Alexandria. Only there did it dawn on him that he had not the slightest notion of where he was going.

But the pleasure of being on the road was intense. He loved the sense of spaciousness, of land reaching away to a far horizon, green with barley and rye. He loved the sweet stink of the river, moving beside him in a muddy swirl. He loved the fishermen in their reed boats, the watermen lifting the Nile bucket by bucket into a thousand agricultural ditches and the women flogging grain on threshing floors of sun-baked clay. This was the unseen hinterland that made city life possible, the unvarying drudgery of the hundreds of dirt-poor Egyptians who supported his own bookish existence. He did not feel any injustice in this arrangement, nor did it seem to him that these impoverished peasant drudges were any less happy than himself. Rather, as someone who had begun to call himself a physician, it seemed to Valentine that the farm and fisherfolk he met along the river had firmer bodies and a healthier cast than the pale and flabby plebs of the city—and a better grip on the long stick of nature than the scholars holed up in the scroll-lined crevices of the Alexandrian Museum.

At Nucratis he hired passage on a ship heading upriver, lateen rigged for catching the breezes off the sea. He slept on deck and lay awake most of the night as a nearly full moon arched overhead, making the river shine like burnished bronze. At dawn the sky turned a brilliant orange, then pink, and as the sun edged its disk over the distant horizon he swore he saw a flash of green. Then he saw what he had only read about, far away on the southern horizon: the tombs of the Egyptian kings, colossal pyramids of stone arrayed like angry teeth against the sky.

Valentine spent the following night near the base of the largest of the pyramids. He had purchased shelter with an Egyptian trader who plied his wares up and down the Nile by camel caravan, carrying iron ingots and alabaster from the regions near Syene to the markets of Alexandria, and the cloths and trinkets of the city back to villages of Middle Egypt. The trader's name was Pjol. As the moon rose, the mountain of stone cast a long triangular shadow across Pjol's many-tented stopping place.

Valentine shared the evening meal with Pjol and his entourage: a brother, cousins, nephews and, outside the dining pavilion, a dozen female slaves and concubines. The food was basic but plentiful: dried and salted camel meat, goat cheese, dried apricots, dates and an unidentified fermented liquor that caused Valentine to gag with his first sip, to the amusement of his dining companions. Traveller's fare. He ate ravenously, and as he ate he shared with Pjol his vague plan of a desert hermitage.

His host snorted with derision. "What would possess you to want such a life?"

Valentine shrugged.

"Are you a Christian?"

"No."

"Some sort of religious fanatic?"

Valentine shook his head gravely.

"Then why? No women. No wine. No companionship with those who can entertain you . . ."

Valentine stammered to explain, but realised that he did not have a convincing rationale for his action.

Pjol sneered: "I've seen these desert hermits. We have passed near their cells. They are like rats dragged up out of holes, with filthy skin and matted hair. Their hovels stink of urine and semen. They beg piteously from passers-by and leer at every pretty boy in our entourage. These are not men, my friend, they are . . ." Pjol switched into his native tongue and addressed his companions. They laughed.

Valentine knew there was more than this to desert flight, that solitude was not without refinements of the mind, but he also knew that to continue along this line of thought with Pjol was pointless. He turned the conversation to the three great mountains of stone that loomed over their encampment, and in particular, of course, the largest of all, the pyramid that according to legend was built by and for the pharaoh Khufu.

"There were giants in those days," said Pjol, the only one of the entourage who spoke a passable Greek.

"Giants?" queried Valentine, uncertain of his host's meaning.

Pjol stretched both arms over his head. "A hundred handspans tall. Men who could lift a stone the size of this tent as easily as I might lift this fig." He tossed the fruit into the air and caught it cleanly.

This naive theory seemed dubious to Valentine, but he had seen the blocks of stone of which the pyramid was built, each one more than an arm's length long and weighing, certainly, ten or twenty tons. He had estimated nearly two hundred and fifty stones in the bottom step of the pyramid along one side. Even roughly this must yield more than a million stones in all. In this single structure, there was surely more cut stone than in all of the buildings of Alexandria.

"When?" asked Valentine. "When was it built?" He had read bits of Egyptian history in the library of Theophrastus. He had some vague notion of the various dynasties who had ruled this land before the coming of Julius Caesar.

Pjol laughed. "That is not a question one can answer," he said. "It was before human time, in the time of the gods. The gods put the pyramid here to mark the centre of the world."

"Wasn't it built in the time of the pharaohs, as a tomb for Khufu?"

Pjol laughed again and translated Valentine's remarks to his brother, cousins and nephews. They laughed together.

Pjol leaned towards Valentine and spoke with great seriousness: "This place was never a habitation for men. No race of men could have made these monuments."

Valentine cautiously challenged Pjol. "Caesar Augustus brought the great obelisk of Rameses all the way to Rome. It is said to weigh much more than any stone of this pyramid."

"Have you seen it, this obelisk?" asked Pjol, sceptical.

Valentine had to confess that he had not.

Pjol placed his cup on the rug and stood up, his colourful robe falling in folds to his feet. "Come," he said. "It is one thing to chatter and talk of obelisks. You intellectuals think too much. You must *experience* the gods, not talk about them. The gods are not matters for philosophy. They must be *felt*. Come with me."

Valentine followed Pjol outside the tent. The Great Pyramid of Khufu loomed not a hundred paces from where they were standing, drenched in moonlight, seeming to fill half of the world with its intimidating presence. Pjol led his young guest to the base of the pyramid and then, following a path that he had clearly taken before, began the arduous ascent. From step to step they climbed, moving along each narrow terrace to a place where a stone or pile of stones gave them purchase upward to the next level. Pjol, though aged, moved without apparent effort, his loosely strapped sandals flip-flopping against the stones. Valentine followed behind, breathing heavily, stopping every now and then to rest. An hour passed before they achieved the apex.

The moon was high now. The pyramid cast no shadow. Pjol said nothing. He sat on the penultimate step with his back against the highest block of stone and let Valentine ascend to the very summit to absorb the splendour of the scene. All of Egypt lay about them: the endless dark gardens to the north, the cluttered town of Memphis, the river, the desert escarpments to the west, the mysterious carpet of mottled sand to the south that spread away into the hot interior of Africa. Looking down along the western slope of the monument, Valentine saw the tents of Pjol's encampment, the corralled camels as small as the toys of children, and the prick of light that was the campfire where the women sat huddled against the chill. He was swept by vertigo, an intoxication, as if Pjol's strange liquor had at last reached the innermost core of his being. The stars seemed within hand's reach. He sensed the presence of another equal, inverted pyramid, crystalline, invisible, reaching down from the sky, touching *this* pyramid tip to tip, or *almost* touching, with only room for himself and Pjol in the gap between aether and stone. His mind was in a whirl.

And just at the moment when he thought he was about to faint, Pjol spoke to him from below.

"Strip," he commanded, with a voice both gentle and persuasive.

"What?"

Pjol smiled up at him. "Remove your garments. You must be naked to feel the pyramid's fire."

Valentine was frightened, but he did as he was told. He shed his sandals, cloak, and tunic, handing them to Pjol. Then, wearing only the thin undergarment that wrapped his genitals, he closed his eyes and reached up his arms, standing on his toes, until every sinew of his body was stretched between earth and sky. He felt, or imagined that he felt, a current of fire flow up and down through his body, from earth to heaven and heaven to earth. He stood at the nexus between mortal and immortal realms, and if it was the gods that he felt, as Pjol insisted, then it was a power too real to be denied. There was a palpable silence, the silence of a million blocks of cold stone in deep repose and of a million stars in their crystalline turning. Then, from below on the desert floor, he heard—or thought he heard—a plaintive melody played on a flute, each note ascending like a dying ember from the campfire of the women, like a call or a prayer from the faraway human world.

XVIII

In the dark hour before daybreak he was still awake, thinking of the *capaciousness* of the world that he had experienced at the top of the pyramid and of the Jovian thrill that seemed to flow up and down through the nexus of his flesh. Perhaps Pjol was right. Perhaps one should forego philosophy and simply accept the world in the spirit in which it was given to us by the Olympian gods, with their brave machinations and wanton desires. He remembered the meal the previous evening in Pjol's pavilion: the prayers the men had mumbled before lashing into each course of food, the heaped fruits, the beards running with juices, the dark fingers pulling, tearing, breaking and being licked clean by desiccated desert lips. And the women sitting around the fire outside, with only the glint of reflected moonlight on their golden rings and bangles to betray a feminine presence within their voluminous black robes. What did analysis have to do with any of this? Hippocrates and Galenus with their endless speculations, their anatomical experiments, their talk of "general principles" and "natural faculties"; and Lucretius, who had the hubris to call his poem "The Way Things Are"; did they know anything at all of beauty? What scroll in Theophrastus's library could explain what he had felt as he stood naked on the pyramid's apex, stretched between heaven and earth? What philosophy could explain the fierce sensual appetites of these Egyptian caravanners or the mysterious geographies of flesh that hid beneath the black robes of their women? Or, for that matter, what in all of the thousands of scrolls in the Museum of Alexandria— astronomy, geography, mechanics, botany, mathematics and all the rest—could explain the chill of longing and desire he felt as he lay unsleeping in Pjol's tent, with the moon beating down on the desert sand outside, stars blazing, and the muffled rhythmic breath of Pjol's sleeping concubine not an arm's length away, her closed eyelids dusted with gold? Was all of this just a swirl of particles, as Lucretius said, corpuscles colliding, momentarily coalescing to give life and spirit, then dissolving away, going hither and yon, so that nothing of the self remains? Could it be that simple? And if it were—if it were all just a random wind of particles—would he, Valentine, *want* to believe it? He thought, too, of the pharaoh Khufu, whoever he might have been, whose embalmed corpse presumably lay even now in the bowels of the pyramid—if his rest had not been violated by thieves—in a sealed chamber that might as well be at the centre of the earth, surrounded with the accouterments of gold, jade and sandalwood that he would require in the afterlife. One could imagine no more confident assertion of immortality than this spectacular mountain of stone, which must represent (thought Valentine) the orchestrated effort of an empire—the compelled labours of a million or ten million slaves. Each block of stone that had so laboriously been lifted into place was a refutation of his philosophers.

As he dreamed thus, the camp began to wake. The light of the sun reached over the horizon and into the shadow of the pyramid to touch the sleeping faces. First one, then another stirred. And soon men and women moved about, rolling rugs, striking tents, drawing the camels into a line, restoring the animals' burdens. Valentine had made a decision. His meeting with Pjol had been fortuitous. There would be no hiding in the desert; he saw now that no authority, religious or secular, called him to *that* parody of a life. He would return to Alexandria with the caravan. And then he would take passage on a ship for Rome. Pjol had called the Great Pyramid the axis of the earth and sky. That may have been true in the time of Khufu, but today the axis had shifted. If Valentine was going to make a choice between the gods and the philosophers, he would do it at the new centre of the world. Rome.

XIX

Valentine,

As you see, dear friend, I am far from home. You may not have heard of this place; it is not much more than an oasis, a few mud houses, a muddy well, date palms. A red cliff hangs over the village, placing it permanently in shadow. The wind blows incessantly. The nights are bitter cold. I have dated this letter "winter", as I am uncertain of the day or month. I have been sick. It is only now that I am well enough to write. I am living in the house of an old woman who took me in while I was indisposed. Now she is frightened of my presence. She has been told that I am a fugitive and has asked me to leave. I have nowhere to go.

Val, I write because I must confess to you a terrible sin and give you news that should make you happy but which I fear will sadden and anger you. Let me begin at the beginning.

As you know, these are not safe times to be a Christian. The prefects of Cyrenaica are competing for Valerian's favour by seeing which of them can be most diligent in his persecutions, and the prefect of Apollonia seems determined than none should be more diligent that he. Our little church at Apollonia had been growing strong under the leadership of Cornelius, whom you met. I was one of his first converts. Your sister became one of us, too. It was I who introduced her to Cornelius, and for that I rejoice; I tell you this so that you will see that I evade no responsibility. Your parents were distressed when Helena was baptised; they tried mightily to dissuade her from becoming a Christian, your father especially. They saw no good of it. But Helena was happy. And I was happy. You will know that I loved your sister, and not only as a sister in Christ. I had never seen her so full of joy as when Cornelius prepared her for baptism. It will sound a cliché, but her face had the radiance of a bride. She had fasted, as we all did, for two days. On the evening before the sacrament, she was with Cornelius for the reading of scriptures. Then, at first light, she went with our congregation to the Goat's Well—you will remember the place, on the road to Darnis. She put off her clothes save for her shift, discarded her bracelet and ring, and let down her hair. She turned toward the west to renounce Satan, then towards the east to confess Christ. Cornelius anointed her head and back and shoulders with oil, then led her three times into the pool. When she emerged she took on the new white garment of her salvation.

It was soon after this that the persecutions began. Anyone who openly professed Christ was invited by the authorities to offer sacrifice to the gods; any that refused were beheaded. It was a bloody time, Valentine. All of Cyrenaica lived in fear. Cornelius told us that these trials were a joyful occasion. The Christian must die to live, he said. Twice he must die. First he must die to Satan at baptism, when he puts on the life of Christ. And then he must die a mortal death to gain eternal life. Martyrdom is a second baptism—a baptism of blood. Tertullian spoke of the day of a martyr's death as his "birthday", a time to be celebrated, for the Christian who dies for his faith gains immediate entry into paradise. Nothing, said Cornelius, is more to be sought for than dying for Christ.

The denunciations began. Neighbours accused neighbours. None of us knew which of our friends might betray us. Helena was accused. I was with her when the soldiers came. It was a bright afternoon. Helena had spread a cloth on the ground in your father's orchard. We were reading from the Gospel of Thomas, or rather Helena was reading; I was lying on my back, watching the clouds scud the sky, occasionally glancing at Helena and thinking how beautiful she was—unworthy thoughts, I know, and perhaps not unrelated to what followed. I remember the last words she read: *Jesus said, "Split a piece of wood and I am there. Pick up a stone and you will find me there."* The soldiers walked towards us between the olive trees. Helena saw them first and stopped reading. I looked up and saw them, too. One tall, one short, in steel and leather, with short swords strapped at their waists. They stopped before us; for a moment it seemed as if they might join us beneath the trees. They asked if she were Helena, the daughter of Stephanus. She said, "Yes." Her eyes were alive with green fire. They asked if she were a Christian. She said, "Yes." She said to them, "I have been waiting for you." The soldiers seemed embarrassed, as if loath to do what they must do. She stood up and smoothed her tunic against her thighs. With both hands, she gathered her hair at the back of her neck and fixed it with a clasp. There was nothing more the soldiers needed to say; she knew why they had come. She fixed her sandals. As they led her away, she turned to me and said, "Antonius, will you not come, too?" Valentine, I did not follow her. I was frightened. I could see that Helena *wanted to die,* that she *welcomed* what was about to happen. I was frozen in my place, desperately in love with her and cowering with fear. I watched them disappear behind the wall by the well, Helena between the two soldiers. The soldiers did not touch her or force her in any way to follow. She might have been their sister.

She was in prison for a week, but refused to offer sacrifice. Your father tried pulling every string he could to win her release, to no avail. There were other Christians in prison with her. They prayed. They sang. None recanted. None offered sacrifice. I cannot tell you of her death, Valentine, without weeping copious tears. When I heard what they had done to her, I fled the city, in fear and shame. At every moment I thought I might be next, that the soldiers would come for me. The shame! That your sister was so brave while I was such a coward. I cannot understand my fear. I knew that if I died I would be instantly with Christ—and with Helena. The words of Jesus were constantly in my ears: *This day, you shall be with me in paradise.* I should have followed her and been beside her when the sword . . .

I wept. I wept incessantly for days, until I was physically sick with weeping. I had walked five hundred stadia into the desert. The old woman found me unconscious at the side of a desert track, my tunic covered with vomit. Not only have I lost paradise, but I have damned my soul to hell. Nothing can save me now, Val. I keep thinking: if I can find Cornelius, he will tell me what to do. He will stiffen my backbone and grant me absolution. But still I am afraid. I know that if I am asked to offer sacrifice to the Roman gods in order to save my neck, I will do so—and spend all of eternity in hellfire. Can you imagine what that must be like? Endless torment, without release. I am terrified. Terrified to live and terrified to die.

I am giving this letter to a tradesman who camped here last evening. He is going to the coast. I have asked him to put it on a boat for Alexandria. Do not reply to this place. I will be gone. Pray for me, Valentine. If you can find it in your heart to care for me at all, pray that I will find the courage to bear witness for Christ.

Do not grieve for Helena. Hate me, Valentine, if you must, but don't grieve for your sister. She is safe in heaven. Origen told us that Christianity must be true because people are prepared to die for it. Her beauty is now one with the beauty of Christ.

Your wretched friend,
Antonius

XX

Antonius's letter was waiting for Valentine at the house of Theophrastus when he returned from his journey into the desert. He read it without weeping. He had seen so much suffering during the time of the plague that not even the death of his beloved sister could make him cry. He was sorry, of course, but a weariness in his heart stopped his tears. The letter smelled of sweat and salt. It had perhaps been held against a sailor's breast as it made its way from Cyrenaica to Alexandria, three thousand stadia along the coast. Sun, wind and spray, the creaking of the ship's timbers, the crack of the sail slapping in the wind, the whine of windlass and tackle. The tiny folded scrap of papyrus, bearing on the outside the simple address *Valentine, in the care of Theophrastus the physician, Alexandria.* With its terrible message. He could not quite grasp the import of the message: the keen blade severing Helena's thin white neck. How could any man, no matter how debased, no matter how much emboldened by the edicts of Rome, commit so heinous a crime? He had seen horrendous deaths, bodies corrupted by disease, scabrous and black with decay. But at least what he saw then was a person, whole and entire, and when death came it was as if a candle were going out, as the person's spirit evaporated into air. But to be *decapitated.* Instantly. With the spirit still intact in the frame of the body. The head in the dust, dead and not dead. The eyes still open, ablaze with light. The heart still pumping blood.

Mostly what Valentine felt was anger, a cold indignation against Antonius. Not for abandoning Helena, but for introducing her to the Christians in the first place. *A bride.* He said she had been as happy as a bride. A bride to deceit, a fanatical dream. Origen, Cyprian, Tertullian and all the rest. Procurators to a feeble empire of the spirit, a cult of weakness and shame. And Cornelius. He had distrusted the man from the moment he had met him, all full of sweet talk and condescension. The unflinching eyes, the hard certainty. The pocks on his otherwise handsome face. He could imagine Cornelius in the Goat's Well with Helena. Pouring the water over her body, full of self-importance, speaking magical incantations and pious platitudes, his prick rising in his loincloth. Cornelius was the villain in this sorry story, thought Valentine. And where was Cornelius now, this charlatan of Christ? Had he, too, taken the quick passage to paradise? Or was martyrdom only for women? It is said that Cyprian of Carthage, during the persecutions of Decius, claimed that the glory of all martyrs accrued to the bishop—himself—as representative of God in the Christian community. Like an emperor, Cyprian gathered his treasure from the wretched poor; meanwhile, he kept himself safely out of reach of the emperor's wrath. It occurred to Valentine that he might go to Cyrenaica and seek out Cornelius, drag him to a magistrate's court, denounce him for the Christian that he was and let him feel for himself the kiss of the sword on his neck. He would look for Antonius too and shake some sense into his friend, make him see that the only god worth worshiping was whatever was beautiful and good in the here and now. But no, that would be a waste of time. Sooner or latter Antonius would make his own way back to sense, if his cowardice kept him from the sword. And Cornelius, too, would have his comeuppance, if it had not happened already, the blade falling like lightning on his neck, then, eyes wide open, the spirit still trapped behind the eyes, looking out into this world and the otherworld simultaneously—that instantaneous cusp between not-death and death—when Cornelius would realise with a stunning and unexpected clarity that what the next moment will bring is not bliss but oblivion.

XXI

Valentine took passage on a freighter sailing from Alexandria to Rome with a cargo of three hundred amphora of oil and five hundred ingots of iron. The ship was thirty-five passus in length, with a high-masted sail and crew enough to row if needed. At the vessel's prow a great swan's head and neck arched gracefully into the future. Valentine shared deck passage with two dozen other paying passengers. He was twenty-one years old. He carried an iron box full of gold coins (a modest initial stake for a young doctor in Rome), a dozen medical books laboriously copied from the library of Theophrastus, provisions for a journey of several months and portable shelter for night and rain. At the insistence of Theophrastus, he had hired a servant, nicknamed Rufi, a red-haired boy of fourteen who seemed to have no family or fixed address and who was willing to travel wherever Valentine might take him. ("No one but paupers and fugitives travel without a servant," said Theophrastus.) The two young men boarded the ship at the Obelisk Quay and claimed a corner of the deck that was out of the way of the working crew. As they settled their things, they watched the spectacle of the loading of a hippopotamus, a monstrous beast with rolls of flesh hanging from its flanks and legs like the pillars of an Egyptian temple; it was the first hippopotamus Valentine had seen, although Rufi professed to have seen one before as it passed through Alexandria on its way to Rome. The beast was confined within a stout timber cage which was manhandled on to the deck of the freighter with the aid of rollers and cranes, with much shouting, cursing, creaking of timbers and the angry roaring of the hippo. A crowd of spectators watched from the quay. This magnificent animal had been transported up the Nile from a river marsh in the land of Nubia, clearly with enormous difficulty. Its journey was far from over yet. Its destination, Valentine supposed, was the Flavian Amphitheatre in Rome, where, after its long (and expensive!) journey, the animal would be slaughtered by bestiarii for the amusement of the populace. He had heard that five thousand animals—leopards from Asia Minor, lions, elephants and rhinoceroses from Africa, bears and wild bulls from northern Europe—were killed in a single day during the games with which the emperor Titus inaugurated the great many-tiered arena that dominates the city of Rome. The splendid animal with which Valentine and Rufi now shared a journey would presumably be part of a less magnificent extravaganza, if for no other reason than that nearly two hundred years of Roman games had rendered the provinces and their hinterlands mostly devoid of wild beasts.

"Can we go to the games at which the hippo will be killed?" asked Rufi.

Valentine shrugged and smiled. "We'll see," he replied inconclusively. He had no desire to see the animal butchered.

"How will they kill it?"

"Beast-men will do the job," guessed Valentine; he spoke in Rufi's patois, a mix of indigenous languages and Latin. Few animals other than lions were used in the games at Cyrene or Alexandria; larger animals were consigned to the capital. "Perhaps archers will shoot the hippo from the safety of the stands. Or perhaps the beast will be let loose to run amok in an arena full of Christians." He added this last as a sort of joke, for he guessed, incorrectly as it turned out, that Rufi might be a secret follower of the Nazarene. If so, the boy betrayed no fear at the prospect of being trampled in the arena by a hippopotamus.

Rufi said, "The Romans must be very rich if they can bring animals from Nubia for an afternoon of fun."

"The money is not the half of it," ventured Valentine. "Think of the organisation it must take to ensure that day after day there are sufficient criminals, slaves and animals to fill the arenas—the dozens of arenas of the empire, but especially those in Rome—and to train the gladiators and bestiarii to slay them. The amphitheatre's victims, both human and animal, are a commodity, like oil or iron. You need warehouses. Lines of supply. Training schools. Only the Romans have that kind of organisation. Or power."

"It's an ugly sort of animal," said Rufi, looking toward the hippo. "It deserves to die."

When at last the hippo's cage was lashed firmly to the deck and passengers had taken up their places, the ship slipped its moorings. The crew heaved at the dozen oars, and the craft moved away from the quay and across the harbour at an excruciatingly slow pace, the hippo bellowing all the while. The sun stood high above the mast when the ship at last cleared the breakwater near the Pharos light. Now the great canvas sail was unfurled, much patched but still majestic in its billowing. A waning land breeze gave the ship a gentle push away from shore. As the lighthouse dropped below the horizon in late afternoon, the breeze faltered and the sails flapped forlornly. It was fortunate that there were no landmarks by which to mark their forward motion, or Valentine and Rufi might have wondered if they would ever reach their destination. The prevailing winds in the eastern Mediterranean are from the north; a voyage from Rome to Alexandria might take only two weeks, but the opposite journey could sometimes require six times as long.

The master of the ship provided the passengers with drinking water, nothing more. The water was rationed, and in the heat of afternoon both Valentine and Rufi wanted more than their stingy allotment. It occurred to Valentine that he might buy an extra ration for himself and Rufi, but he resisted this impulse when he saw that less affluent passengers were thirsty, too. As the sun set, the air cooled and their thirst abated. Valentine broke out a simple evening meal. He had decided to provision himself with the same sorts of foods that Pjol and his entourage had carried in the desert—dried meats and fruits, bread, goat cheese, dates—food that required little preparation. At two places on the deck, iron containers were provided for cooking fires, and at these the servants or slaves of the more affluent passengers prepared pancakes, vegetables or broth. Prominent among the passengers for the luxury of their provisions and accommodations were a Roman official and his family—a wife and two young daughters. They dined on mats and cushions under a crimson pavilion at the front of the ship—as far as possible from the stinking hippo's cage—perfuming the sea air with honey, spiced broth, fruit and wine to the distraction of those with less to eat, while their several slaves busied themselves preparing course after course of delicacies.

Toward the middle of the night, the wind picked up a bit from the north-east, with just enough transverseness to their course to gain purchase on the sail. Rufi took what warmth he could find by curling between Valentine's pile of travel parcels and Valentine himself. Valentine lay awake, lulled into contentment by the gentle slap of waves against the side of the ship. He counted six falling stars during the hour it took to fall asleep.

XXII

From Alexandria the ship sailed westward along the coast towards Cyrenaica, searching for a following wind to push it north. For a time Valentine was concerned that the ship might put into a Cyrenaicean port, perhaps even at Apollonia; he had no hankering for a homecoming. But the wind, such as there was of it, turned easterly, and the ship put its stern towards Cyrenaica and reached towards Greece, the first of two long crossings of open sea. For days the ship was out of sight of land, until it seemed as if they must be for ever at sea. At night the skies were clear and posted with a million stars. Valentine taught Rufi the constellations that he knew and Hipparchus's system for numbering the brightness of stars.

"Why would anyone want to number the stars?" asked Rufi.

"Not just numbers for their brightness," answered Valentine. "Eudoxus and Hipparchus also impressed upon the heavens circles, meridians, angles and degrees." He knew a smattering of astronomy.

"I would rather count coins than stars."

"You are a true Roman," laughed Valentine.

"And you are a Greek, with your head in the air," countered Rufi impudently.

"It is all a matter of how you wish to live your life. The Alexandrian astronomers cared more for eternal things—the immutable element of the heavens—than for earthly possessions that rust and rot." Valentine remembered the moment his body had been suspended between heaven and earth at the pyramid's apex.

Rufi gestured toward the place where the Roman official and his family were sleeping. "I would rather have a canopy of silk than a canopy of stars."

"When you are dead, what will they say that you did with your life?"

"They will say that I married the pretty daughter of a rich Roman and lived happily ever after."

Valentine caught the spirit of his jest. "Which of the girls do you prefer?"

Rufi gazed dreamily at the sleeping forms of the daughters. "Both," he said. "I'll marry the one and keep the other as my mistress."

"I want something more," whispered Valentine. Then he spoke more forcefully, although perhaps not yet with full sincerity, "I would like to be remembered as Hipparchus or Galenus are remembered, for having nudged mankind away from fear and superstition." The hippo rumbled in its cage. Valentine's eyes swept the dome of night from horizon to horizon. "When I get to Rome, I will try to live as Epicurus taught us to live—fully in this world, but chastely, wisely, moderately, well."

"I'll take the girls," laughed Rufi, and the two young men slumped happily against each other on the gently rolling deck.

At last, after days of featureless horizons, land appeared to the north. The passengers crowded to the prow of the ship and gaped at the hills of green and brown that rose from the sea. The ship put in at a small island on the southern coast of the Peloponnese for fresh water, and Valentine sent Rufi ashore to buy figs, olives and salted fish. He resisted the opportunity to put his own foot on Greek soil; he was fatigued by the long crossing—two weeks out of sight of land—and anxious that the ship get on with its voyage to Rome. Many inhabitants of the island came to the quayside to gaze at the hippopotamus, which now rested on its fat belly in its stout cage. The ship's crew took advantage of a supply of fresh water to wash the great beast down; out of its element, it had become desiccated and lethargic.

The ship's master wasted no time in port. With water casks topped off and bunged shut, the vessel was rowed out of harbour and waited for the whiff of air that would move it eastward to Sicily.

Days passed of tedious inactivity; three weeks to cross the Ionian Sea. Valentine tired of his books, tired of watching seabirds and flying fish, tired of the stars. Tired even of watching Rufi making harebrained excuses to be near the daughters of the wealthy Roman; there was no possibility, of course, that those haughty creatures would take notice of a servant. Valentine, in his ennui and weariness, quoted him Lucretius: *It is easier to avoid the net of love than to escape it once you are snared.* There were only seven years difference in age between Valentine and his servant, but to Valentine the difference seemed like a generation. The thought of Rufi's irrepressible enthusiasm and his own dispirited lassitude depressed him. He kept his awning up by day and lay sprawled on the deck, his mind blank, as the hours passed with the same dozy languor as the wind.

By the middle of July the ship took port in Syracuse, offloaded iron and took on more amphora of olive oil. This time Valentine went ashore, forcing himself to leave the ship. He walked the streets of the city with Rufi, perhaps, he thought, along the very cobblestones where Archimedes had trod. Even that—even exploring the place where the great mechanician confounded the Roman fleet—did not excite him. That night he slept in a proper bed, at an inn near the quays, with Rufi on the floor beside him. The next morning, with their food supply replenished and with two goatskins of good Sicilian wine, they reboarded the ship for the last leg of the journey. As they coasted northward, Mount Etna began to dominate the landward horizon, more than twenty stadia high and smoking like a chimney. The wind was westerly and a gentle rain of ash fell upon the ship, dusting the sun-warmed planks of the deck, infiltrating the eyes and nostrils of the passengers, adding a seasoning of grit to every bite of food. The passengers huddled under their awnings. The hippopotamus grew restless and noisy. The ship's master ordered an offering of fish to the god Vulcanus; the fish were wrapped in a red silk cloth and thrown into the sea.

A sultry morning became a torrid afternoon as the ship entered the Strait of Messina, hugging the Sicilian coast. Towering black clouds built up over the active mountain, as if distilled from the shadowy steam that erupted from the bowels of the earth. As the afternoon passed, ominous clouds filled the sky from horizon to horizon. At the fifth hour past midday, rain lashed down and lightning flashed. Thunder reverberated from shore to shore, roiling the sea. In its cage the hippo stood unsteadily on its massive legs and heaved its heavy haunches backwards, again and again, like a ram, into the stout timbers of its cage. The wind swung to the south, and the ship's master could not resist throwing up sail to run before the storm, the first chance on the entire voyage to make good time with the wind at the stern. Terrified sailors clung to the rigging as they raised the great patched sheet. The passengers heaped themselves on to the foredeck, rich and poor, slave and master, taking some small comfort in their collective mass. Their individual awnings, of canvas or of silk, had been ripped away by the wind.

The lightning was nearer now and more constant. It became clear to the master and officers of the ship that the hippopotamus was in an acute state of fright and in danger of shattering its cage. Orders were shouted, and the crew abandoned the rigging to bring ropes and props to reinforce the great beast's cell. Too late. With a massive thrust of its rump, the hippo shattered the timbers at the rear of the cage and backed out on to the deck, snorting and roaring with terror. The sailors fled to the stern or foredeck of the ship, resisting all shouts of the officers to confine the beast. The crew had the sense to know that reconfining the hippo under these conditions was impossible and that anyone who approached the animal was likely to be trampled. Undeterred by the cowardice of the crew, the officers prodded the hippo with grapples, hoping to manoeuvre the animal back into what was left of its cage, but this only excited the beast further. It stumbled forward along the gunwales, causing the ship to list severely to starboard. From below deck came the sound of smashing amphora and shifting iron. As the hippo bellowed towards the ship's prow, the passengers scattered in terror. Valentine grabbed Rufi by the arm and tried to drag him into the rigging, but Rufi's attention was fixed on the daughters of the Roman official, who cowered petrified in the path of the animal. He broke away from Valentine's grip and ran to help them.

There was a terrible rumbling sound below deck, like a volcano awakening, as three hundred iron ingots shifted in the hold of the listing ship. Just as Rufi reached the girls, the port side of the vessel lifted from the sea, and waves washed over the starboard gunwale. The hippo stopped its forward progress not two strides from Rufi and the girls. There was a terrible instant when time stood still and it seemed the ship must capsize—like a coin balanced on its edge. As Valentine watched open-mouthed, the hippo slipped sidewards down the sloping deck and crashed through the gunwale into the sea. Rufi lost his footing on the rain-slicked deck and tumbled after it. Valentine gaped in horror from the port rigging as his young servant disappeared into the churning water. Without thinking, as if moved by a will not his own, he leapt from his place in the rigging into the sea. The ship settled somewhat back towards an even keel, though waves still lashed through the broken gunwale. At the master's frantic command, the crew entered the hold and began shifting ingots to port. Two hours later, the ship would be safely balanced and underway with tattered sail.

In the black sea Valentine swam, rising and falling with the waves, to where he thought Rufi might be. In the troughs, he saw nothing. On the crests he scanned the sea and shouted. Down with the swell into ashy darkness, then up into the Jovian light of the storm. Down. Up. Down. Up. To a frightening vision. The hippopotamus's two bulging eyes loomed from the sea, like the eyes of a leviathan. The great maw opened with ivory teeth, seemingly swallowing the sea. Then, as quickly as it appeared, the apparition vanished. Something pulled at his tunic, and Valentine thought he would be dragged to the bottom by the sinking hippo.

XXIII

Julia's childhood was spent in the company of gladiators. Our school in the Alban Hills was private and highly select. Unlike the imperial gladiatorial schools of Rome, our fighters were few in number—never more than one hundred—and mostly freemen. The gladiators of the imperial schools included prisoners of war, convicts and slaves. These men had no choice but to fight in the arena or die a less ceremonial death under the executioner's sword; training at least gave them a chance for life and glory, perhaps even freedom, slim though that chance might be. By contrast, our men came to us of their own free will and asked to be admitted. It was known throughout the empire that our training programme was unequalled. For a generation, our gladiators were favourites of emperors and spectators alike. It might seem odd that men would freely choose a profession that included the virtual certainty of injury or death. Most of our recruits were poor or desperate men who saw in the gladiator's life a period, no matter how brief it might turn out to be, of security and camaraderie, with comfortable quarters and plenty to eat. But there were others, too, less needy: adventurers and ex-soldiers, foreigners seeking attention in the capital of empire, debt-ridden sons of good family. They came seeking the romance of combat and the thrill of adulation by thousands of cheering spectators—the glorious focus of the blood lust of Rome. Our men had a better than even chance of victory against the fighters of the imperial schools. The best of our gladiators became rich men, sought after by women, and, if they won the rudis, the wooden baton that released them from the obligation to fight in the arena, free to retire with fame and glory.

Security at our school was minimal. Once a potential recruit was screened for health and physical stamina, he signed a binding contract for a period of four years of training and combat. Some few lost their will along the way and left the school illegally. If they were caught—and they usually were—they were turned over to one of the imperial schools and forced to train and fight with a lesser breed of men. To a large extent, our experienced gladiators, the primi pali, maintained discipline among the newcomers, the tirones. They brought the less experienced men into the guild of gladiators, instilled in them a sense of pride and taught them the legends of the guild. All of the men participated in the sacrifices to Mars that preceded and followed combat in the arena. Our school had it own small shrine to the god of battle.

Julia was a favourite of our champions. They adopted her as their tiny protégée and spent some part of their idle hours teaching her their skills. They equipped her with a child-sized wooden sword and shield and, at the age of eight, with her own leather tunic. I had mixed emotions as I watched my little girl playing at combat, but I could see that the gladiators were teaching her skills that would serve her well in her lightless world. At she play-dueled with one or the other of our swordsmen, she relied on her heightened sense of hearing. Touch, too. Her skin was supremely sensitive to a kick of dust or currents of air. And smell. Julia's sense of smell was extremely acute, lupine even. She could identify each gladiator by his odour alone, even before she heard his voice. She could discern the number of men in a group by the variety of their scents. When a new man came to take her under his wing, she was sometimes able to identify the place of his origin by the scent of his sweat; it had never occurred to me, or to anyone else of my acquaintance, that a Celt and Syrian might not smell the same. Outside the walls of our villa was a dusty circle that became Julia's own miniature arena. Gladiators would come down from the school in their leisure and teach her tricks of thrust and parry, offence and defence. As time passed, the men made fewer concessions to her blindness, and in our own little world of the gladiatorial school she made her way with remarkable agility. In her leather tunic she bobbed and weaved in feigned combat, and swung her wooden sword with uncanny skill. Several of our teachers, who no longer fought in the arena, had families, and among the children mock gladiatorial games were a favourite pastime. Boys and girls engaged with toy weapons, always minding not to seriously hurt their companions. Each child adopted the kit of his favourite kind of fighter: samnite and hoplomachus with helmet, sword and shield, or retiarius with net and trident. In play, little Julia gave as good as she got, and someone watching the children's games might not immediately guess that the dark-haired, blue-eyed girl in leather tunic fought in darkness. Only when they saw her wooden sword occasionally widely miss its intended target would they realise her impediment.

Given the circumstances of her upbringing, it was inevitable that Julia would acquire boyish habits. Ours was a male world of brawn and sweat. Our men trained five hours each morning and four hours in the afternoon, with an hour's respite at midday. Each new recruit took the gladiator's oath: *I undertake to be burnt by fire, to be bound in chains, to be beaten by rods and to die by the sword.* It was not often that our teachers or guards needed to resort to chains or rods, but there was nothing soft about our regimen. The gladiators were treated with firmness and physical rigour, especially the tirones. Our teachers were tough men, who had killed often and well; their teaching authority was backed with superior strength and shouted oaths. Even from the distance of our villa, Julia's ears were daily filled with the clash of weapons and profanity, but the gladiators and their trainers could be surprisingly gentle when they dealt one-on-one with the assistant master's little girl.

The tirones among our gladiators began practising against each other with wooden swords, to learn the basics of thrust and parry. They graduated to iron swords, blunt and heavy. These more accurately simulated the weapons of the arena and had the added advantage of building strength and muscle. The men lived according to rank and experience. The primi pali, who had fought and won in the Roman arena, had special privileges: comfortable quarters, fine food, access to women and the occasional freedom of the city. They were often very rich men, who had won many plates of gold as prizes. The newcomers' accommodations were more spartan, but they always had before them the example of the proud and content champions, whom they sought to emulate in swagger and skill. Our school provided all armour and weapons, of the best make; the helmets and shields of our primi pali were works of high art and craftsmanship, and contributed mightily to the flair of the warrior's presence in the arena. It is important in this sort of work for the trainers to keep aloof from the students. Many of our men who went down to Rome did not return from their first combat, and even a champion who had been with us for a long time, and who felt he was charmed to live for ever, might meet his superior on the dusty floor of the arena. Our instructors maintained an emotional distance from their charges.

In such a hard and masculine environment, I thought it important that Julia be given the feminine arts. I hired tutors to teach her music, poetry and spoken Greek. She had Homer, Euripides, Sophocles and Meanander read to her by slaves. In Latin, she heard Virgil, Horace and Terence. But it must be said that Julia was not a keen student. She preferred her boyish games and the company of gladiators. It was as if she were determined to show that her blindness was no excuse to be confined to feminine pursuits. Desso, her nurse, tried to plant in her mind the notion that there was something immoral about the premise of our school; I had to caution Desso that I would not tolerate such nonsense.

We were ten years in the Alban Hills, between my imperial tours of duty in Alexandria and Rome. It was there that Julia's character was shaped—a girl of surpassing gentleness yet capable of a firm resourcefulness. In summers, she ranged the woods, fields, orchards and streams with her young friends, gathering flowers, climbing trees, wading in limpid pools. There were few activities of the sighted children that Julia could not follow. She had difficulty catching a thrown ball. I kept her from riding for fear that she might be trampled by the school's massive horses, but she loved the animals and, with proper supervision, loved to lay upon their backs. She avoided games with dice because she refused to depend upon others to read the spots. But in many ways, she outshined her companions. She could identify an astonishing variety of plants by their smell: all of the local herbs, of course—basil, garlic, lavender, rosemary, hyssop, sage, savory and rue—but also juniper, broom, gromwell, spurge, heather, rockrose, daphne and a hundred others I cannot remember. In winter, she could track a fox or hare through the barren fields. Sometimes when snow blanketed the mountains, wolves came down into the lowland hills seeking prey in the environs of farms; she could detect their presence in our neighbourhood by their odour long before the farmers found a wolf in their traps.

Julia was a happy child. She lived as if she did not know she was different from other children. Her outer darkness never affected her inner spirit. My greatest worry was that in her vigorous explorations of the world she might injure herself. Her blindness was a constant shadow in my life. Sometimes I closed my eyes and tried to move in Julia's darkness; I never endured sightlessness for long. She ran circles around me—her thin white arms and dancing hands playing the role of eyes. When she scanned my face with her fingertips, she often discovered a tear.

XXIV

Dear Valentine,

As you see, I am in Alexandria, having made my way here from Cyrenaica. I sought out your mentor, Theophrastus, who gave me your address in Rome. He also told me of the misadventure that befell you on your way thence and of your courage in rescuing your servant. I cannot help but think that God must have some great plan in store for you to have saved you from what seemed certain death. Pray to him, Valentine, and ask him for his guidance, that you, too, will enjoy the light of our Lord and Saviour, Jesus Christ.

The persecutions have abated in Egypt. I came to Alexandria with Cornelius that we might have freedom to worship the One True God. There is now a flourishing Christian community here, and I have been ordained a deacon. Our bishop Gaius is an old man and very frail. It is expected that Cornelius will succeed him. If so, then I, too, will certainly acquire more responsibility in ministering to our congregation. Between Gaius and Cornelius there are several issues of contention. The old man has ordained women to be presbyters and deacons. This Cornelius will not allow if he becomes bishop and, of course, he is right; Paul said that women in the church should be quiet and respectful, because Adam was formed first and Eve afterwards. Cornelius teaches that women are more likely to be possessed by the Devil than are men, again on the basis of scripture—and our experience here shows that to be true. On more than one occasion I have been asked to pray over women who spoke in voices that could only be those of the Evil One himself. Gaius is more lenient in matters of the flesh than Cornelius. Cornelius believes with Paul that sexual abstinence is appropriate for Christians, especially for any who might have authority over the congregation. But do not think, Valentine, that he is not a loving man. He kisses me often, although chastely, and so, too, the others, men and women both. He is full of the spirit of Christ, and the Christians of Alexandria will be fortunate to have him as their bishop.

Many of the Jews of Alexandria have seen the error of their ways and have accepted Jesus as Messiah. We have letters from churches in other provinces which also speak of growing numbers of converts. Cornelius is convinced that the time of the Messiah's second coming is near. The idols of Rome will be tumbled, and the elect will establish a New Kingdom on earth. Christ will separate "the sheep from the goats", and those who have been baptised and believe will be ushered into paradise. Valentine, I cannot bear to think of your soul being cast into hellfire. I beg you to seek out the Christian community in Rome and ask to be instructed in the faith. I pray that when we meet again we will be brothers in Christ.

Please let me hear from you. Theophrastus has volunteered to receive your letter for me.

Your loving friend,
Antonius

XXV

Antonius,

It grieves me to hear that you are still in the thrall of the Christians.
I would think that after the terrible mischief of my sister's death
you might have the sense to see that nothing good comes of
superstition. The Roman gods are silly enough, but at least a
Roman does not claim that his particular deity is One and True,
and that all other gods are false. Here in Rome, temples of Saturn,
Concord, Vesta, Castor and Pollux, and deified emperors ring the
forum. The Temple of Jupiter Optimus Maximus looks down from
the Capitoline Hill. At other places about the city are temples of
Venus, Mars, Minerva, Mercury, Apollo, Luna and a host of other
gods. Isis and Cybele have been imported from the outposts of
empire. In this crowded pantheon there is no room for fanaticism.
All of these petty deities—these images of the human self—coexist
comfortably in the Roman imagination. They stand as symbols of
Roman unity and serve the needs of politics and patriotism rather
than an afterlife. It is hard to imagine any Roman dying for Apollo
or facing the lions for Isis. Only Christians have the arrogance to
believe that God has singled them out of all people to be saved. I
have seen enough of the world, my friend, to know that the gods—
if they exist—have nothing to do with the lives of men. No caring
deity would loose plagues among us. What god worth worshiping
would snuff out the life of a city with volcanic ash? What sort of

god would demand that my sister should surrender her life for him, the sword falling on her slender neck? To worship such a god, Antonius, is not wisdom but madness. You have surrendered your most precious gift—your reason. Epicurus or Lucretius would smile at your infantile notions of heaven and hell. The gods most certainly do not care about our concerns. They do not ask "something for something", nor do they instigate fear and suffering. As Epicurus said, *True religion is the contemplation of things as they are in a spirit of repose.* If we can achieve that, then we are lucky. How foolish to throw away the possibility of natural wisdom and equanimity of spirit to follow an upstart eastern magician who imagines himself the Messiah.

I have not stopped loving you, Antonius; we were too close for that. But I do hold you responsible for Helena's death. The life of an innocent girl has been lost because you took it upon yourself to save her soul. Helena's soul was her own; it shined in her eyes. She was born into goodness; she did not need "saving". And now you worry, too, that my own soul stands in danger of hellfire. What is the source of this unwarranted and pernicious fear? On whose authority do you worry about Acheron's realm? Among the Greeks and Romans the underworld is but a quaint story; you Christians turn Hades into an instrument of fear and oppression. Lucretius says that fear of hell stains everything with death's black darkness, leaves no pleasure pure and clear, and drives men to violate honour, break friendships, overthrow all decencies. And surely he is right. Helena is dead. Antonius is at risk. For what? For the ravings of a madman. Heaven and hell are illusions, dear friend, born of fretfulness. Stop worrying about the afterlife and learn how to live in this world with dignity and equanimity of spirit. Embrace beauty. Enjoy love. And when war and sickness and famine and tempest threaten our contentment, let us use our rational faculties to find ways to alleviate the darkness.

You say that my survival in the sea near Sicily was a miracle, that God has some plan for me for which he preserved my life. I do not know how I survived that storm, and surely I would have drowned had I not found a floating piece of the hippo's shattered cage. I was in the water with Rufi for three hours before we reached the shore.

A dozen times I thought we were finished, but somehow I managed to keep Rufi afloat and moving shoreward. Our survival was an astonishing bit of good fortune, but it was not a miracle. *You* taught me to swim, Antonius. It was with *you* that I practised the skill that saved my life and Rufi's in the shadow of Etna. You say it was God's will that I survived. If I had drowned, then presumably that, too, would have been God's will. Why not just accept that whatever happens is the course of nature? We are buffeted by fate. There are circumstances of our lives over which we have no control. It was certainly through no action of my own that our ship was racked by storm, or that the mountain chose that particular day to spew forth its fiery venom into the sky. No decision of mine brought the great beast aboard our ship, nor set it loose from its cage. Fate cast Rufi into the sea, and unthinkingly I followed. What happened in the water was by my action, not God's. We have within ourselves some modest capacity to hold our destinies on course. If I am alive today, I do not thank Providence. Rather, I thank my friend Antonius who taught me to swim in the sea at Apollonia.

But enough. I have lived long enough to know that religious practice is not amenable to logic. Let me tell you instead of my present circumstances. It has been three years since I came to Rome. Antonius, nothing I could say could help you imagine this city. You could not walk its perimeter in a day. One million Romans live within its walls. Marble buildings and monuments stand on every side. Forums, temples, theatres, stadia. Magnificent thoroughfares. Palaces. Statues. Buildings three, four, even five storeys high. Our home town would nestle snugly into the Circus Maximus. The streets are crowded from dawn to dusk. Every sort of people are to be seen: citizens, freedmen and slaves, rich and poor, from every part of the empire. I have an apartment of two rooms in a multi-storeyed building between the Campus Martius and the Tiber which I share with my servant Rufi. My apartment is on the second floor and looks out at the Theatre of Pompey, which rises at the end of our street like a mountainous wall.

I have established a small but growing practice of medicine, mostly among the shopkeepers and Tiber dockmen of my district. The doctors here are mostly Greek. The great majority of them are faith-healers and quacks. Since they cannot read, they know nothing of Hippocrates and Galenus, although these illustrious names trip easily off their tongues. Some of them practise the healing arts after an apprenticeship of only several weeks. They carry with them many mouldy concoctions of herbals and smelly poultices which they prescribe indiscriminately for whatever injury or disease they encounter. They seem to rely upon the fact that their patients will believe in the efficacy of any remedy that smells sufficiently obnoxious. I am confident that these so-called healers seldom effect a cure, but at least their fraudulent remedies do little damage. They have no theory of disease and therefore no justification for prescribing one cure rather than another, and no knowledge of internal anatomy other than what they have seen hanging in a butcher shop. Of the natural causes of diseases they are ignorant, ascribing most maladies to the influence of gods or evil spirits. Their therapies are as often as not religious purifications and incantations. For epilepsy, one of these charlatans prescribes lying on goatskins! Another forbids baths. Yet another insists on immersion in water. Following Theophrastus, my own practice is to intervene as little as possible, but rather to facilitate for my patients the conditions in which the body can muster its own curative powers. Of course, most of my patients are reluctant to believe that my minimal therapies can be effective and would rather pay exorbitant fees to Greek charlatans to drain their blood or fill their stomachs with foul tasting medicines. Only slowly has word begun to get around that Valentine's record of success is better than that of the mongers of superstition. Balance and harmony of the humours is my touchstone. Fresh food and water, clean air and healthy thoughts can do more good than all the prayers and incantations in the world.

When I am not working, I read. Whatever extra money I have I spend on books to replace those I lost at sea. I ignore the theatre and I have not set foot in the arena. Once each week I visit the Baths of Agrippa. But, Antonius, note this: in this most populous city of the world I find that I am lonely. You are in my thoughts often. Sometimes I think of you with anger, for having led Helena into superstition. More often I recall the good times we had as children and the firm friendship that sustained us. Keep yourself safe, dear friend. I do not know how it is in Alexandria, but in this city Christians are in constant danger.

Valentine

XXVI

When Valentine and Rufi washed up on the Sicilian shore, they were found and cared for by a family of peasants who gave them rest and food and drink. Valentine was anxious to move on to Rome, but first his curiosity about the flaming mountain drove him to Etna's slopes. Rufi balked, terrified, as they approached the lava stream, and as they climbed through acrid smoke and falling ash, Valentine steadied Rufi's nerve. For those who live in Etna's shadow, the mountain's fury is thought to be the work of a local god of the underworld, a cousin, I suppose, of Vulcan. Valentine scoffed at supernatural theories of the fire and wanted to discover the cause for himself. Lucretius spoke of winds rushing through honeycombed hollows of the mountain, fast and furious, heating the rocks to incandescence and causing them to gush from the mountain's throat with fire and brimstone. But Valentine wondered if Lucretius had ever seen Etna in eruption or if his speculations were based on hearsay only. As he climbed the mountain with Rufi, the earth shook beneath their feet; surely something stirred below, but whether it was winds or not Valentine could not say. He wondered if the rumbling might be caused by currents of molten rock coursing through subterranean channels, seeking escape from a cauldron at the mountain's root. What was the source of the mountain's heat? And why was the heat concentrated here and not in some other place? Why in Sicily and not in Egypt, say? Was the heat a fever of the earth? Did the body of the earth suffer from an imbalance of humours, as might the human body? Perhaps the earth, across which he had been sailing for weeks, could itself be likened to a living organism, subject to fits of fever and distemper, and he and Rufi upon the mountain's flank were as lice upon the body of a man. The river of molten rock that streamed down the mountain resembled blood from a wound; the mountain's tremors were like the shaking of a man with fever. How might a physician minister to the earth to restore its balance? Perhaps cool waters from the sea might be sent through underground passages to quench the source of the mountain's fire. Of one thing he was certain: the fiery eruption was not the work of gods.

When at last Rufi could not be made to go a step further, Valentine relinquished his study of Etna's fury and descended to the mountain's base. Now he had to consider how to continue his journey. He had lost his money and his books. Rufi had a few coins secreted in his tunic. With these they purchased grapes, olives and cheese and made their way along the coast road to Messina. There in the harbour was their swan-necked ship, undergoing repairs, cleaning and reloading. The gunwale had been shattered by the hippo, the bulkheads cracked by shifting iron. The hold was awash with oil and the shards of amphora. Valentine and Rufi were welcomed by the master and crew of the ship and by the other passengers as if risen from the dead, their survival acclaimed a miracle. Some treated them as ghosts and kept their distance. Others offered food and drink, as if to gods. Since their passage had been paid for in advance, the two returned passengers were assured a continuation of their journey when the boat was ready.

Three months after leaving Alexandria, twenty-two-year-old Valentine and red-haired Rufi arrived at the Roman port of Ostia at the Tiber's mouth, the magnificent harbour begun by Claudius, completed by Nero and expanded by Trajan. Valentine knew some Roman history from his books, and all of this he communicated to Rufi as their vessel slipped past the lighthouse into the outer basin, then between walls of finely figured stone into the hexagonal inner harbour. Rufi was altogether ignorant of history; to him Claudius, Nero and Trajan were as fabulous as Jupiter and Hercules. But Valentine was deeply impressed by all that the harbour represented—the labours of architects and engineers of what seemed to him an age of heroic grandeur and, of course, majesty of empire.

He stood at the prow of the ship, hands fixed firmly upon the gunwale, as the vessel manoeuvred into position with other ships awaiting a place at the quays.

Everything about Ostia was new and grand and made the harbour at Alexandria seem provincial and small. Vessels from Egypt, Carthage, Iberia, Gaul, Britain, the Greek Isles and the Black Sea jostled prow to stern and side to side, unloading goods to satisfy Rome's insatiable taste for luxury. Slaves sweated on the quays, shifting cargoes from ship to dockside, then into the rows of warehouses that stretched back endlessly from the harbour. Among the sweating labourers moved merchants, bankers, ship-owners, warehousemen, trans-shippers, customs agents, tax collectors, soldiers and people seeking passage to and from all parts of the world. The iron-rimmed wheels of carts rattled on the stones; cranes groaned under their loads. Valentine was not insensitive to the greater meaning of the scene. As his ship rose and fell on the gently pulsing tide, he wondered at this race of men whose might and ingenuity had subdued the world. These Romans were not a subtle people; they cared nothing for nuance or grace. They were a people who felt the masculine pulse of continents, who plundered the tops of mountains and the bottoms of seas to increase their wealth, who could fling roads and sea lanes like spider's silk across a universe of space and time. What was at work here was not an idea, he understood, but a feeling; not something cerebral, but sensual. The hubbub, energy and scale of Ostia's harbour seemed the very antithesis of all that he had learned from Epicurus. There was no repose, no equanimity of spirit; rather what he saw at work here was sweat, muscle, force, clamour and the sweet smell of money. Valentine was both attracted and repelled; attracted to the beauty of irresistible energy, repelled by its unyielding *single-mindedness*. He sensed *even then* that honour bade him return to Alexandria, but a more powerful attraction, obscure and visceral, drew him body and soul into the heat of the commotion.

XXVII

What most struck Valentine about Rome was the contrast between grandeur and squalor, between great wealth and abject poverty, and these extremes I, too, have noticed as if through Valentine's eyes. Grand monuments of marble rise next to crumbling tenements of brick and concrete. Splendid temples and public baths harbour in the midst of slums. Affluent merchants live on the bottom floors of buildings whose upper storeys are jammed with poor. Triumphant arches and statue-capped columns might give the impression that our city is built for eternity, but every day somewhere in the city a shabbily constructed tenement collapses into its foundations, and every night another goes up in flames. Windows in the apartment houses are open or shut: if open in winter, the occupants freeze; if shut, they cower in darkness; if open in summer, the occupants suffer the stench of the city; if closed, they swelter. Heat is provided in winter only by an open brazier—if the occupants can afford fuel—and no provision is made for the escape of smoke. Lamps, too, fill the tiny rooms with soot and grime. Aqueducts bring fresh water into the city, but this is distributed only to the public fountains and homes of the rich, or occasionally to the ground floor of a building. Anyone who can afford the expense employs a servant whose sole task is to bring water for drinking, cleaning and fire prevention.

Every neighbourhood has public latrines, but within the tenements no provision is made for the removal of night soil. Chamber pots fester in the corners of every room, occasionally to be dumped into the nearest cess trench for eventual removal by a manure merchant. The sewers of Rome are one of the glories of the city, but only a fraction of the human waste generated by the teeming thousands makes its way through the sewers to the Tiber; most goes into the streets and gutters. Every alley stinks with ordure; the acrid smell of urine is pervasive. All of this within a few steps of gleaming public spaces immaculately maintained by the civil authorities.

Expansive vistas along the avenue and in the forums invariably give the visitor to our city a sense of spaciousness, but most of the streets that Valentine and Rufi walked as they searched for lodging were zigzag passageways hardly wide enough for a single cart. During daylight hours carts are banned from most quarters of the city, and the streets and lanes are jammed with pedestrians, hucksters, money changers, barbers, beggars, schoolmasters and their students; at night the noise of rattling wagons is incessant. On moonless nights the neighbourhoods of Rome are cast into Stygian gloom, the streets are dark defiles, and only the bravest or the foolhardy venture out. At sunset rich and poor alike take in their flower pots from windowsills, bolt their doors and wait out the night in the safer confines of their own apartments. Carters and footpads inherit the darkness.

Among the teeming tenements, Valentine had no trouble finding patients. Sickness was endemic; accidents and injuries frequent. He ministered to the poor because he lived among them and took what they could afford to pay for his services. It gave him pleasure to serve with skill those who could otherwise win with their pitiful coppers only the ministrations of quacks and astrologers. And he led a chaste life: no chasing after whores as he had done in Alexandria. After his narrow escape at sea, he had decided most fervently to follow his master Epicurus, who wrote that *Sex never benefited anyone*, and took seriously Lucretius's dictum that *Passion plants the seeds of madness*. Valentine thought himself sufficiently armoured by his principles against the common cravings of men—for luxury, extravagant entertainment, sex. He had, after all, the example of his former master Theophrastus, a man who in all things cultivated moderation.

But ideals are notoriously fragile things, especially in a city teeming with greed and licentiousness, which is probably why certain Christian zealots and oracular augers betake themselves to wooded isolation or desert caves. Principles are like marble; they are not easily shattered, but they are subject to slow erosion. There was no time during his time in Rome when Valentine made a conscious decision to renounce his abstemious life. Rather, his ideals of service and temperance were imperceptibly abraded away by rubbing against the rough grain of the city. Within half a dozen years his circumstances changed considerably. He moved into the second storey of a handsome house in a fashionable neighbourhood near the Palatine that turned a blind facade to the busy streets and opened on to a sun-filled courtyard. A dozen chambers: fauces, atrium, alae, triclinium, tablinum and peristylium, plus rooms for servants.

Rufi left his service to join the Imperial Guard, but Valentine brought four new servants into his employ: porter, cleaner, water carrier and cook. His patients were now mostly wealthy merchants, lawyers, magistrates, army officers and their families, who expected to be received by their physician in gracious quarters, and Valentine was unfailing in his hospitality. His earlier commitment to the poor had slipped away as his reputation grew and wealth nibbled away at holy poverty. But to give him his due, no temptation was greater than the opportunity afforded by his new affluence to build up his library again. His house was filled with books. He haunted the stalls and shops of the book merchants. Excess income that others of his class might have spent on lavish entertaining, Valentine spent on the acquisition of fair copies of Roman, Greek and Alexandrian texts.

His chastity, too, was at risk. Increasingly he found that his most avid patients were the wives, mothers, sisters and daughters of the notable men with whom he socialised at the baths. He became, in spite of himself, an authority on hysteria, inflammation of the womb, wandering womb, abnormal menstruation and other female maladies, following in his treatments not only Hippocrates and Galenus, but also Soranus of Ephesus and Aretaeus of Cappadocia. It became evident even to Valentine that many of the women who sought his diagnosis were motivated as much by the desire to be in his company as by any actual symptoms. He must surely have been aware that he was dangerously attractive to his patients. His dark eyes and boyish curls attracted the attention even of women in the street, but it was his distracted intellectuality and disengagement from wanton conduct that women found irresistible. The more he ignored their flirtations and attempted seductions, the more his practice and his library grew. As time passed, he found that invitations into their beds were too enticing to resist. He rationalised these excursions in the service of Eros as a kind of inquiry into the psychopathology of his patients. It was also, he told himself, so much a part of the common behaviour of their class that it was silly to reject their enjoiners.

Meanwhile, Julia's life moved along the path that would bring her and Valentine together. Most decisively, when Julia was twelve years old, I left my post as assistant master at the gladiator school in the Alban Hills to become a jailer for the prefect of Rome. I was given charge of the Tiberian Prison near the Pinciana Gate, with cells enough for five hundred men, mostly common criminals, but with a sprinkling of Christians and runaway slaves. The job was easy enough—I had ample staff—and I was paid a more generous salary than had been mine at the school. To be honest, it was a sinecure provided for me by a friend in the civil administration. However, I brought Julia to the city with considerable misgivings. In our country villa she moved about with an ease born of a dozen years of practice, and she was safe there from the physical and moral contagions of the city. But there were other considerations regarding Julia that inclined me towards Rome. Julia's environment at the gladiator school was excessively male and violent. She had few friends of her own age or sex. As she entered puberty her striking beauty became apparent to all, and the brotherly affection previously shown to Julia by the gladiators became tinged, I observed, with a less filial interest. The last thing I wanted for my Julia was that she might become involved with a man whose life expectancy was measured in months—a few years at most. In the city we were provided a fine house not far from my place of work and sufficient salary to maintain a villa in the country if and when I chose to find one. In the city, too, would be the opportunity for Julia to learn the womanly arts and, when the time came, to make acquaintance with a man of substance and character whom she might marry.

XXVIII

Not until his eighth year in Rome did Valentine attend the games. Rufi, now an officer in the urban cohort, invited him to the Flavian Amphitheatre to view a gladiatorial combat pairing a slave partly owned by Rufi against an Egyptian. On the evening before the games, the two friends visited the banquet at which the fifty fighters of the morrow were feasted by the procurator of games, a certain Quintus Mimmius. At this meal, Rufi's champion, nicknamed Aptus, and his designated opponent ate side by side. Neither spoke the language of the other, but between them there was a fatal camaraderie. Each knew his survival depended upon the other's death, yet he bore no animosity against his rival. There was much laughter and morbid humour. Rufi joked with his man, urging him lightheartedly to moderate his drinking so that he might not be addleheaded in the arena. Valentine sensed an unspoken frisson of hope and fear as each of the many gladiators sought to dispel with loud bravado the possibility of death in the sand.

"Why do they do it?" asked Valentine as he and Rufi returned to Valentine's apartment through the dark streets.

Rufi answered, "For glory. For money. In the case of Aptus, for freedom. He has fought successfully a dozen times. If he wins tomorrow, we have promised him manumission. Then he can continue fighting or not, as he pleases."

"But these men must know that sooner or later their luck will run out. The risk of death seems a high price even for freedom."

"It is a risk worth taking. Consider our man, Aptus. He is strong and agile and prepared for combat. We have given him the best training, and he knows it. He has made his owners a tidy return on their investment"—he rattled the coins in his purse—"and he has enriched himself. Women throw themselves at him. When he fights and wins, fifty thousand people stand to cheer him. Imagine what it must be like to accept the adulation of the arena. To take into his hands the dish of gold and silver coins that comes to the victor. To bask in the emperor's or the prefect's smile. Sometimes I envy him."

"But would *you* fight?"

"It is part of my training as a soldier to fight and kill, and for considerably less reward than might come to Aptus. But no, I would not fight in the arena. The odds are short. I love life too much—the life *you* saved, my friend."

Valentine was silent. Then he said, "It seems a barbaric practice. Those men tonight, they have become friends, some of them. Yet they will kill each other. For . . ."

Rufi interrupted, "Don't be sentimental, Val. Death is the foundation of the empire. Think of how many tens of thousands of men, women and children have died in our wars of conquest. Think of how many Roman legionnaires have fallen in battle. Every block of marble in this city has the price tag of a human life. Every paving stone might as well be the skull of a Gaul or Briton or German or Sythian whose life and fortune was absorbed by Rome. The glory of this city is steeped in blood."

"But we do not revel in the killing of war. Not the way we applaud the slaughter of the arena."

"Of course, we revel in war. The city celebrates every conquest. We raise triumphal arches in memory of our victories. We march our defeated victims through the city streets to the sounds of trumpets and drums and declare holidays whose gaiety and duration are measured by the number of our enemies who were left dead on the field of battle. Make no mistake, Valentine. The expansion of the empire feeds the affluence of Rome. Your own fortune has been taken from peoples of distant places whom our soldiers kill. Ultimately, every sesterce in your pocket has its origin on the bloody perimeter of the empire. When the killing stops, the city dies."

Again, Valentine lapsed into silence. What Rufi said made perfect sense, but still he fished for a flaw in the argument. After a while he said, "Tomorrow will be my first time to the ganes here or in Alexandria."

"Your first?" Rufi was not surprised. He knew his friend was a man of strange philosophies.

"Theophrastus taught me to heal—"

"At least the killing in the arena is honest," said Rufi. "No moralising to hide behind. No cloak of self-righteousness. Our Roman bloodlust is unvarnished. And not just the bloodlust of the audience who cheer the gladiators. Aptus, too, will thrill when his sword slips up under the Egyptian's helmet and the blood gushes downward like water spilled from a bowl." He paused. "Do you believe in an afterlife, Valentine?"

"You know that I do not."

"Then what does it matter?" asked Rufi. "Against the oblivion of eternity, our lives are brief flashes of light. A flurry of atoms, according to your beloved Lucretius. What does it matter if we live for an instant or half an instant if we are destined to be consumed by darkness?"

That night Valentine slept little. His mind kept drifting back to the banquet of the gladiators, to the long, laden tables lined by men whose bodies and minds had been honed to kill. They seemed so ordinary, these gladiators. So likable. It might have been a banquet of tailors or costermongers. Or a feast at the palace of the princeps. These champions had their roles to play in the life of the city, and if it meant that half of them would not survive the morrow, then at least they seemed to willingly accept that terrible prospect. But if death was so much a part of the city's life, if tomorrow fifty thousand Romans would applaud the killing of good men who might in their ordinariness have been tailors or costermongers, then what was the point of his own healing arts? Why struggle to save the life of a child dying of fever when in the arena a hundred lives are snuffed out in one grand entertainment. Galenus insisted that nature, not the heavens, was the basis for medicine. But if an appetite for killing—the doing of it and the watching of it—is part of human nature, then the healing arts have a paradox at their core. The physician saves what the patients squander.

In the morning Valentine made several house calls to patients on the Palatine, then met Rufi at the Temple of Venus in time to enter the amphitheatre during midday intermission. The morning's entertainments had been taken up with various animal hunts and the execution of criminals who had committed capital offences. These last would have been armed as a group and set against one another, without training or preparation of any sort, until all but one lay dead in the sand; the survivor had his sentence commuted from death in the arena to the gladiator school. Some of these condemned men fought to the best of their ability; others simply cowered in terror and waited for the sword to lop off their heads or the trident to plunge into their breasts. Aptus and other professional gladiators, including the famous Flamma, were scheduled to fight in the afternoon.

As Valentine and Rufi approached the oval splendour of the amphitheatre, they encountered a group of Christians, two men and three women, beseeching the milling crowd to forego the games. These zealots prattled on about the teachings of their Messiah, ignoring the taunts and buffets of the jostling thousands who disgorged from the amphitheatre in search of midday refreshment from the many vendors of food and drink. Rufi, mindful of his responsibilities as a captain of the urban cohort, waited to be certain that the Christians were arrested, and indeed soldiers were not long in coming.

"Those Christians have their own tickets to the arena now," said Rufi with a wink.

Rufi and Valentine took their seats in the podium, those rows of benches reserved for patricians and others of special privilege in the city. High above them sailors rigged into place the vast awning, suspended from hundreds of masts, that would shade the audience from the afternoon sun. The scale of the amphitheatre was breathtaking. Valentine had often seen this structure from the outside, but now it seemed as if the great bowl might hold the sky itself. It rose celestially in tiers of marble benches from the blood-soaked sand to the columns that supported the roof of the highest gallery. As Rufi engaged in speculations with his partners—two other officers of the urban cohort with whom he shared ownership of Aptus—Valentine simply gaped at the scale of a building that might be the work of gods, not men.

A fanfare of trumpets announced the prefect's arrival in the imperial box, and the crowd rose to its feet and shouted adulation. Gallienus Narcissus Syrus was a man of immense popularity, a simple and dignified patrician who lent the games an air of refined sensibility. The emperor's seat remained vacant; Claudius II was a soldier rather than a statesman, away tending to problems on the empire's frontier. The first combat on the afternoon card matched the brilliant Flamma against *two* Thracians. Flamma was a tall, muscular Nubian whose black skin glistened in a sheen of oil. His celebrity was ensured by his many and glorious triumphs in the arena. He rode about the streets of Rome in a chariot drawn by matched white horses. Now, as he entered the arena, admirers in the lowest rows tossed flowers and silver bangles into the arena. Flamma bowed graciously to the prefect, then turned to meet his adversaries. The battle was quick and decisive. The two skilled Thracians were dispatched as readily as if they had been unarmed Christians. These were the first men Valentine had seen killed in combat. Their deaths were less disturbing than he had thought they might be; he had after all attended many hundreds of gruesome deaths in his capacity as a physician. But his tolerance for arena violence was now to be tested.

The second combat on the afternoon card pitted a woman gladiator against a male dwarf—an entertaining diversion that appeared to be much to the liking of the audience. The dwarf was armoured as a hoplomachus, with heavy rectangular shield, helmet and short sword. The woman was more lightly armed, with a small, circular shield and long sword. She wore no helmet so that her long hair might fly free, but her right arm was protected by a chain link sheath and her upper body was covered by a leather tunic. She was a young woman, and it quickly became clear to Valentine that both she and her opponent had been trained for their encounter. With her fair skin and flaxen hair, the girl was probably a slave from one of the recent battles on the German frontier. The dwarf was apparently well known to the crowd; he had fought and won in previous games. The two opponents stood side by side and raised their weapons to the prefect. Then they moved to the centre of the arena and began a series of tentative thrusts, sizing up their adversaries. The bets, said Rufi, were on the dwarf, who had easily defeated previous opponents.

But this time it would not be so simple. The woman knew how to use her shield to deflect her rival's blows, and the strikes he directed at her legs she blunted with her sword. Her strategy was defensive, and this she made good; she bided her time, waiting for the dwarf to make a mistake. The minutes passed, and the crowd grew impatient with what seemed to them a spiritless encounter. The dwarf was their favourite, and they wanted a quick kill. Roars of encouragement for the diminutive battler cascaded down from the terraces until the whole bowl of the amphitheatre reverberated with sound. Against his expectations, Valentine found himself emotionally taken up with the dance of death unfolding in the sand. He could not take his eyes off the girl, and his heart stopped with each thrust of the dwarf's short sword. Then she drew blood. The dwarf had glanced briefly toward the prefect, and in that instant of inattention her sword nicked flesh on his upper thigh. He glanced down disbelievingly at the flow of blood, and as he did so she struck again, drawing a gash across his chest; this potentially mortal blow was blunted by the iron ring that connected the leather straps of his sword-arm armour.

The crowd was on its feet, and Valentine held his breath, waiting for the strike from the girl that would finish the awful spectacle. But now the dwarf went mad with pain and anger. He thrashed with fury, driving the woman before him, at last knocking her shield from her grip. She was finished, and her face took on a mask of fear, but still she held the dwarf at bay for a few agonising seconds until his short sword plunged into her belly. She managed a last blow that clanged against his helmet, knocking him momentarily senseless. But it was too late to press home her advantage. She fell forward in a gush of blood. This was what the crowd had come to see, and they poured down approbation on the tiny man, who now pranced, limping and dazed, around the arena, waving his weapon triumphantly above his head. Valentine vomited, soiling the person in front of him, and hurried embarrassed from his seat.

The dwarf was presented with a dish of coins by the prefect and escorted from the arena through the Gate of Life. The body of the woman was dragged with an iron hook through the Gate of Death, and the place where she fell was spread with fresh sand. Trumpets and drums announced the main events of the afternoon. Twenty gladiators marched into the arena pair by pair, each splendidly attired. They lined up before the royal box with empty throne and shouted the salute that had echoed in this amphitheatre for two hundred years: "Hail, Emperor! We who are about to die salute you!"

XXIX

"We shall have to toughen you," said Rufi when next they met.

"I can't explain what happened," said Valentine. "It was involuntary."

They were disrobing in a dressing room of the Antonine Baths.

"You very nearly caused a riot. The man whose toga you soiled turned on me and my companions and demanded satisfaction. I managed to fob him off with a few coins . . ."

"I'll repay you," interrupted Valentine.

Rufi laughed. "No need. The day was profitable. Aptus displayed his usual talent in dispatching the Egyptian. And the victim of your weak stomach quickly realised that it would be foolish to take on three captains of the guard, even if we were unarmed."

"I am sorry I did not stay to watch your Aptus fight."

"I think it was just as well that you departed. If the girl's clean death upset you, some of what followed might have been more unsettling. You have lived too long with your books, Valentine."

"Have you ever killed a man?"

Rufi folded his garments and placed them in the cubicle provided for their storage. His hard soldier's body was much changed from that of the thin boy Valentine had hired in Alexandria. As they stood naked together, Valentine felt soft and unproved.

"No," admitted Rufi gaily. "But I am prepared to kill if I must. I might be transferred to the provinces at any time. We are hard pressed near at home by the Alamanni, in the Balkans by the Goths and in Egypt by that wretched harpy the Queen of Palmyra. How I'd love to relieve Zenobia of *her* head."

"The woman in the arena . . ."

"Not bad." Rufi shook his red curls. "The managers of the games know what they are doing when they recruit the best looking female slaves for these diversions. Every cock in the amphitheatre was stiff when she went down."

Valentine was speechless.

Rufi laughed. "Are you embarrassed? Don't be. Admit that you are normal, Valentine. Give up your Epicurean ideals and join the human race. Why do you think the emperors have endowed the amphitheatre and the baths? To give their subjects an outlet for their normal instincts. So that we don't channel our sexual and bloodlusts into sedition. What other nation has endured so long and with such prosperity?"

Valentine had no answer. He knew that his own emotional reaction to the combat between the woman and the dwarf had had an erotic edge, and he did not know how to separate his disgust with his own carnality from his condemnation of the bloody extravaganza in the amphitheatre. He thought of Nibi, his Nubian whore, dying of plague in her darkened chamber, made putrid and pustular by disease, and of the beauty of the woman warrior in her shiny leather tunic cut down in the sun-baked dust of the arena. He had no context, no scale of values, to reconcile the two images.

They walked silently from the dressing room into the warm tepidarium, and stood for a while watching naked men and boys at games in the gymnasium. Rufi said nothing, but he knew from previous experience that Valentine was made uncomfortable by the voluptuousness of the baths. This mammoth structure, inaugurated by Caracalla and completed by the last of the Antonines, is a monument to sensuality, to the primacy of flesh. The heat, the cold, the wafting vapours, the huge volume of clean water carried by aqueducts from faraway hills, the nakedness, the idle athletic activities, the masseuses, the winding sheets and plush cloths, all convey the same message: the physical supremacy of Rome. No god's temple rivals this hedonistic basilica that celebrates raw corporeal power: sinew and muscle, youth and beauty, skin scraped clean with strigil and rubbed with glistening oil and wax. Yes, flab too, rolls and folds of aged skin, drooping jowls and purple veins, toothless grins and balding pates, but these on men who assert their consequence by airs of wealth and influence. These fat patrician elders swagger with the rest, their shriveled genitals covered by a towel, always in a group of peers. They move confidently among the beautiful boys and fit younger men as if their whispered conversations might consign the fates of all the others.

"*Vina, Venus, balnea corrumpunt corpora nostra—sed vitam faciunt,*" said Rufi, quoting some forgotten Latin source, then added in the dialect of Alexandria, "Wine, women and baths corrupt our bodies—but make life itself."

"Surely there is more to life than this," said Valentine. He visited the baths only in the interest of hygiene, or at least he had convinced himself that this was his motive. But if there is more to life than sensual pleasure, what might that other thing be? Not an afterlife, surely; no reasonable person could hold that view. His books and his work occupied his time, but what might those heady pursuits mean in the grand scheme of things. The Romans gave place of honour in their libraries to Horace, Ovid and Marcus Aurelius, but the teachings of philosophers were ignored in the Senate, the marketplace and on the battlefield. Here, in the library of the Antonine Baths, the treasured volumes rested in their wooden chests, available to all, but seldom read. What bather cared to peruse the musings of some ancient sage when he might instead watch beautiful young men wrestling in the gymnasium, their bronzed bodies perfumed and polished with oil. And as for work—what difference did it make in the final accounting if Valentine relieved a single old man of the pain of gout on a day when one hundred men were butchered in the amphitheatre and thousands more were put to death in Rome's many other venues of execution. Only recently Valentine had heard reports of fifty thousand Goths cut down in a single day on a Danube battlefield by the legions of Claudius; all of Rome celebrated; coins would be struck in all the mints of empire and shields of gold erected in the Senate to celebrate the slaughter. And with this melancholy arithmetic another fact stood firm: most of Valentine's work as healer now consisted of ministering to the imagined ailments of the rich.

Rufi did not press his friend. He knew Valentine had no satisfactory answer to his query.

They repaired to the hot dry bath of the sudatorium, where in steaming mist men of consequence sat side by side talking quietly. One of these was a man whom Rufi had often been assigned to guard, Quintus Mimmius, procurator in charge of the city's entertainments. Quintus was a Greek, a former slave who had risen high in the administration of Philip the Arab, won his manumission and continued to make himself indispensable in the service of all the governments that followed. He lived in an opulent palace on the Esquiline Hill, surrounded by gardens admired even by the emperors, and worked out of spacious offices on the Via Labicana. His responsibilities included all theatrical productions, games and races subsidised by the public treasury. It was said that his salary was a fabulous three hundred thousand sesterces a year, but this was surely only a fraction of the riches that came his way as administrator of a budget of tens of millions. More than anything else, Quintus was a master of the restrained exercise of power; he knew how to insinuate his influence into every quarter of the governance of Rome, without overreaching to such an extent that he excited jealously among those who might cast him down. His many enemies were invariably to be found among his lessers, and to protect himself and his family from these jealous rivals, he availed himself of the services of imperial guards, of which Rufi had been one, as even now a soldier in uniform stood watching at the door of the sudatorium.

"Ah, my red-headed protector," said Qunitus on recognising Rufi. He was a man in his fifties, still fit and lean, darkly handsome, but with a dropped lid on his left eye and a curl to his lip that made his face oddly asymmetric. His shoulder was scarred with an old wound, the long line of a blade. His posture made no concession to his nakedness. His penis was short, thick and semi-erect.

Rufi offered greetings with appropriate deference.

"Your friend?" inquired Quintus, nodding toward Valentine, who stood nakedly vulnerable to the procurator's gaze. Quintus dominated his less physically impressive companions, men whose loose and sallow skin marked them as merchants or administrators.

Valentine was introduced. "He is a superb physician," added Rufi, "one of the best in Rome."

"What does he know about the maladies of women?" asked Quintus.

"As a matter of fact, that is his specialty," replied Rufi. "But it is not his only skill."

Valentine stood embarrassed, by his nakedness and by Rufi's praise.

"Have him come to my house tomorrow at the ninth hour," said Quintus, and turned back to his companions without addressing a word to Valentine.

Valentine and Rufi distanced themselves from the procurator and his friends. They moved to a bench at the opposite end of the sudatorium and maintained a deferential silence. In a few moments, Quintus and his companions moved to the caldarium.

When they were gone, a grinning Rufi broke the silence: "Now, my friend, you have a chance to become a wealthy man."

XXX

Dear Valentine,

A new year. How many years has it been since we exchanged letters? Five? Six? I have forgotten. Much has happened, but first the news you will not want to hear. Your mother, father and Olivia are dead of the plague. This news comes to me in Alexandria by your son, Philip, who was here in search of you. It seems that Olivia on her deathbed told him who was his father. He found me here, God knows how, and asked for you. I told him you had left the city, but that I did not know where you had gone. I honoured your wish to let him be, but wondered if you might now have changed your mind. I have no more news of him. He seems earnest and serious, and full of anger, and except for the anger he reminded me of you. More bad news: your friend and mentor Theophrastus is also dead at the age of sixty-three. I passed his house several months ago and saw that the door was sealed and marked with a notice of the city magistrate. Asking about, I discovered that he had died three days previously. He passed away in the night, apparently without suffering, and left behind no family, although among his neighbours many grieve his passing.

So much has transpired here to make it difficult to think of old friends. As you have no doubt heard in Rome, Alexandria is in turmoil. Our governor, Probus, went off as commander of a Roman fleet to counter a force of Gothic ships that was ravaging the Aegean.

Zenobia, the Palmyrene queen, took advantage of his absence to attack Egypt, with her allies the Syrians. Some Egyptians under a local rascal named Timagenes also took up arms against Rome, and together the invaders and the insurrectionists have occupied much of lower Egypt. Only Alexandria remains under Roman control. The city is awash in intrigue and revolution. Probus is said to be returning. Everyone fears for his life and fortune.

I have much to be fearful for. I am married and have three children, a boy and two girls. I make my living as a clockmaker. You would marvel, Valentine, to see what your old friend is up to. My water clocks are among the most accurate of those made in Alexandria, with cylinders engraved for every month of the year and for the degree of elevation of the sun at whatever city they will be used. A system of floats activate chimes that ring the hour, a feature of my own invention. Many of my clocks have been exported to Rome; perhaps you will see one there; look on the cylinder's base for my stamp, a circled "A". My shop is in the forum near the Temple of Serapis, and until the recent turmoils it was visited by one and all. Now I must keep the shutters closed and the door bolted. The magistrates are unable to maintain order in the city, and looters and troublemakers roam the streets.

I met my wife, Justine, six years ago. She was not a Christian but adhered instead to the cult of Isis. I was not successful in bringing her to the Christian faith. It was then, as now, a dangerous thing in Alexandria to confess Jesus Christ, and Justine was frightened for herself and her family. Afraid for me, too, and for the child of mine that she carried in her womb. Cornelius, our bishop, forbade me to see her. She was unclean, he said, not only with the sin of Eve and with a child conceived in sin, but also with the stain of false gods. I was torn, Valentine, between my love for Justine and my love of Christ. I chose Justine. I worried that by choosing her I had damned my soul to hell, and Cornelius said as much when he cast me out of the Church, but now I have come to understand that God, if he is good, will welcome me to paradise. I am a faithful husband and father; I work hard; I am happy. Justine continues to make sacrifice to Isis, and I wait until such time as the Christian Church in Alexandria accepts me back into its company. That time may be coming soon; Cornelius has departed for Rome and has appointed a new bishop in his stead. Perhaps the new man will be more forgiving.

I have not been back to Apollonia since I came here. I do not even know if my own parents are alive or dead. It is my earnest prayer that you are in good health and that this letter will somehow find its way into your hand. I address it simply "Valentine, Physician, Rome".

Your loving friend,
Antonius

XXXI

a.d. iv Kal. Aprilis
Rome

Dear Antonius,

Your letter has been received at last, although how long it has been in transit I do not know. More than a year, certainly, as the person who finally put it into my hand has held it since November. I wish it had borne better news. I grieve for my parents, although it has been so long since I have seen them that they might as well have been already dead. I grieve, too, for Theophrastus, who was like a father to me; it was he who set me on the journey that I continue to travel. As for Olivia, I can hardly evoke her face. A thin girl, serious, who surrendered her virginity to mine, and whom I abandoned. The boy. It is just as well that you did not tell him where to find me. He will make his own way in the world, as I did. Let us hope that he has better luck.

I envy you, Antonius, for your wife and children, for your craft and for the steadfastness of your life. My own life has taken an untoward turn, and for the first time since I came to Rome I find that I am powerless to control my destiny. For a long time I lived according to the principles of Epicurus, eschewing the pleasures so dear to Romans. I avoided the theatre, the races and the games, and kept to my medical practice and my books. But this is not a city in which to live as an Epicurean. There is no restraint among the Romans. They are a debauched people, preferring excess. Against my will and better judgment, I find that I am slipping into their habits.

It began innocuously enough. From being physician to the poor, I found myself increasingly ministering to the affluent. It was easier, required less attention and was more remunerative—more money for my library, more time for my studies. Most of my new patients suffered trivial complaints or imagined their maladies. I treated them as often with placebos as with medicines. Seldom was I required to intervene surgically. I struggled, however, to be honest and true to the principles of my masters, Hippocrates, Galenus and Theophrastus. I cured when I could and otherwise did no harm. I had few friends, and none as close as my former servant Rufi, who came with me from Alexandria. He is now a centurion in the urban guard. It was he who introduced me to Quintus—and thereby added another turn to my career.

Imagine this, Antonius: a house of forty-seven rooms, constructed entirely of marble. A peristyle with a pool large enough for swimming. Gardens flowing down the Esquiline Hill, surrounded by a high wall and containing plants and animals of every continent. An aviary filled with exotic birds. So many servants I cannot give you a count. This is the house of Quintus Mimmius, procurator of the public entertainments of Rome, and it is to him that I now dedicate my services as private physician. I minister only to Quintus, his wife, his mistresses, his family and servants, and for this I am paid more than double what I previously earned from my general practice among the affluent of Rome.

One might think that in these new circumstances I have yet more time for my studies. But alas, Antonius, the opposite is true. I seldom read. My library goes untended. I spend my time at the baths, the theatre, even the amphitheatre, with Quintus and his companions. And the irony is this—I do not particularly like these people. They are crass, presumptuous, decadent and cruel. But I find that I am reluctant to cut the tie that binds me to them, and perhaps also a bit afraid. If I were to leave the service of Quintus without his permission, he could make my life difficult in the city. He might even have me killed. But I would be dishonest if I said that fear is the only thing that binds me to him. I find that I *like* the luxury of my present position. I am attracted to the beauty of these people and to the beauty of their surroundings. Against all my former principles, I find that Roman decadence is seductively attractive. And one more thing: Lycisca, the wife of Quintus, has become my obsession.

It is a dangerous path that I am on. Was it Juvenal who wrote: *What does Venus care when she's drunk? She can't tell head from tail when she eats big oysters at midnight, and when her perfume foams with undiluted wine, and when in her dizziness the roof turns round and the table rises up to meet the lights.* I am bound to Lycisca by a thousand delicious threads. The games we play are like a drug. Even if I wanted to leave her company, I could not. Ostensibly my task—assigned by Quintus—is to treat her "frigidity", but I assure you, Antonius, that there is nothing to treat. She is certainly not without passion. She is simply bored with her husband and tired of being called into his bed when he wearies of his many mistresses. She is an intelligent woman, high born, with more gifts of heart and mind than her husband—a former slave!—might ever dream of. She is not yet my lover, but every day we move closer to that consummation. I know that she is as intent as I to bring our affair to its inevitable conclusion. Quintus suspects nothing.

My employer has one child, Maxi, a boy, upon whom he dotes. The lad is only fourteen years of age, but already Quintus takes him everywhere—to the baths, to the races, to the gladiator barracks of the imperial schools and to the emperor's menagerie outside the Praenestine Gate. The boy is sickly and pale, to the father's chagrin, and Quintus bids me bring the lad to robust health and stamina. This I try to do by a strict regime of exercise and diet, but in the miasmic air and general filth of the city, I fear there is not much I can do. I beg Quintus to let the boy go to live in one of the procurator's country villas, but he will not be parted from the child. The boy is greatly attached to his mother, which is, I suppose, along with her family connections, one reason Quintus keeps Lycisca as his spouse.

You see, Antonius, why I envy your quiet domesticity. And why I earnestly wish you safety and peace. The turmoils of Egypt are repeated on every side of the empire. Even in Italy the army is pressed. No sooner is insurrection quelled in one province than it flares up in another. It has been a long time since the emperor was in Rome; he knows that his survival as princeps requires him to keep the enemy far from our city walls, so that his subjects can continue to live as if war and insurrection did not exist, enjoying the spoils of conquest and learning new ways to indulge their taste for extravagance and impudicity. Yesterday I saw—with Quintus and his son—two tigers, sent as tribute to Rome by a potentate of India! Tigers, Antonius! The question was what to do with these magnificent beasts. To what imperial entertainment might their slaughter be put? Some among Quintus's lieutenants wish to stage a re-creation of an imperial tiger hunt in India, with elephants and a hundred eastern slaves dressed in the splendid regalia of that region. Quintus leans towards a more subtle contest—the two tigers versus a single champion armed only with a knife. As we departed the animal compound the issue was not resolved, but think, Antonius, of what power exists in the hands of this man who can squander homage from the rulers of distant empires to satisfy the Roman desire for momentary novelty.

I am glad to hear that you are no longer keeping the company of Christians, even if your separation from them is involuntary. Here in Rome it is still dangerous to announce oneself as a follower of the Nazarene. Each week we see further executions, some in the arena. The severity of the persecutions waxes and wanes with the fates of our armies abroad. When Roman legions are defeated in Egypt or the Danube, more Christians lose their heads in Rome.

Be well, my friend,
Valentine

XXXII

As one of the chief suppliers of criminal candidates for the imperial gladiatorial schools, it was inevitable that I would have frequent contact with Quintus, the procurator of the games. It was through this contact that the threads of fate binding Julia and Valentine were drawn more tightly together.

Julia was late reaching puberty; she was fourteen when she first menstruated, at least a year behind her contemporaries. Desso had prepared her for the flow, but still the first bleeding evoked a drastic change in the girl's behaviour. Whereas before she had been an unfailingly cheerful child, full of life and curiosity, now she became moody and depressed, rising late in the morning and spending long hours of the day sulking in her room. She lost her appetite and became dangerously thin. Or so I thought. In any case, I became concerned for her health, and once, in the company of Quintus, when he commented on the weakness of his son, I mentioned that my daughter, too, was frail. He was immediately curious. Why he might be interested in the health of my child I did not know. He volunteered to send his personal physician to examine her. I accepted only because it was wise to accept anything Quintus suggested. I had no wish for Quintus to have contact with Julia. He was a man with a reputation for soiling any girl who took his fancy, no matter how young or inexperienced, and he had the power to make these abominations happen without consequence to himself. Quintus was a man who took what he wanted from the powerless, leaving wrecked lives in his wake.

And so it was that Valentine came to our house. He was gentle and well-spoken, not at all the sort of person I associated with Quintus and his circle. He apologised for intruding and gave me to understand that Quintus had *insisted* that he come. We talked for a bit, and our conversation turned to Alexandria and Theophrastus. It was with some happy surprise that I recognised in Valentine the boy who had been present at Julia's birth those many years before. Immediately, my misgivings disappeared and I invited him to examine Julia. I told him of the changes that had accompanied the coming of her menses and led him to her room. Desso, Julia's nurse, came with us. Julia, of course, did not welcome our intervention. She huddled into a corner of her bed, her knees drawn up under her chin. Her dark eyes glowered under long lashes. It took Valentine only a moment to realise that she was blind.

He spoke quietly. "Julia, I am Valentine. I am a doctor, and your father has asked that I have a look at you. He is concerned for your well-being."

I added, "Valentine was present at your birth, Julia. In Alexandria. He was assistant to the doctor who brought you into the world."

She spoke nothing but wrapped her body more tightly with her thin white arms and shrank against the wall. Her eyes seemed to dart about the room, as if she were looking for a way of escape, but of course Valentine understood that she saw nothing. Her fine dark hair was uncombed. The bedclothes in disarray.

"I don't want to inconvenience you," said Valentine. "Perhaps we could talk. I am sending your father away. Your nurse . . .?"

"Desso," I said.

". . . Desso will stay with us."

"Please go away," Julia whispered.

"Yes, I will, of course, go away if that is what you wish. But can't we at least have a talk first? You father is leaving . . ."

"I know he is leaving."

"Yes. Desso is with us . . ."

"Please don't condescend to me," said Julia sharply. "I know who is here."

And that was the last of what I heard. I resisted my curiosity and left them to it. Valentine was with Julia for half of the hour. When he emerged from her room I queried him.

"I did not examine her physically," he said. "We talked. Or rather, I talked and Julia occasionally responded." He smiled. "She was not forthcoming. She is a strong-willed girl, even in her unhappiness. She is angry that you brought me here."

"Is she ill?"

Valentine considered for a moment. "No, I don't believe there is anything *organically* wrong with the girl, nor does there seem to be any unbalance of humours. She is confused and frightened. I believe it may have something to do with the onset of her menses, the realisation that she is no longer a little girl. She is frightened of the city and homesick for whatever place it was you lived in the country. Make sure she is confident of your love. Help her find a friend if she doesn't have one, a girl of her own age. Encourage her to go out."

None of what Valentine said was particularly useful. He merely stated the obvious. Julia showed no interest in the few friends she already had. She refused to go out. Certainly, there was no reason that she should not be confident of my love. And so Quintus's illustrious physician departed, and I put him out of my mind.

Two days later a Gallic pony was delivered to our house. It was from Valentine, and it would be the last I would see or hear of him until he was placed in my custody two years later.

XXXIII

Did something pass between Julia and Valentine during those few moments they spent together, some ineffable communication that would make their amour inevitable? There was no sign of it then from Julia. Only later, much later, did she tell me that Valentine's voice had lodged itself in her ear—*Perhaps we could just talk. I am sending your father away.*—lodged itself there and continued whispering during all of the following weeks and months until they met again—*Perhaps we could just talk. I am sending your father away.*—and always she sought to invent a face for the voice, until finally Valentine's dimly remembered voice and the voice that spoke to her in her religious ecstasies became the same voice: *In a short time you will no longer see me, and then a short time later you will see me again.* And the pony? Why would a physician, out of his own purse, gift my daughter with the animal? Something about his interview with Julia had lodged itself with Valentine, too. Perhaps he did not realise how much my pretty daughter had caught him in her spell. Did her image, dishevelled upon the bed, lovely in her dishevelment, trouble *his* dreams, too? When he saw her again, in his cell at the Tiberian Prison, I recognised in his startled eyes the re-emergence of something lost, now found.

There is no way to explain these things, these choosings by Eros. Fate, we say: the gods, the stars. Or accident, silly chance. Explaining love is best left to poets, not to philosophers or astrologers, or, least of all, to the father of a wounded heart. The pony, of course, was Julia's salvation. It took our garden as its domain, and I arranged for fodder to be brought from the imperial stores. There was hardly room in our small space to ride, but Julia loved to climb upon the pony's back and lay her body along its neck. She named the pony Mel, for I told her of the animal's honey-coloured coat. Occasionally, on days when I was not occupied at work, we would lead the pony out of the Pinciana Gate into the countryside north of the city. There Julia could ride to her heart's content, with no equipage but a bridle, and between herself and Mel there developed a mutual affection that alleviated her unhappiness and sent her flying back into her carefree childhood, with her hair streaming in the wind and a pony for her eyes. Once I borrowed a horse and we rode together to the sea. On the long soft strand, she galloped with abandon and took her pony deep into the licking tide until she felt the warm sea on her calves and thighs. The sun warmed our faces, Tyrrhenian breezes cooled our bodies, and the tumult of the city was forgotten as I waited, holding my steed by its bridle, as Julia galloped along the shore. I felt that if her moment of happiness could be extended for ever, I would surrender my own future happiness for that prospect.

XXXIV

The garden of Quintus was vastly more spacious than our own. It stepped in terraces down the Esquiline Hill. Nothing so ordinary there as a Gallic pony. To the imperial zoo came animals from all over the world, and Quintus had his pick of these for his private garden. Peacocks from the East with regal fans. A pair of red deer from Germany. Monkeys from Africa. Hedgehogs from Britain. These many animals wandered among the fruit trees and flowering plants that overhung the pools and streams that kept the garden cool even in the heat of summer. Eight aqueducts brought hundreds of millions of gallons of water into the city every day, but little of this immense supply found its way to private houses, and none at all into the homes of the poorer sections of the city. But Quintus and other high officials had as much water as they desired. The cisterns of his palace were always full. These fed the basins of the atriums and peristyle, which overflowed into the garden streams and pools and finally emptied their contents, still clean and fresh, into the sewer at the foot of the Esquiline Hill.

The apartment of Quintus's wife Lycisca opened on to the highest terrace of the garden, where blackbirds and nightingales sang in a netted courtyard. It was here that Valentine first visited his "patient". He had been apprised by Quintus of his wife's "complaint". But he had also been advised by Quintus to treat Lycisca without her knowing that it was her husband who had sent the physician to her. When Valentine was ushered into the courtyard, Lycisca was being read to by a female slave, the poetry of Ovid. He apologised for interrupting her and introduced himself as Quintus's personal doctor.

"For what does Quintus need a physician?" asked Lycisca. "He has never been ill a day in his life."

She was an attractive woman, some years older than Valentine but much younger than her husband. She wore a gown of yellow silk, and her hair was braided with blossoms from the garden. There was firm resolve about her mouth and eyes, which were inclined to intimations of smiles but gave little away. Her most striking feature, observed Valentine, were her long and graceful fingers, which moved continuously against the silk of her gown as she spoke.

"He wishes to make me available to his family—to yourself and to your son—and to his servants and slaves," replied Valentine. Then added hesitantly: "In case of need."

"What you will mostly be asked to do is abort his many illegitimate offspring," said Lycisca without a trace of embarrassment or irony.

It was Valentine who was embarrassed. He glanced involuntarily to the slave girl. Lycisca caught his gesture.

"Don't worry about *her*," she said. "There is not a woman in this household whom Quintus has not debauched at one time or another." That flickered smile, the flowing fingers. "I have long since ceased to keep track of the mistresses he keeps in apartments all over town."

"I know nothing of that," said Valentine.

"Well, you will know about it soon enough," replied Lycisca. She shooed away the slave girl and spoke more intimately. "Where are you from?"

"Cyrenaica. By way of Alexandria. I have been in Rome for eleven years."

"It doesn't show."

"What?"

"You seem much too naive to have been in this city for so long. No one in Rome blushes. You blush."

Lycisca rose from her couch. She smoothed her gown against her legs.

"Come," she said. "Let's walk in the garden."

Valentine found that he was pleased to be near her. She was unlike any woman he had known before—confident, intelligent and subtle, regal in the way she held her head and shoulders. Her breasts were full and firm, her belly flat.

"What does Quintus want of me?" she asked.

Valentine shook his head as if he did not understand.

"Again," she said. "Blushing. You need not be embarrassed. Quintus is always suggesting that there is something wrong with me because I do not share his insatiable appetite for perversity. What has he told you? That I am frigid? That I am nonorgasmic?"

They stopped by a pool as two tame red deer came up to Lycisca. From the folds of her sleeve she took out small lumps of sugar which she fed to the animals.

"He asked only that I treat any complaints that you might have."

Lycisca laughed, for the first time out loud. "I assure you, dear Valentine, that I am in the best of health—as you can see. It is Quintus who could use a doctor—to cure him of his concupiscence."

"Why do you . . .?"

"Why do I stay with him?" It was not the question he was about to ask, but it was appropriate. "The answer is obvious. Look around you. I want for nothing. For all of this I need only put up with his occasional connubial maulings. The question you might rather ask is, 'Why does he stay with me?' And the answer to that is also obvious. It was *my* family who placed him in his position of power. And *my* family has the power to ruin him."

"You need not fear that I will betray your confidences," said Valentine, suddenly apprehensive.

She touched his cheek with a long finger. "How did a person such as yourself get mixed up with Quintus? His friends and accomplices are usually as priapic as himself." She paused. "Why have you never taken a wife?"

Was it that *obvious?* wondered Valentine, but he answered honestly, explaining himself as best he could.

Lycisca laughed. "I've never understood philosophy. Ideas are such insubstantial things. Daydreams, really. Sooner or later one wakes up and realises that what seemed so real was only an illusion." She spread her hands. "Why would anyone prefer the *supposings* of philosophers to flesh and blood? The Christians, for example; they are so eager to surrender their lives for an idea, giving up *all of this* . . ." She stroked the deer's fine downy nose. ". . . for an illusion of immortality. And you, Valentine, give up the satisfactions of a woman's love for the abstractions of Epicurus."

"Ideas are perhaps more substantial than you think. I have spent the past dozen years reading Greek philosophy. Mathematics, astronomy . . ."

"Tell me, Valentine, what did philosophy do for the Greeks? Rome made short work of them. I have Greek slaves." She laughed. "Greeks comb my hair, bathe me, dress me. And I haven't an idea in my head of mathematics or astronomy."

"Rome couldn't exist without an idea—the *idea of Rome,* if nothing else."

"Rome is not an idea," she laughed. "Rome is Quintus. Rome is steel and stone. The Caesars *invented* Rome. Not out of an idea, but out of marble. This city has a dozen gates, and what goes in and out of those gates are not ideas, but material things, weighty things, things you can hold in your hands." She gently cupped the deer's face in her hand.

Valentine was silent. The appropriate arguments to refute Lycisca hesitated at the tip of his tongue. He thought of a dozen relevant quotes from Epicurus and Lucretius. But he was silent. He was silent because suddenly his philosophy did seem weightless. It was not the profundity of Lycisca's cynicism that silenced him. It was the force of her beauty. Not a girl's beauty. She was not *pretty.* Her beauty was hard and sure. It showed in the way she held the head of the deer, firmly, possessively. It manifested itself in the unembarrassed curve of her exposed breast when she raised her hand to her hair. It showed in the golden straps of her sandals and the matching paint of her toenails. It showed in the refractory light of her eyes that seemed to burn his cheek.

"What do *you* want, Valentine?" she asked.

He walked away from her and sat down on a bench of fine black granite. *What do* you *want, Valentine?* No one had asked him that question before. He had not even asked it of himself. If anyone other than Lycisca had asked the question, he might have answered: *I want to master the healing arts because the secrets of human health are hidden in the world. I want to understand warmth, cold, dryness and moisture, and how these reside in the atoms, and how to achieve balance in their mixture and expression. I want to understand the innermost machinery of nature, by close observation and reflection.* But he understood that if he answered thus to Lycisca she would laugh, and he knew that she would be right to laugh. Even as he rehearsed the answer in his mind, he had begun to laugh himself. The words did not match the person he had become. True, he still bought books compulsively, but they mouldered on his shelves like gold shut up in chests. He had not performed an anatomical dissection in years. He now spent more time at the baths and in the forum than at the practice of his craft.

She came and sat beside him on the bench. He was suddenly conscious of intense fragrances of orange blossoms and another plant he did not recognise. She pressed his silence. "Do you *know*, Valentine? Do you know what you want?"

He thought that she might be offering herself.

He returned the question, "Do *you* know what *you* want?"

She laughed without hesitating. "Oh, yes. I want to wake in the morning in cool silk sheets. I want to look in the mirror and like what I see. I want to feel warm water sluice down my legs when I step from my bath. I want a pretty girl to be waiting with a clean dry towel. I want her to braid fresh flowers into my hair. I want a handsome young doctor to sit beside me on the bench. I want Quintus to stay away from my bed."

And what would I answer? thought Valentine. *I attend the baths for hygiene's sake only. I eat and drink to be nourished. I have committed to memory the three books of Galenus, but I have no real patients to treat. If I look into the mirror, I see a man who has grown soft and unprincipled.*

Lycisca leaned toward Valentine so that she almost whispered in his ear. She said, "If Quintus saw us sitting here he would know immediately that I desire you, and your life would be forfeit." She stood up and smoothed her gown against her belly. "I would seduce you, Valentine, but I like you too much to wish you dead. An unusual sentiment on my part, since I am used to having what I want. In that way, I suppose, I am like my husband."

"What makes you think I am seducible?" It was his first gambit in a game she was defining on her terms.

She looked at him with bemused condescension. "*Every* man is seducible. I have not yet met a man who does not think with his cock. You are all so terribly predictable."

"Perhaps I am the man who is the exception to your rule."

"Then you would be either a eunuch or a child, and therefore of no use to me at all," she said. She turned and walked back to the courtyard. He was bewildered as he saw her go, her golden feet flashing on the marble steps. He knew that he had been inextricably drawn into her life. And he knew that an affair with Lycisca would be a dangerous sport.

XXXV

Valentine asked Rufi to accompany him to the theatre. He had heard that the *Laureolus* of Catullus was on offer at the Pompey. He did not know the play, but he understood that it was a glory of Roman literature, and he was acquainted with certain other works of Catullus. Since his visit with Lycisca he had decided to engage more fully with the life of the city, to become a proper Roman. Lycisca, he knew, was a frequent theatregoer. It might sit well with her if he were seen at a public entertainment in the company of the popular Rufi.

As they entered the theatre, Valentine was struck by the size of the structure. Thirty thousand seats rising like the slopes of a vast hemispherical valley. The plebs in the highest terrace could hardly see the stage, he imagined, much less hear the spoken words.

"Have you ever wondered how it is that our Roman government has lasted so long?" asked Rufi. "Longer than any other state in the history of the world."

Valentine laughed. He had heard all this before.

"Your Quintus is the most important person in Rome. More important than the princeps, more important than the Senate, more important than the magistrates. Emperors come and go, but the public entertainments endure, and with them the state."

"Aren't you forgetting the army? Without the army the empire would be crushed from the outside, like a tent collapsed by the wind." Valentine was pleased with his analogy.

"Rebellious citizens are of more danger to the state than a horde of half-civilised barbarians ten thousand stadia away. There will always be ambitious men like myself to wield the sword on distant battlefields. But let there be idle and disgruntled citizens at home and the tent would collapse from within, as if someone pulled down the supporting pole."

Thousands of people streamed with them into the theatre. The well-to-do took seats with Valentine and Rufi in the lower tiers; the poor climbed to the highest benches.

Rufi gestured about him. "The genius of government is to provide the people with what they think they need. Romans have become addicted to these extravaganzas, as to opium or wine. The government exploits their addiction."

"The people also need to eat," said Valentine.

"They have their bread. Ships full of grain from Africa clog the Tiber wharves."

"Yet they die by the thousands of disease."

"Romans have a keen sense concerning what is the responsibility of government and what is the responsibility of the gods. If a child dies of plague, the parents do not blame the emperor; they blame themselves for failing to say their prayers or for making insufficient sacrifice. But if the child dies of hunger, not even cheap theatre seats will save the government from their discontent."

"The government abets malevolent gods when they allow the poor to live in excrement."

"You are too gloomy, Valentine. Surely excrement in no more unhealthy *outside* the body than inside. Stop thinking about medicine for a change and enjoy the spectacle of the crowd."

In this Rufi gave good example. He seemed to salute everyone, bantering with the men, flirting with the women. Valentine envied his guileless friendliness, his easy repartee. As Rufi played the charmer, Valentine scanned the crowd for Lycisca. So intent was he upon finding her face that he hardly noticed when the play began. There was no immediate diminution in the hubbub of the crowd. Only slowly and distractedly did the audience turn their attention to what was happening on the stage. The voices of the actors were drowned out by the chatter of the audience. When at last he turned to the performance, Valentine found himself almost alone in giving his full attention to the drama of Catullus.

What he now saw and heard at the stage was an apparent chaos of actors, a cacophony of shouted voices and chants. He certainly did not recognise the play he had heard so much about, a supposedly dignified entertainment on the merits of good government and the certainty of justice. His expectations for the theatre had been shaped by reading the plays of Terence, Plautus and the Greeks—actors speaking parts, a chorus. What he saw instead was a single actor pantomiming the story in dance and gesture, surrounded by others, men and women, who swayed to and fro, chanting and singing, and musicians with lute, flute, trumpet and cymbals. Characterisations were signalled by a code of colour and dress that was, he assumed, understood by the audience through long experience: white for an old man, multicoloured for a youth, yellow for a strumpet, purple for the rich, red for the poor, and so on. A short tunic signified a slave, a short Greek cloak a soldier, a rolled cloak for the hanger-on. The hands of the mime articulated every nuance of horror, fear, joy, sorrow, hesitation, repentance, abandonment, transformation. Only upon close attention to all of this did Valentine get the drift of the story, but always there was some exaggerated thing to grasp the audience's attention—a lascivious gesture, a bared breast, a ludicrous pratfall. Inexorably the play wound towards its climax, with actions and voices becoming ever more fabulous—the rough and tumble of simulated violence. As the play approached its conclusion, the brigand protagonist was put to the torture. His anguish seemed unfeigned.

Rufi noticed Valentine's puzzlement and discomfiture. "If you had been watching more closely, you would have seen the switch," he said. "The actor has been replaced by a condemned criminal."

At first Valentine did not understand Rufi's meaning. But then he became aware of a sudden stillness that had come over the audience as they gave their full attention to the action on the stage. The instruments of torture were not props. The blood was real. The terror of the victim genuine. The mime, now stripped to a loincloth, body glistening with sweat, whirled with fevered ardour, coughing out his words. The company of dancers and musicians convulsed in ecstasy. Women in the audience gasped their delight.

At that moment Valentine caught sight of Lycisca, some distance across the theatre. She had her arms about her slave girl, whose head was turned to Lycisca's breast. Without any volition on his part, Valentine's attention pendulumed between Lycisca and the excruciating agonies being inflicted upon the screaming counterfeit actor. Lycisca's eyes were unwavering—they followed the mime, who signalled by his frenzied gestures the cruel denouement—her hand meanwhile gently stroking the slave girl's head. Then a swelling hum went up from the audience, rising tier by tier, growing in intensity, practised by habit, until it seemed it must fill all of the air above Rome, and broke—crashed in a descending roar, as at the intersection of twenty thousand rapt gazes a knife was plunged into the throat of the condemned brigand.

In the chaos that followed the drama's end, Valentine lost sight of Lycisca. Rufi noticed how his eyes swept the crowd.

"Who is it you are looking for?" he asked.

Valentine shook his head. "No one."

"Some girl, no doubt. And about time, too. Tell me who she is."

"I thought I saw Quintus's wife."

"Quintus's wife! Lycisca! Val, you play with fire."

"I met her only once . . ."

"That woman has been responsible for the disappearance of more young men . . ."

"There is nothing between us."

"Val, for your sake, stay on the good side of Quintus. Take his money. Enjoy the good life. But don't entangle yourself with Lycisca."

They stood in their places, waiting for the crowd to thin.

Valentine nodded towards the stage. "Did I see what I thought I saw?"

"Are you surprised?"

"Nothing about this city would surprise me."

"Condemned criminals have been used in the theatre for hundreds of years. I believe it was the emperor Domitian who first allowed it. Some emperors have been more approving than others, some less. Our Gothicus Maximus is too busy to care. He leaves such things to his procurator of games."

"Does it happen often?"

"Often enough. A few weeks ago on this very stage we saw Prometheus nailed to his cross and torn by the claws of the Caledonian bear. It was an astonishing spectacle—insofar as Romans are able to be astonished by anything. The pressure is on Quintus to provide ever more titillating amusements. And Val, I wouldn't be surprised if one of these poor fellows we see killed on the stage had committed no more crime that slipping into Lycisca's bed."

"She doesn't strike me as that sort of woman. She is intelligent. She comes from a noble family. She is appalled by Quintus's excesses."

Rufi laughed as he led Valentine down the ramp that opened on to the street. "If you are interested in women, Valentine, I can introduce you to the finest courtesans in the city. If you have a brain in your head, you will stay away from Lycisca."

XXXVI

Julia was suddenly very grown up. The Gallic pony given to her by Valentine became her consuming passion. For the first time she had responsibility for another creature, and this overflowed into a keen new sense of self-responsibility. Desso was getting old and frail and not so able as before to run our household. Julia therefore took up some of Desso's duties, cooking, washing, seeing to it that a fresh toga was laid out for me each morning. She refused to let me hire another servant, knowing that Desso would feel put aside. Also, Julia became more interested in my work—and she did not like all of what she learned.

It was I, for example, who supplied the condemned man for the play attended by Valentine and Rufi. The requirements of the Pompey Theatre were provided for by *my* jail. A docket would arrive from the office of the procurator: *One capital male, of medium height and build, to be delivered to the Pompey at the eighth hour of the morning on Id. Jun.* A simple transaction. The man was condemned to die anyway, perhaps with no less torment at the hands of the public executioner than on the stage of the Pompey. As often as not, the man—or occasionally woman—that I sent to the theatre was the perpetrator of a heinous crime and unworthy of compassion. In any case, it was not my task to question the custom of ages. I was a civil servant, and a good one. My jail was clean, efficient, orderly. We played our part in making Rome the safest and best regulated city of the empire.

But Julia did not approve. She heard from her new young friends—attracted by the pony—about the violence of the theatre and amphitheatre, and questioned me closely. I answered her as honestly as I could. "These things are decreed by history," I said. "Fourteen-year-old girls do not change the course of time's river." She had spent most of her life in the company of men who would die in the arena, but it had never occurred to her until now that their combats were anything but childlike games. The gladiators who befriended her at the school in the Alban Hills were volunteers, who embraced their fate with bravado, occasionally feigned but more often real. Now she discovered that for every volunteer who fought in the arena, a dozen or a hundred more went unwilling to their wretched fates. On the emperor's birthday, one hundred of these gladiatores meridiani were driven into the arena, not true gladiators, but common criminals and runaway slaves, many of them supplied by the jails of Rome, including my own. Two men of the hundred were chosen by lots. One was given a sword and ordered at spearpoint to kill the other, who was unarmed. His job complete, the executioner was disarmed and killed by the next man. And so on, until at the midday intermission one hundred bodies paved the arena floor like so many cobblestones. This spectacle was the talk of the city, and Julia, of course, heard of it. She refused to accept these public amusements as just or right and was deeply distressed by the part her father played in making them possible. And so a tension grew up between us for the first time, a narrow but very real space of alienation. I did not doubt her love for me, but for the first time her love was not offered as a matter of course but grudgingly. Her affection was hedged about with an unarticulated cloud of doubt, and I began to feel somehow sullied.

To some extent Julia's alienation was perhaps normal for a girl of her age. There was nothing to be done for it but to soldier on and love her more unconditionally than ever. I did not share her scruples about the games. My professional career had been premised upon violence—its execution and its enjoyment—as part of human nature. No priest or priestess of the temples refused to accept my offerings on account of my job. My record as a trainer of gladiators and jailer was frequently rewarded by official commendations. After one particularly satisfying games at which the gladiators of our Alban school excelled, the emperor himself sent me a leather pouch of gold coins bearing his likeness. But once Julia got it fixed in her head that the arena and theatre were places of debasement, nothing could shake her from that conviction. She might have outgrown this girlish tenderness had she not heard that a sect of dissenters called Christians shared her views.

But where was a blind girl to find Christians in the immensity of Rome? Julia could not go about the city except in the company of Desso or myself, although we now let her move about the immediate neighbourhood with her new girlfriends. She queried her friends about the Christian faith but had no satisfactory answers. She heard from them half-mythical tales of the Nazarene and of the deaths of Christians in the arena, but they knew nothing of the tenets of the Christian faith, or why Christians objected to Roman ways. Months went by, and the answer to her quest came from an unexpected quarter. Against Julia's wishes, I hired a new servant to assist Desso. Desso could no longer manage on her own, and it did not seem fitting to me that Julia should engage in menial household chores. Her friends were daughters of other civil administrators, waited on hand and foot by slaves, and I had no desire that they should take home stories of my Julia busy with a servant's tasks. And so I brought into our household a young servant woman, twenty or so years of age, surprisingly literate for a person of her class, named Margarita.

Julia, naturally enough, resisted the friendship or even the help of Margarita, who she saw as Desso's rival. And truth to tell, I did not blame her. The new girl was sullen and uncommunicative. She did her work efficiently enough, but made no effort to ingratiate herself into our family circle. She was frightened of Julia's pony and stayed well clear of Mel's domain. When not engaged about her tasks, she harboured in her cubicle with the curtain closed. During her free time, she left the house without any explanation of where she might be going. Julia was accustomed to know what her acquaintances "looked like" by examining their faces and bodies with her hands. But she refused to touch Margarita, nor did our new servant invite her to do so.

"What does Margarita look like?" she asked, after the new young woman had been in our house for some weeks.

It was a difficult question to answer. There was nothing particularly distinctive about the girl. "She is a bit taller than you," I began awkwardly.

"What colour are her eyes?"

I could not remember. Nor could I understand what the answer might mean to Julia. She was always interested in the colour of things, but how she envisioned different colours was beyond my understanding. "Brown, I think," I answered tentatively.

"Her hair?"

"Also brown. A kind of rusty brown—seldom combed."

"Is she pretty?"

"I—I really can't say. I haven't given it a moment's thought. I guess the answer must be 'no'. If she were pretty, I suppose I would have taken notice."

This last answer seemed to please Julia. She knew by now that she herself was pretty, because everyone told her so. Although, again, what she understood the word to mean was a mystery.

In spite of Julia's initial antipathy to Margarita, it was inevitable that sooner or later she would ask the question she posed to everyone: "Do you know any Christians?" These were the first words Julia had addressed to her servant directly. Margarita was in the kitchen, preparing vegetables for a broth. Julia entered the room quietly and stood at the opposite end of the table where Margarita worked. She could tell what sort of vegetables were being cut from the smell and the sound of the knife—leeks and turnips.

"Why do you ask?" replied Margarita.

"I have heard that Christians oppose the games," said Julia. "That they oppose the taking of life."

"And what do *you* think?" asked Margarita.

"I think the Christians are right."

It was a casual beginning, but after that unrevealing exchange Margarita went out of her way to cultivate Julia's friendship. She brushed and braided Julia's hair, helped her bathe and dress. And Julia, too, lessened her antipathy toward Margarita. It was as if each knew what was in the other's heart and where their friendship was taking them, until at last Margarita confessed her Christian faith to Julia.

"My secret name is Thecla," she said. And she told Julia the story of the person from whom she took her secret name, a Christian martyr condemned to die in the arena whose life was saved by a lioness that defended her against the attack of a he-bear and a lion. "Then Thecla was tied to bulls and their testicles were heated, so that they might pull her to pieces, but the flame spread around her and saved her," said Margarita. "The flame was Grace, the ever-Virgin, she who is before all things."

"Who is this 'she'?" asked Julia. "I thought Christians worshiped Jesus, the Galilean."

"Jesus is the incarnation of God, the visible sign on Earth."

"Was he not God himself?"

"He is with us always. He is the Father. The Mother. The Child. He is the incorruptible and undefiled, the pure light that no one can see."

"But who was the 'she' who appeared as the flame?"

"She is the first power, who came forth from the Father's mind as the Forethought of all. Her light is the Father's light, the spring of pure luminous water surrounding the Perfect One."

Julia struggled to understand these strange words. The images were vague and confusing; what did these images of light mean in her pure unseeing?

"We cannot know, cannot understand, what is unmeasurable, unspeakable, were it not for the One who came from the Father and told us these things," said Margarita. Then she added, conspiratorially, "When we are together, you may call me Thecla."

Of course, at that time, I knew nothing of these conversations. Julia did not confide to me her new enthusiasm for Christianity. I only knew that a friendship had been established between my daughter and Margarita, and that the tension in our household had diminished considerably. The gulf of suspicion that had opened between Julia and myself also seemed to measurably close, although our relationship would never again have its former warmth and spontaneity.

XXXVII

Is it ever possible for a sighted person to understand the world of the blind? As I have said, I often closed my eyes and moved about the house trying to grasp the nature of Julia's experience. But, of course, my experience was not the same at all. Although temporarily I could not see, I carried memories of the world of sight. I have seen a blue sky, a green sea, a white cloud, a red sunset. Even my dreams are coloured. But what is the world that resides in Julia's mind and in her dreams? Not a world of black and white, surely? Nor a world of darkness? It is a world founded without the sense of sight. Certainly it is true that Julia's other senses, especially her senses of hearing and touch, are more acute than my own, so perhaps her dreams are of subtle sounds and tactile sensations. I do not know. Nor can I ever know.

Julia had a keen sense of her own body; it would be impossible if it were otherwise. But what of men's bodies? She was now of an age at which many Roman girls were married, and sighted girls had ample opportunities to see the naked bodies of men—at the baths or athletic contests, paintings, sculptures, siblings and infants. But none of these were available to Julia. On the wall of our atrium were paintings of the household gods, and these included male nudity, but Julia could not fully grasp what a painting was, much less its content. To remedy the situation, I brought into the house a sculpture of naked Apollo, and this she explored with her hands, but never in my company did she touch the genitals. It was as if she knew she must not let her hands go there, at least not in my presence, perhaps because she already knew what she would find and did not wish to be embarrassed. What she had learned from Desso or her young friends I do not know.

Like most adolescent girls, she spent time "in front of the mirror", except that she had no mirror. She would sit on the side of her bed and explore her face and body with her fingertips—eyes, nose, lips, cheeks, neck, shoulders and breasts—the hands moving with infinite tenderness, as if she were memorising every pore of her own skin. And when her girlfriends were in the house, she sometimes explored them too, with the same care, as if she were trying to understand which of her own features were unique, and thus to frame a self-image in her mind. A self-image must surely come as much from knowing how one is *different* from others as from knowing how one is the same. And for Julia, the most important signifier of self—her blindness—was the most difficult thing to understand because she had so little notion of its opposite.

I knew nothing of Margarita's secret Christianity, but as she and Julia began to spend more time together, I did notice changes in Julia's personality. Throughout her childhood Julia had been physically brave, even reckless; she had thrown herself into the world as if it were impossible that she might be hurt. But now she became cautious and moved with care. Her hands floated in front of her in a way that revealed her blindness more quickly to those who saw her. I took this change to be part of her transformation from girl to woman, an attempt to define for herself a sense of grown-up grace, or perhaps simply a more mature reflection upon the physical dangers of darkness. But, in fact, it was something else altogether. Margarita had introduced Julia to a religion of spirits, immaterial powers, unworldly presences. Julia's darkness was now inhabited by angels and demons. These "invisible beings" were perhaps more real to Julia than to other Christians because *all* of her conceptual world was invisible.

They went out together. They told Desso they were going shopping for the table. But Margarita was taking Julia to Christian gatherings in secret rooms about the city. There they prayed together, or listened to the rants of the priests, or read their scriptures, or broke the bread of Eucharist, which they took to be the flesh and blood of their Galilean god. And what, I wonder, did

Julia feel in the presence of these subversives? Conspiracy is a creature of darkness and shadows. It feeds on fear and alienation. And these desperate emotions fed back into Julia, augmenting her own darkness, exaggerating her own sense of otherness. *You shall know the truth and the truth shall make you free,* said Jesus. But this so-called "truth", this bodiless stew of eastern miracle-mongering, was Julia's prison, a wrap of guilt and impotence that separated her ever more thoroughly from the world of taste and touch and smell and sound and pushed her ever deeper into the shadowy spaces of fantasy and fear.

XXXVIII

Dear Antonius,

Greetings from Valentine. We have reports of terrible strife at Alexandria under pressure of the Palmyrenes, and naturally my thoughts turn to you. I pray that you and your family are safe and well. But, if truth be told, concern for your welfare is not the only reason that I write: I find that my sense of foreignness in this city continues to grow, and I reach out for any connection with home. Forgive me if I indulge your patience in prattling on about my self-doubts and apprehensions.

I believe I told you in my last letter that I have become private physician to Quintus, the procurator of public games and amusements. But I fear it is not only as a doctor that he has engaged my services. I am also, it seems, his pet intellectual. He drags me out whenever he wishes to project an air of philosophical detachment. I am an accessory; when I am on his arm, it is as if he carried the works of Juvenal or Ovid. *See,* my presence conveys to his friends, *I am a man of culture. Refinement. Valentine carries with him all of the learning of the Alexandrian library, and he does not disdain my company.* But, of course, Quintus has not the slightest interest in philosophy or literature. He is articulate and affable in his public presence, affecting the finest dress and grooming, but underneath the polished exterior is a man of infinite coarseness. I do not believe I know the half of his private vices, but of what I do know there is to be found no harmony with philosophy.

You will rightly ask why I continue in his service. I have no good answer. I find that I am carried along by a kind of impetus, as a projectile expends in flight the force of its projection. I can no more interrupt the course of my present life than a spear hurled through the air can abruptly halt its own passage. It is as if I am determined to know, as by a kind of morbid curiosity, the depth and extent of Quintus's perversions. The lives of people with such power as his are not like our own. You and I cannot even dream of the evil (or good!) such power can effect. And this I am determined to know—not necessarily to experience, but at least to know—so that I can more fully understand the nature of human volition.

Most striking of Quintus's hypocrisies is his religion. Like many civil administrators of his class, he worships in the cult of Mithras. He once invited me to join him at that sect's sacred rituals, as an initiate, I suppose, although by the Mithric code I had no right to be there. The chapel to which I was taken by Quintus was long and narrow and covered over with a barrel vault. At one end was a shrine decorated with sacred scenes, especially that of Mithras slaying the bull. The initiates sorted themselves according to rank. The lowest order is that of Raven; then, in ascending dignity, the Hidden One, Soldier, Lion, Persian, Sun-Runner and lastly Father, who presides over all. Each rank has its appropriate costume, and during the course of the ceremonies, the initiates cawed or growled or made other appropriate sounds.

Now, Antonius, what was I to make of this? Here were some of the most influential men of Rome, men upon whose wisdom depends the well-being of the city—the empire—cavorting as children, dressing up, cawing like ravens, growling like lions. I will admit that the Mithric stories are no more or less absurd than those which occupy most other Romans or those which you Christians profess to believe. But what astonished me was the ritualised *indignity* to which these august men subjected themselves. Even Quintus, who in other circumstances carries himself with haughty pride and affects an utter cynicism, hummed and cooed in the Mithric cave like a puppet on the Father's string. A Sun-Runner himself, I had no doubt that if he had sought the highest rank he would have found a way to remove the Father. But I saw that here, as in most circumstances, Quintus sought the slightly subsidiary role, as if he knew that his power was best augmented and maintained if he did not draw attention to himself.

I learned enough of this curious faith to understand that Mithras makes stern demands upon his devotees. They are supposed to be morally pure, resolute and ascetic, like the god they serve. Whether the other initiates in that claustrophobic chapel were of upright character I cannot say, but I would guess they were no more moral or ascetic in their private lives than Quintus. The neophytes cultivated the favour of Quintus and the other men of influence, fawning in their presence, mouthing obsequies. The worst of it is that I did the same, pretending to take the rituals seriously even as I forced my mouth to shape the idiotic sounds.

When afterwards Quintus asked me what I thought of the ceremonies, I professed interest and admiration, but I have found reasons to excuse myself from further excursions to the "cave". What I cannot grasp, Antonius, are the *contradictions* of Rome. Juvenal pokes fun at the gods and laughingly dismisses the *kingdoms below ground, and punt poles, and Stygian pools black with frogs, and all those thousands crossing over in a single bark*; these things, he says, *not even boys believe, except such as are not yet old enough to have paid their penny bath*. Any Roman, closely pressed, will hem and haw and say, "Well, of course, I do not believe *literally*," but still they troop up to Jupiter's temple on the Capitol to pray for rain for their crops or for safe voyage of the ship that carries their fortune. The baths have libraries containing the loftiest thoughts of the great philosophers, but these go unread as the potbellied captains of empire cluster gleefully in their white wraps to watch young boys cavort naked with the scrimmage-ball. Orators expound on official public occasions about the dignity of man, and then the crowd rushes off to the arena to watch men slaughter other men as if they were animals in an abattoir. We are a nation that lives a lie. Our national dress is white, but our souls are black, and none blacker than that of Quintus, who rules godlike over a vast bureaucracy and in secret satisfies his every diabolic whim.

Not long ago he sent me to a certain address in the city to treat "a friend". I know, because everyone knows, that Quintus keeps a dozen mistresses in the city and at his country villas, but to visit the apartment of one of these poor creatures was a revelation. The girl's mother greeted me at the door in tears, fearful to admit me until I convinced her that I was indeed a doctor. Her daughter was no more than thirteen year of age. I will not describe, Antonius, the fearful abuse this young girl had suffered at the hands of Quintus and which I tried to mend as best I could with salves and ointments. The girl herself didn't cry. Her attitude was one of dumb resignation. "Why?" I asked the mother. She did not answer, but I could see in her eyes that Quintus had purchased her connivance and possessed it still, even in the face of her daughter's suffering. She loved her daughter, that much was clear, but even more she loved not having to work in some rich person's scullery or clean their slops. How Quintus reconciled the hurting of another parent's child with his solicitation for his own son's well-being, I do not know.

I do know that he owns *me* as much as he owns the mother of the girl. I am his medical pimp. I tell myself that as long as I do not collude with his mischief then I have no reason to turn my back on the comfort and affluence which I have by his generosity. I look back on those years when I lived an austere life among the poor of Rome and wonder what it was for. No gods kept my moral accounts. My ministrations to the poor made not a whit of difference in the grand total of human suffering. Take any consumptive from the slums of Rome, put him in my fine house, give him my iron chest of money, and he would look back upon his former fellows without a whit of solicitation. The longer I live in this city, the more I realise that sweet Nibi, my Nubian whore, knew more than my philosophers. She found quite simply a life that suited her and used what gifts she possessed to indulge herself with beautiful things. And if in the end she suffered a terrible fate, it is no less than what awaits Quintus or Valentine. I wake now in the morning in a room that is clean and bright. A servant brings me a toga freshly laundered and smelling of sunlight and rosewater. My sandals are of the softest leather. My hair is trimmed and curled by the best barber in Rome. If I choose to do so, I am carried in a litter to any destination in the city. For this, Antonius, I need only strive to bring the son of Quintus to hearty health and salve the bruises of an occasional misused girl.

I hear your voice: *Valentine, why do you strive so hard to justify yourself?* And, of course, that is why I am telling you these things: I *want* to hear your voice. I remember the way you cautioned me as a child whenever I took an unnecessary risk—jumped too long, climbed too high, swam out too far. No boy ever had a more faithful friend than I had in you, and although it has been more years than I can remember, your voice is as clear to me now as it was in Apollonia. I don't know what I want to hear you say. I would hope that you would neither bless nor condemn the road that I am on, but simply say: *Valentine, take care.* I am on a journey I cannot interrupt, and I will only know the journey's end when I come to it. But I know I will not find my heart's content unless I look in every place where human happiness might hide.

Your loving friend,
Valentine

XXXIX

Once, years ago, when I still imagined that Julia might gain her sight, I visited an astrologer. I did not give much credence to those starry fiddlers, but neither did I dismiss the possibility that they might have something to say that would give me hope. After all, I also visited the temples of every god or goddess in Rome and in the countryside round about, leaving small offerings with the priests and priestesses, covering every bet. Flocks of doves went up in smoke at my behest, and occasionally a lamb or goat was offered at the urging of a particularly persuasive priest.

I visited, too, interpreters of dreams, oracles, casters of bones and, of course, the doctors, who, it seemed to me then, had no more power than the readers of the stars. At that time, before the Christianising edicts of Constantine, every street in Rome had its practising astrologer. There is something seductive about the idea of an all-encompassing fate ruling heavens and earth. Fate has ordained correspondences between the movements of the heavenly bodies and events on earth, say the astrologers, and therefore the lives of men are pushed this way and that by peregrinations of wandering stars. A sceptic might well ask how it is that men born under different signs and therefore fated by the stars to die at different times all go down together in the same shipwreck, or why one should pay the astrologer's fee to hear what is spelled out in advance in any case. The hope, I suppose, is that by knowing what the stars have in store we can somehow elude their influence. *I alone may prolong the span of life allotted by fate*, boasts Isis, and so her priestesses and the astrologers depend upon each other to keep their customers coming.

What did I hope to hear the astrologers say? That Julia's stars were lucky and that someday she might see? Or that her blindness was a star-crossed fate that only the gods might contravene? My astrologer, I remember, was a Persian, who professed to know the uncorrupted secrets of the ancient astrologers of that land, "before they fell into the hands of Egyptian charlatans", he said. He asked for the particulars of Julia's birth and consulted his ephemerides—scraps of papyrus scribbled over with incomprehensible signs—and sketched out a zodiac with planets, sun and moon. He prescribed that Julia should dress in the colour of Jupiter and wear an amulet that bore a certain plant—what was it? heliotrope? so long ago, my memory fails—and a flake of amethyst, or some such thing.

None of this had the slightest effect on Julia's sight, but I do remember that the astrologer said—upon extracting an extra sesterce—that a man from the East would "help Julia see the light". It was a fragile prognostication on which to hang a hope and so vague as to be ostensibly satisfied by almost any subsequent event, but it remained with me, and when at last the physician Valentine came into our lives, I was heartened by the possibility that Julia's darkness might at last be lessened. And so it was, although not in the manner for which I prayed.

Looking back now, there does seem to have been a predestined quality to the lovers' terrible fate. When Valentine first appeared at our door, at the suggestion of Quintus, I did not imagine that he might be "the man from the East". If I had been more perceptive, I might have noticed that of all the doctors, priests, priestesses and practitioners of occult arts he was the first who did not offer false hope or prescribe some useless remedy. When the pony showed up at our garden gate, I was initially baffled and a bit annoyed, but it soon became apparent that the young physician had perceptively read Julia's melancholy. And so, when next I met him, when he was brought in shackles to my jail, I did not treat him as just another prisoner. But neither did I show him any conspicuous privileges, for I knew that he was sent to me by Quintus, a man whose favour I did not wish to abuse. Quintus was the steering demon of Valentine's and Julia's story: it was he who unwittingly nudged her towards Christianity by imposing his official and proper requests upon my office; and it was he who sent Valentine into my care. The next and fatal step was mine alone.

But I am getting ahead of myself. There are intervening scenes yet to play.

XL

If one had asked Valentine why he became involved with Lycisca, I doubt if he could have given a persuasive answer. She was attractive, certainly, in the way that any woman with money, taste and breeding is attractive. What physical gifts Venus gave her at birth, she knew how to conserve and show to best advantage. Although she was in her early forties when Valentine met her, she still turned heads in the forum, as much by her bearing and dress as by her face and figure. She was one of those women who project an attractive force, as rubbed amber draws to itself bits of chaff, and Valentine was drawn into her aura. But there was more. Lycisca's allure partook of Quintus's power. There was an element of delicious and compelling danger about the possession of Lycisca's favours: the treasure guarded by monsters is always more to be desired than the treasure that lies open for the taking. Valentine found excuses enough to be in her presence. If nothing else, he could pretend that it was Quintus's son Maxi whom he came to visit, and for the boy he always had on offer an ever-modified regime of diet and exercise. The slaves and servants of the household, too, had their occasional complaints to be treated, and these Lycisca immoderately exaggerated to draw Valentine to the house. This time it was Quintus who called for Valentine to visit the boy, who had become more sickly than usual. But when Valentine arrived at the house, the servant who admitted him had been instructed by Lycisca to bring him directly into her presence.

"I saw you at the theatre," he said.

"The theatre?"

"The *Laureolus*."

"Ah, the *Laureolus*. I did not see you there."

It was the day following his visit to the Pompey with Rufi. Lycisca was in her bath, a pool of travertine in the courtyard of her apartment. Her hair was bound upon her head, her nakedness covered by floating petals of roses and gardenias. As he was led into the courtyard, he flushed with embarrassment. She laughed and bade him sit beside her bath on a canvas stool.

"I have a medical request of you, Valentine. But first you must tell me what you thought of the play."

"I did not think it a play at all, nor could I recognise the hand of Catullus in what I saw. It was rather the chaotic parody of a play, raucous and uncivil."

"You have no taste for theatre?"

"I have no taste for public excess. There was a time when the arts were graced by nuance, when the death of a villain, for example, might be suggested through the talents of playwright and actors, not turned into the spectacle of a public execution. When art merges with reality it ceases to be art."

"My husband is not paid to provide the public with nuance. You will agree that he has a shrewd sense of what the plebeians want?"

"Then why were you there? And others of your rank?"

Lycisca stroked scented water across her cheeks. Her lips were rouged a full ruby red. "Ah, Valentine, you are so exquisitely naive. We are at the theatre so that the plebs will not forget that we exist. If they had nothing to aspire to, their lives would be even more miserable than they are. Our presence at the theatre or games is our gift to them, part of our civic responsibility."

"Aren't you afraid that they might simply decide to take . . ." He circumnavigated the lavishly appointed courtyard with his eyes. ". . . all of this from you? Certainly they have the power to do so should they choose to exercise it."

She raised her pencilled eyebrows. "It is Quintus's job to see that they don't have time to think seditious thoughts. The most dangerous of the plebeians are the Christians. They are not distracted by public entertainments."

"But surely the Christians are not about to grasp your riches. Their Messiah preached a philosophy of abnegation."

"They will not tear us down to take what we have. They will tear us down because their 'abnegation' is so sublimely self-righteous."

"They are weak and few in number."

"Perhaps not so few as you believe." She beckoned with her finger and her slave came forward with a wrap. "Beware of the self-righteous, Valentine. You have a tendency yourself towards arrogance."

He stood, uncomfortable, and changed the subject. "How's the boy?"

"More sickly than ever."

"I'll go to him."

"Not yet."

She rose from her bath with her arms crossed over her breasts. Water streamed down her hips and belly. He saw that her pudenda was shaved. He turned away.

She teased him. "Oh, come now, doctor. Surely you have seen your patients naked."

He turned back to face her, as her servant wrapped her in the soft white cloth. He said, "My friend Rufi warned me to stay away from you. He said that our friendship will bring me nothing but trouble."

She fixed him with her steely gray eyes. "Quintus? Are you worried about Quintus?"

He did not acknowledge the question, but kept her gaze.

She laughed. "You flatter yourself, Valentine. But yes, I suppose you should worry about Qunitus. He is jealous and unpredictable. He knows nothing of loyalty. His so-called 'friendship' can turn to vengeance in a flash. You might never know why he has turned against you. Some imagined slight, perhaps." She sat in a sandalwood chair and let the soft towel fall low upon her breasts. Her maid stood behind her and began to brush her hair. She said, "There is only one thing that Quintus respects: power. And you have none."

"What is this medical request that you have for me?"

"Oh, yes. You see, Valentine, you do after all have something to offer a woman such as myself. Your skill as a physician. I have a bit of a problem, and if you take care of it for me I will reward you handsomely, out of my own pocket. Quintus will know nothing of our transaction."

"I don't need your money."

"Then what do you want, Valentine? To come into my bed?"

It was true. Against his better judgment, he desired her. With a fierceness he had not felt since Nibi. The thought of being naked with her upon her silken sheets had become an obsession. And he understood that it was not mere sexual heat burning within him. It was an attraction to danger. Possessing Lycisca would be walking a tightrope. Above the abyss. Embarrassed, he looked away.

"Don't turn from me, Valentine."

He turned back to face her. Her maid was applying a golden cosmetic to her left nipple. And Lycisca, too, touched herself, with the tips of her long fingers, tracing soft circles on her yet untended breast.

He asked, "What do *you* want?"

"Can you guess?"

"An abortion?"

"You are perceptive, Valentine."

"Quintus's child?"

She laughed. "That would be dangerous, wouldn't it? Aborting the seed of the great procurator himself, perhaps the fit son he so longs for. But, no, nothing so ordinary as that, and far more dangerous for me than for you. The child in my belly belongs to Flamma . . ."

"The gladiator?"

"Yes, Valentine. Flamma Africanus."

He knew, of course, who she was talking about. Flamma was the toast of Rome, the most successful gladiator in the recent history of the games. A tall, strikingly handsome black man. Owned by Quintus himself. Valentine felt his body shake with an emotion he could not define. Jealousy? Fear? Or was it lust, coupled with a sense of his own inadequacy?

She stood. She moved into her dressing room and beckoned him to follow. There she let her servant dress her in a gown of white silk. Over her shoulder she said, "So you will understand why this thing inside me must not be born."

"How long?"

"Six weeks."

"The Oath of Hippocrates proscribes a physician's use of abortifacients."

"Hippocrates . . .?"

He shrugged. He thought of Theophrastus's scrupulous adherence to the highest principles of his profession.

She came to him and held his cheeks between her hands. Then she kissed him full and hard on the mouth, her tongue darting between his lips. Before he could raise his arms to embrace her, she moved away. Without turning to face him, she said: "You are not the *only* physician in Rome."

Flustered, he said, "I must prepare the proper concoctions. I will return tomorrow."

She approached him again. She drew a long finger down the bridge of his nose. "And now, Valentine, you must go to the boy. I am not the only one of this household who requires your ministrations."

"What is wrong with Maxi, that Quintus would send for me with such urgency?"

Lycasia shrugged.

"You haven't seen him?" asked Valentine.

"Why should I?"

"He is your son."

"He is Quintus's son, and the only thing wrong with him is that he is terrified of his father. Terrified of becoming what his father wants him to be. I'll tell you what I think, Valentine. I think that Maxi prefers the company of boys. And he knows that his Greek tastes will anger his father, who constantly harps on manliness." She observed the perplexity in his face and returned a look of blank dismay. "Go away, Valentine; your self-righteousness is oppressive."

At Lycisca's instructions, her maid led Valentine through the seemingly endless warren of rooms and courtyards to Maxi's chamber. The boy lay prostrate in his bed, under heavy cotton coverlets. Someone, the servants perhaps, had set up shrines to those gods and goddesses who look after the health of children: Cunina, Fabulinus, Paventia, Ossipaga, Vagitanus. Valentine could see at once that Maxi was gravely ill. The boy's skin was chalky white, his thin body shook convulsively. Valentine felt Maxi's forehead, his pulse, examined his extremities. Something in the boy's constitution was frightfully amiss, but he could not discern an organic cause.

XLI

As Valentine left the palace on the Esquiline Hill, he noticed a boy of about Maxi's age, or a bit older, sitting on the step of the house across the street. As he walked along the street, the boy followed. At the bottom of the hill, the boy was still behind him. Valentine turned and accosted him.

"Are you following me?"

The boy was thin and dark, his hair unkempt. He did not respond, but neither did he avert his eyes from Valentine's inquisitive gaze.

"Why? Why are you following me?"

The boy spoke, with a Roman accent: "I am Maxi's friend. I know he is sick. I wonder how he is?"

Valentine was surprised that this ragtag boy, with flapping sandals and threadbare tunic, might be a friend of the son of Quintus. Where was the toga praetexta that a boy of Maxi's class would wear? Perhaps Maxi made friends outside of his class to annoy his father.

"How is it that a boy such as yourself is a friend of Maxi?"

"I was hired by Quintus's steward to work in the kitchen. I met Maxi when I served him."

"Served him?"

"We became friends."

"A child of Maxi's station would not be allowed to befriend a servant."

The boy hesitated. "He has no friend but me."

Valentine was uneasy. The boy seemed in earnest.

"Maxi is very ill."

"Will he die?"

Valentine shrugged. "It is too soon to tell. I have treated him as best I can. I will bring him medicines when I return." He turned to continue along the street. The boy tagged behind.

"Are you a doctor, then?"

"I am."

"I want to be a doctor."

Valentine stopped and considered the youngster at his elbow. The boy seemed bright, alert. He wore the faint scars of pox on his neck and chin.

"Why do you want to be a doctor?"

The boy answered, "A doctor saved me once when I was very sick. My mother died."

They quickstepped along the street.

The boy asked, "Might I be your apprentice? You could teach me."

The request stopped Valentine in his tracks. He searched the boy with his eyes and saw at once that the request was sincere. Valentine remembered his own apprenticeship with Theophrastus and how the older man had taken him kindly under his wing and shown him every confidence.

"I wasn't much older than you when I began my own study of medicine," he said. He thought with affection of Theophrastus. Then asked, "What is your name?"

The boy's eyes went to the ground. "Nilus."

For a brief moment Valentine entertained the thought of taking Nilus into his care as a young apprentice. The boy seemed likable and quick, and Valentine thrilled at the possibility that the child might be just the stimulus he needed to get his own life back in order. But then he thought of Lycisca and Quintus and the complications of negotiating that tangled arena of seduction and revenge with a friend of Maxi's under his care. And he thought, too, of how far he had removed himself from the ideals that had guided Theophrastus and felt shame at the thought of exposing his own suborned principles to this innocent youngster.

He turned on Nilus and spoke with an anger that surged up from some unexpected reservoir of bitterness. "Get off with you. I have better things to do than wipe the nose of a snotty urchin."

Even as he said it, he knew it was a lie. But by the time he reached the forum, he had put the the boy out of his mind.

XLII

It was of some concern to me that Julia now seemed less interested in her young friends than in Margarita, her maid. There were certain unsettling changes in Julia's habits and disposition. Margarita, too, seemed transformed by the friendship between them; she was less sullen, more commanding, more willing to show attention to her young charge. All of this I accepted as natural. Only Desso was dismayed by the growing bond between Julia and Margarita. This I attributed to jealousy—after so long a time as Julia's exclusive minder, it would be surprising if Desso did not resent the intrusion of the younger woman. With little now to do, Julia's former maid kept to her room and took upon herself Margarita's former sullenness. I was disappointed for Desso, but knew that Julia's blossoming womanhood required a younger companion.

I count myself derelict that I was not more aware of what was going on—Julia's consortings with Christians—but my work demanded that I be away from home for much of the time, and I was grateful that Margarita now seemed eager to care for Julia's welfare. Unfortunately, at those times when I thought Margarita was taking Julia shopping or to the women's baths or to visit the temples of the Palatine, she was in fact guiding her to private houses where Christians celebrated their agape. As a catechumen, or apprentice Christian, Julia was not allowed to receive the bread and wine which were reserved for the baptised; she received instead what was called "the bread of exorcism", a lesser form of the sacrament which was supposed to drive the demons from her soul. Why these fanatics believed that my innocent Julia might harbour demons is more than

I can understand. As I later learned, these Christians imagine angels and demons everywhere, as actual presences, not mere shibboleths. The most devout among them pretend to *see* these spiritual beings, in dreams and visions. They told my darling Julia that she, too, might have such visions, in spite of her physical blindness. This, I believe, was part of her attraction to the Galilean faith.

There was at that time in Rome a Christian bishop named Cornelius, the same person Valentine had met in Egypt and who had converted Valentine's friend Antonius. This Cyrenean out of Alexandria preached an uncompromising faith that emphasised the soul's disembodied nature. Sex was proscribed by Cornelius as the consequence of Adam's sin; in accepting Christ, the new convert was expected to forgo every pleasure of the flesh. Even married Christians were urged to live as brother and sister. Cornelius was unique among the Christian preachers of Rome in his obsessive rejection of carnality, and certainly his message went against the grain of the Roman character. The games and theatre, too, Cornelius rejected, as diabolical and cruel, and the public baths he proscribed as occasions of sin, most especially the Greek sin of homosexuality. While Christians of other congregations continued to enjoy the public amenities of the city, those who followed Cornelius might as well have been living in an African desert for all of the urban pleasures they allowed themselves.

It was to this sect of Cornelius that Margarita took Julia, and my daughter embraced his preaching with enthusiasm. Everything Cornelius said about the "immorality" of the theatre and arena confirmed her prejudices. And his prudish attitudes on matters of the flesh somehow confirmed her discomfort with her own newly awakened sexuality. If I had been more perceptive, I might have noticed the transformation in Julia's behaviour. Her appetite for food diminished. She dressed with less care for the tricks of fashion she had learned from her well-bred friends. Her toilet and ablutions became careless. At home she lazed about in a kind of dreamy idleness that I ascribed to adolescence. The little shrines of household gods and goddesses that had decorated her room vanished. Most surprisingly of all, she truncated her lovely hair, cropping it with little regard for fashion or comeliness. It was with some consternation that I observed these transformations; at the very time when I had hoped to see Julia take pride in her appearance and perhaps attract the attentions of some young man of good family, she seemed to lapse into a slovenly disregard for her natural beauty.

Cornelius took a particular interest in Julia. Her blindness was a goad to his pride as a healer and a visionary. He held her face between his hands and covered her eyes with his fingertips.

"Have you been blind since birth?" he asked.

"I don't understand," she replied.

"Do you have any memory of light?"

She shook her head.

He said, very quietly, "Your blindness is a species of possession. The Evil One has taken up residence within your body and obstructs your vision. We must pray for Christ to vanquish the Evil One's power." And with that he closed his own eyes and quietly prayed, all the while holding Julia's face in his hands, invoking with others of the assembly the intercession of Christian martyrs to drive the perverse spirits from Julia's body. What she imagined to be her state of being, I do not know.

He asked her about her dreams and her menses.

All of these obscenities, which I later found recorded in Margarita's journal, I might have forgiven this monstrous acolyte of Christ, but for his glorification of virgin martyrdom.

It was mostly women and girls who were attracted to Cornelius's preaching. As Margarita brought Julia to the assemblies where Cornelius spoke, so did other women bring their friends. To these women, and especially to those who were not married, he exhorted a life of virginity. By practising virginity, he said, they participated in a union with the Godhead such as existed before the fall of Adam. Whereas sex distracted a person's thoughts from God, abstinence made her a ready vessel for God's love and perfected the redemption of Christ.

"Virginity makes itself equal to the angels," preached Cornelius. "Rather, it excels the angels, because it must struggle against the flesh to master a nature which the angels do not possess. Virginity is a magnificent contemplation of the life to come, an anticipation of the perfection of heaven when the virgin takes up her role as the bride of Christ."

And then he uttered the greatest obscenity of all. "The virgin's martyrdom is especially blessed, because it allows the virgin to die in the unblemished perfection of Christ.

"We are smeared with sins as if with pitch," said Cornelius. "Why should the martyr fear the sword of martyrdom, which is painless and quick compared to the everlasting fires of hell. I have seen the river of fire in a vision. I have seen the souls tormented by flames, but unperishing. In heaven, the rewards of a virgin are sixty times greater than those of an ordinary Christian, but a *virgin martyr's* rewards are a hundred times greater."

What did poor blind Julia made of this madness? She stood in those assemblies full of women and girls (with a sprinkling of men), her hair cropped short like a boy's, and shuddered in her skin. She had heard stories from her young friends of Christian executions and of Christian men and women dying in the arena with criminals of every sort. She knew that some of these Christian martyrs had been discharged to the arena by her own father, in his capacity as jailer. An even deeper wedge of mistrust was driven between us.

I believe I am correct in saying that from the time Julia first heard Cornelius preach she courted martyrdom and secretly plotted her own death under the sword. If it had not been for her blindness, she might have more impetuously and publicly asserted her new faith. As it was, it was impossible for Julia to go about the city except in the company of Margarita, and apparently Margarita did not share Julia's appetite for the hundred-fold rewards of the virgin martyr. Perhaps Julia more avidly anticipated the afterlife because the Christians spoke of heaven in images of light, as a counterpart of the darkness of hades. When the risen Christ showed himself at the tomb, those who saw him were dazzled by the radiance that enveloped him, or so said the Christian preachers. Julia somehow imagined Christ as all that was not visible to her—the sun, the sky, the sea, the fields of wheat. And what did our Roman gods and goddesses offer her? Certainly not luminous immortality.

Then Mel died. Julia's pony lamed itself and had to be put down, a task that fell to me. Not the actual killing, of course, but the calling for the knackers who led the pony away to its unfortunate fate. In Julia's mind this act of humane necessity on my part was all of a piece with my role in sending prisoners to the arena. I had now taken from her the one thing she loved, and a great melancholy fell across her spirit that not even Christian joy could ameliorate. Now she lived only for the times when Cornelius would press his thumbs against her eyes and pray her free from darkness.

XLIII

Among the doctors of Rome there are as many techniques for inducing an abortion as there are women who desire them. Some doctors poke and jab with a sharp instrument, as often as not damaging tissue adjacent to the fetus and causing the patient to die of infection. Other doctors prescribe horseback riding, jumping or vigourous shaking by draft animals. Yet others use baths or suppositories of toxic herbs, or even bleeding. In this matter, as in others, Valentine opted for a less violent approach, always seeking to enlist the body's natural tendencies in achieving the desired effect. What he prescribed for Lycisca was a suppository of linseed, mallow and wormwood, to be inserted in the vagina after a warm hip bath in water containing the same ingredients. It was with this concoction of herbs, contained within several flasks carried by his servant, that he arrived at the palace on the Esquiline Hill on the day following Lycisca's request. He also carried packets of medicine for Maxi.

He asked to be taken at once to Lycisca. To his surprise, he was led instead into the company of Quintus Mimmius, who sat dictating orders in the largest of the house's several peristyles. For long moments, Quintus took no note of Valentine's presence. Valentine stood silent and fearful, wondering why he had been fetched into his employer's presence.

At last Quintus put aside his papers, dismissed his amanuensis with a wave of the hand and addressed Valentine. "Ah, physician, you have come to see Maxi?" The dropped lid of Quintus's left eye and his asymmetric mouth gave his face an air of menace, difficult to interpret in the best of times. Even seated, the man's physical stature was commanding. His toga was immaculate, the purple stripe a bit wider than what was appropriate for a man of his rank.

Valentine was cautious. "Maxi. And Lycisca."

"Lycisca?"

"Yes."

"And for what are you treating Lycisca?"

Valentine knew that his answer must be correct. It would not be enough to say that he had come to see Lycisca for the supposed problem that had led Quintus to employ Valentine in the first place. Nor could he make up a fictitious ailment. He was an employee of Quintus, not Lycisca, and his employer would assume his loyalty. And there was the possibility that Quintus already knew the nature of his mission.

He replied, "I am prepared to induce an abortion, but first, of course, I must ask your permission."

"Of course."

Valentine waited, as Quintus studied him closely.

Quintus repeated, "Of course."

Valentine asked, "Do I take it then that you concur?" He hoped that Quintus assumed the fetus was his own, in which case any quarrel would be between the procurator and his wife. Valentine's hope of bedding Lycisca seemed suddenly more remote.

"Whose child did my wife say she was aborting?" asked Quintus.

The game had become more dangerous. Valentine understood that a misstep now might cost him his life. He lied. "She did not say. She said only that she was pregnant and wished to abort the child."

Again, Quintus was silent. This time he did not fix his gaze on Valentine but rocked slowly in his seat, hands folded against his lips. Valentine focused on the scar on Quintus's shoulder, where the toga was gathered with a golden clasp.

Quintus said, finally, into his hands, "I am disappointed, Valentine. I understand that a doctor might entertain a certain loyalty to his patient, but in this case your loyalty belongs entirely to me."

Valentine quickly interjected, "You will understand, sir, that I am reluctant to intervene in what is surely a private matter between yourself and your wife." Was his fear apparent? It was not so much his life that he now felt to be at risk, but the *quality* of his life, for which he owed everything to Quintus.

"Does the name Flamma mean anything to you?" asked Quintus.

"Of course. He is the most famous gladiator in Rome."

"And you also know that it is his black seed that is in my wife's womb?"

"Yes." It was a terrible risk to admit the previous lie, but there was no alternative.

Another long silence. Then Quintus said, "Go. See to Lycisca, doctor. And to my son. Then join me and my friends for a meal. We will be discussing how best to employ Flamma's unusual talents in the arena."

Quintus rose and departed the peristyle, expressing neither acquiescence nor anger. Valentine had no way of reading the man's mood, so effectively hidden behind the permanently distorted smile, no sense of how adequately he had responded to Quintus's inquisition. He waited for a awkwardly long time in the peristyle, rooted to the spot where he had been standing, and heard for the first time the gurgling fountain and the aviary of songbirds that had been singing there all along.

XLIV

He would put off his encounter with Lycisca as long as possible. He did not go first to her, but to Maxi. The boy was in a cool bath, as Valentine had instructed, his thin body pale and white under the crystalline water, his penis erect, a tiny submarine pillar, white. The boy's face, too, was a deathly chalk, his eyes clouded with dark shadows. The ringlets of his hair were plastered against his forehead. Valentine saw that Maxi was slipping from life, yet he had no idea of the nature of the boy's affliction. Of all the diseases and weaknesses he had previously encountered, none quite matched Maxi's symptoms.

"I am dying, Valentine," whispered Maxi. This melancholy statement was delivered matter-of-factly.

Two servants waited there in the caldarium to carry the boy to his bed. A pantheon of divine statuettes watched from the floor along the muralled wall. Valentine said, "Your father wishes you to be well."

The boy managed a thin smile of irony and doubt.

Valentine bathed Maxi's forehead with a wet white cloth. He said, "I will tell you honestly that I have no certain cure for your affliction. I do not even know what is wrong with you. You must *want* to be well, Maxi. The will is the most powerful medicine for marshalling the body's natural strength."

The boy's lips moved, but no words emerged. It was as if he were whispering some private prayer.

"I met a friend of yours yesterday. A boy named Nilus. He, too, wants you to be well."

Maxi's eyes darkened, his brow furrowed ever so slightly. He whispered, "I have no friends."

"Of course you do. Nilus is your friend. Your mother and father love you and wish you to recover. *I* want you to recover."

"Is there an afterlife, Valentine?" The question was barely audible.

What was Valentine to answer? He saw that the boy wanted affirmation.

"I do not believe in an afterlife," said Valentine. "But if you get well, you will have a long and happy life."

The boy closed his eyes and whispered, "I want to sleep."

Valentine signalled for the servants to lift Maxi from the bath and carry him to his bed. They dried the boy's body and wrapped him warmly in cotton bedclothes. Valentine asked for beakers of water and mixed his herbal concoction. This he ordered to be administered to Maxi whenever the boy asked for drink. Valentine had no more confidence in this medicinal preparation than in the influence of the gods and goddesses whose images the servants now carried from bath to bedroom. Maxi's survival now depended upon Maxi alone.

XLV

"The boy is dying."

Valentine stood behind Lycisca. She sat on the bench at the top of the terraced garden where he had first met her. Two fine peacocks grazed near by. She did not acknowledge his remark.

He walked around the bench to face her, shooing the birds out of his way. Her face was bruised, the skin cut above the right eye.

"What happened?" He resisted the temptation to touch her cheek.

"You might as well have done it yourself, Valentine."

"Quintus?"

She laughed coldly. "Of course, Quintus. What did you expect? That he would welcome the news that his wife slept with a Nubian gladiator?" Her voice was brittle with anger.

"How did he know?"

"Don't be disingenuous. It doesn't suit you."

"You think it was I who told him?"

"You are a treacherous person, Valentine. A wolf in sheep's clothing. Pretending to be the principled physician, taking the confidences of your patient, then betraying her to her husband."

"I swear to you that I did not reveal your secret. He already knew about Flamma when he questioned me."

"I told no one but you. He may have guessed, but surely you confirmed his suspicion."

Valentine thought back to his conversation with Quintus. Had he been played the fool? He parried. "If Flamma seduced the wife of Quintus Mimmius, the news is surely all over Rome. Quintus could have heard it anywhere."

"No one knew that I sought an abortion except yourself."

"And your maid. Sabina was with us when you requested my help." Valentine looked to Lycisca's maid, who now sat across the garden, within hearing. The girl did not look up, but Valentine observed her nervousness, and he thought that Lycisca saw it, too.

"What do you have for me?" There was none of the old flirtatiousness; her voice was contemptuous.

Valentine explained the process. There was nothing he needed to do; Lycisca's maid could provide all the help necessary.

He said, "If after a week the fetus is not expelled, then we will try a more violent remedy."

Lycisca touched the cut above her eye. She said, "You might have had what you wanted, Valentine. I was prepared to give you everything."

He changed the subject. "Your son weakens. Maxi may die."

She answered, "It is nothing to me. He is not my son." Valentine's surprise was apparent. She added, "No child of mine would be so spineless. He is the offspring of one of Quintus's many mistresses, which he fobbed off as my child and his legitimate heir. I was never pregnant by Quintus, in spite of enduring his unremitting lust. So you will understand his anger at my becoming pregnant by another."

"The boy will not live long."

"Then your life, too, will be short. Quintus will hold you responsible. That is his way. He always finds a scapegoat."

"What ails Maxi is not curable by the physician's art."

"Do think think such subtleties will concern Quintus. He has paid you to keep the boy alive."

"That is absurd."

"Poor Valentine. You are either more naive than I thought or more devious. You must surely know that when you entered the service of Quintus you left the world of reason behind." She reached out and took the hem of his toga between her fingers, stroking the perfect stitching of purple threads. "Look at your fine garments, Valentine." She took his hand and drew it to herself. She inspected his nails. "Who does your manicure? And your sandals—of the softest calfskin and finest workmanship. Why do you expect reason? *These* are your rewards for accepting absurdity."

Lycisca's maid had meanwhile slipped away. Lycisca moved his hand to her breast, "Do you still desire me?"

Valentine said nothing. His mind was in turmoil. But his answer was obvious. The more dangerous the game became, the more powerfully he wanted her.

She smiled sweetly. "Not as long as Quintus lives."

He was stunned. He searched her eyes for her meaning. "Are you asking me to kill him?"

"If Maxi dies, Quintus will have you killed soon enough. It is a simple matter of self-preservation. You have the skills. You are his physician."

What she said was true. Valentine was trained in the art of poisons, which he often used therapeutically in moderation. He asked, "You told me once that you stayed with Quintus," his gaze swept the house and gardens, "for all of this?"

"If Quintus were to die now, of an unknown cause, all of this would pass to Maxi. And from Maxi to me. And from me, Valentine, some of it to you. You would be amply rewarded." She pressed his hand against her lips and kissed each of his fingertips separately. The last she took into her mouth.

Thoughts stormed in his head. Lycisca's cold hatred for Quintus was apparent. It was clear, too, the more he thought about it, that she understood Quintus's mind more exactly than he. His life was indeed forfeit if Maxi died. He said, "I am a doctor. I save lives. I do not take them."

"In a single day, Quintus might caused to be extinguished as many lives as you will save in a lifetime. Do you know how many men he has consigned to death in the arenas of Rome? By killing Quintus you will save more lives that you have ever ransomed with your potions."

"Why are you telling me this? How do you know I will not betray you to Quintus?"

"You will not go to Quintus." She laughed. "I understand you, Valentine, better than you understand yourself. There is nothing about you that is hard to read. Your thoughts are written all over your face."

"Then you no longer think it was I who betrayed you concerning Flamma?"

"I saw the truth on Sabina's face the moment you mentioned her name. She is his spy."

Valentine considered Lycisca. Even with her bruised face and the cut above the eye, she possessed a perilous beauty. The milky swellings of her breasts filled the throat of her gown. A thin snake of solid gold coiled on her bare arm. Her eyelids and the nails of her sandalled feet were gilded. He desired her no less than before. No, more. As the risk increased, so, it seemed, did his need.

He said, "Let me tend to that cut above your eye."

XLVI

Dear Antonius,

It has been a long time since I have heard from you, but I write again with a sense of urgency. My life may be in danger, and I have a bequest, for you, my fondest friend, that I want you to be aware of. As you know, I have acquired a modest fortune here in Rome, in the service of Quintus Mimmius, the procurator of games. Most of this I have converted into silver and gold coins, which I have placed in two iron chests and given into the care of my friend Cosa Egyptus, whom you will know from my previous letters as Rufi. In the event of my death, one of these chests will go to Rufi; the other to you. I have instructed Rufi to see to it that you are the sure recipient.

Take care, Antonius, whom you choose to serve. I allied myself with power and wealth and now find I have made a contract I cannot fulfill. Quintus pays me handsomely to bring his son to robust good health, yet the boy slips away. I have no remedy. I urge exercise, sunshine, good food. I have tried every potion in my pharmacy, baths, purgings, even bleeding. I have tried courses of treatment in which I have confidence and, in desperation, those in which I have no confidence. Still the boy withers. His problem, I am convinced, is not organic but psychic. His mother Lycisca, who is not his mother, believes that his sexual predilections are Greek. It is true that he shows no interest in girls, even though he is at the age when most boys think of nothing else. He is terrified of Quintus, who speaks to him only of combat and sport. He abhors the activities that his father urges upon him: archery, swordplay, horsemanship. He *wills* himself dead. And he is dying, ever so slowly but with certainty. He will not last the summer. And if he dies, I have not the slightest doubt that Quintus will hold me responsible. He will as readily take my life as he would slap a mosquito on his thigh. To make matters worse, he believes that I have betrayed him regarding Lycisca. She sought an abortion from me—the fetus was the fruit of an affair with someone other than her husband, Flamma, a gladiator owned by Quintus—and I made the mistake of not informing Quintus before he heard it from another, Lycisca's maid. The abortion was successful, but my relationship with Quintus has been altered. He toys with me. He bides his time. He invites me into his confidence, only to dangle me like a puppet over the abyss before he snips the strings.

On a recent visit to his palace—to provide Lycisca with abortifacients—he invited me to join himself and his friends for dinner. Never before had he initiated such an intimacy; I knew this, too, was part of his game. We gathered in Quintus's private dining room at the eighth hour. In addition to myself there were three other guests, two senators and a general of the urban cohort, Marcus Graecus. Antonius, I wish I had some way to adequately describe the luxury of the room. Porticoes and columns of the finest marble. Statues of disporting gods and goddesses on every side. Frescoes of the most exquisite delicacy and eroticism; not even Ovid could have imagined more provocative scenes. The marble table was round, not square or rectangular as customary, and the usual array of couches were replaced by a single circular couch, forming a continuous arc around the table. Cushions of the purest silk. The food conveyed to our table by the servants was apparently inexhaustible; even before the end of the preliminaries I was stuffed. I will mention only one dish, a gilded donkey, about a cubit high, with silver panniers on either side containing olives, white on one side, black on the other. No, I must tell you of one other dish: a Priapus of Corinthian bronze, holding in his lifted skirt every kind of fruit and grapes.

The talk was seditious, although cautiously expressed; it would have been hard to prove it treasonous. Much fun was made of the absent emperor. The men at table seemed supremely confident of their power; the princeps was far away on the Danube frontier, his local agents easily manipulated. Between Quintus and his friends there was a easy repartee, a sure alliance, although an edge, too, as if each man were cautious not to move too far in front of any other in his treasonous schemes, or lag too far behind. At one point in the meal, after many cups of wine had been poured from golden ewers, Quintus sent for Lycisca to greet his guests. She made a brief appearance, charming, beautiful, but her carefully applied cosmetics could not hide the evidence of Quintus's abuse. He showed no shame and even a little pride that she should be battered so and still answer to his beck.

Upon her departure, he raised with the others the matter of Flamma. He did not, of course, mention Flamma's impregnation of his wife. Rather, he posed the challenge: how might the African gladiator's unparalleled celebrity best serve the people of Rome? After forty-seven consecutive victories, Flamma was rich and arrogant. Soon he would feel himself the equal of a freeman, even a patrician, said Quintus. It was time to cut him down a notch, use his fame to give the people a thrill they had not experienced before. Quintus had a proposal: the two tigers from India, magnificent animals. No tiger had been seen in the arena in the lifetime of anyone now living. Since the animals had arrived as a gift for the emperor from an eastern potentate, they had been kept at the imperial zoo. Now was the time to use them to give Flamma the ultimate test. The senators expressed reservations that these rare beasts should be sacrificed without the emperor's permission or knowledge. "Then we must make sure that it is Flamma, not the tigers, who perishes," said Quintus. The talk turned to how best ensure the desired outcome. First, it was decided, the tigers must be trained for aggression.

What will become of Flamma, I do not know, but I do know that my own fate is linked with that of the gladiator in ways I cannot yet imagine. I believe that Quintus asked me to be present at this conversation so that I would understand his utter power. No court of law will be necessary to arrange my execution; that is the message I was meant to learn. Antonius, if you still worship your Christian god, pray that Quintus's son survives. I rack my brain to find a remedy, a way to entice the boy back to health. And to tell the truth, it is not only fear of Quintus's vengeance that drives me to do so; there is also Lycisca, whose image haunts me day and night—a Circe whose siren song calls me to my final and most abject degradation.

Your true friend,
Valentine

XLVII

Two issues divided the Christians of Rome into querulous factions. The first had to do with the nature of Christ: was he fully divine, one with the great God who creates and maintains the cosmos? Or was he merely first among the prophets of God, holy yet human? Cornelius and his allies held the first view and quoted to their advantage Christ's miracles reported by his disciples, and most especially Christ's supposed resurrection from the dead. They took earlier Christian writers at their word when they called Christ the Son of God by whom all things were made. The opponents of this view honoured Christ as the wisest of men but denied his divinity. The One True God is immutable, they contended, uncreated, eternal, invisible, incomprehensible, and therefore it is impossible that he might become man and partake of the visible creation. Christ is the Messiah who leads all men to God, but he is not God. The second issue which divided the Roman Christians concerned the role of women in the Church. Cornelius and his followers averted to Paul's stricture against women speaking in church. *Let a woman learn in silence with full submission,* the apostle had written. *I permit no woman to teach or have authority over a man; she is to keep silent.* (I read from a copy of these remarks of Paul that was taken down in Margarita's hand.) Other Christians quoted Paul to the opposite effect: *There is no longer Jew or Greek, slave or free, male or female, for all of you are one in Christ Jesus.* These latter Christians welcomed women as full participants in the secret ceremonies of that sect.

These theological disputes divided even single congregations into contending groups, and Julia and Margarita were caught up in the heated debates. Margarita followed Cornelius in all things, accepting Christ as fully divine and holding herself silent. Julia was more deeply troubled. She was drawn immediately to the story of Christ—and especially to his message of peace and charity—but she could not understand how a person who lived at a certain time and place in history could be the sole instrument of salvation. What of those who lived before Christ? Were they denied salvation? Julia's God, as I understand it, was ineffable, a kind of pure light blazing behind her darkened eyes. Later, when I became aware of her Christianity, I watched her pray, sitting on her bed, endlessly rocking, eyes wide open, a kind of soft radiance on her face like the sun shining through morning mist, peaceful, untroubled, and I tried to understand the images that resided in her mind, which she spoke of always as "light". She told me that in these trances she saw Christ himself, in a robe of the purest white (what might this mean to Julia?), his unbearded face as smooth as marble, his long, delicate fingers reaching out to touch her gently. He led her though endless rooms of white marble toward a radiance that always approached but never arrived. *Happy the gentle, for they shall inherit the earth,* he said. *Happy the pure of heart, for they shall see God.* As for the proper place of women in the Church, Julia followed those who believed that all were equal in Christ. Although she remained silent at meetings of her co-religionists, she listened to men and women with equal respect, and she was far less taken by the preaching of Cornelius than was Margarita.

It came to pass that Julia and Margarita had a falling out, not over these contentious theological issues, but over the matter of Julia's blindness. Cornelius asserted that my daughter's affliction was demonic, a manifestation of possession by Satan, to be remedied by prayer. He suggested to her that Satan had stolen away her sight in retribution for *my* role in sending Christians to the arena, and Margarita followed Cornelius in this idiocy. Julia had no sympathy for my practical atheism or for my profession as imperial jailer, but she was not ready to blame *me* for her blindness. She remembered what Jesus said when he cured the man who had been blind since birth. The master's disciples asked: *Rabbi, who sinned, this man or his parents that he should be born blind.* And Jesus answered: *Neither he nor his parents sinned; he was born blind so that the works of God might be displayed in him.* Julia took these words at face value and applied them to herself; she was convinced that she had some role to play in bringing unbelievers to Christ. The tension between Julia and Margarita became increasingly urgent, until finally Margarita refused to bring her charge to Christian meetings. Julia was distraught. She desperately sought baptism and had earnestly studied the mysteries of the Christian faith so that she might be born again in Christ. But how was she to move from catechumen to baptised Christian if confined to her home? She turned to Desso— old Desso, who could hardly move about.

Desso was appalled when she learned of Julia's Christian beliefs and came directly to me. I confronted my daughter.

"Do you know what might happen to you if the authorities discover that you are meeting with Christians?" I asked. I did not yet know how fully Julia had given herself to these eastern superstitions.

"Am I not your daughter?"

"What do you mean?"

"Your jail is full of Christians."

"Exactly! Their faith is seditious. They refuse to give homage to the gods, to endure military service, accept public office or fulfil any of the other responsibilities of a Roman. By elevating the Galilean to divine status, they set up a rival to the one god who watches over the empire. If you overthrow the idea that there is one divine king, then there is nothing to prevent the emperor, too, from being challenged."

"Father, you are trying too hard to justify yourself. The Roman authorities accuse Christians of sedition only as scapegoats for their own shortcomings. If crops fail, it is the fault of the Christians. If the fleet suffers a storm, blame the Christians. A plague? The Christians again. And you know as well as I that Quintus needs to fill the jails so that he can multiply his evil games. He is Satan, and you are a participant in his murderous schemes. You might as well draw the sword yourself against his victims."

My heart was breaking. Never had Julia challenged my authority in this way. Yet she was so young and innocent. What did she know of politics or the administration of an empire? I said, "Religion is the buttress of a city, a nation or an empire. It is the cement that holds everything together. Paying homage to the official gods of Rome is a responsibility equal to paying taxes. The Christians are different from those who worship Bacchus or Artemis or Mithras. These deities are acknowledged by their acolytes as lesser gods, subservient to the one god of empire. Yet the Christians set up an idol that . . ."

I became silent. I could see that no reasonable argument would counter Julia's commitment to this cult of the Galilean. What, I wondered, was the source of its power over her?

The thought that she might be arrested, tortured or killed for a superstition was more than I could bear. I put out my hand to touch her cheek. She jerked her head away from my fingers as if they were a branding iron. I asked, as gently as I could, "What is it you want, Julia? What do you receive from these Christians that I cannot give you?"

"Love," she said.

"But I love you with all my heart."

"If you loved me, you would love the people in your jail. You would love the hundreds of innocents that your friend Quintus . . ."

"He is not my friend."

". . . that your friend Quintus kills in the arena. You would love the poor, the slaves and the thousands who live in poverty so that Quintus and his ilk can have their palaces."

"How do you know what you have never seen?"

"Father, don't condescend to me. Because I am blind doesn't mean I am ignorant. I have ears. I listen."

"And tell me, how will these Christians make things better? They are weak. They have no experience in government. Their followers are mostly women and slaves. Think about it, Julia. Because of Rome, the world is at peace, with relative prosperity, from the Indus to the Pillars of Hercules, from Britannia to the African deserts. Without this hegemony the world would be . . ."

She interrupted. "Free to worship the one true God."

There was no point in trying to show Julia the error of her ways. I had met enough Christians in my work to know that their ignorance is refractory. Any charlatan or trickster can exploit their credulity. It was well known in those days that a whole new class of racketeers had emerged to separate Christians from their money—men who posed as saints and healers.

Julia retreated to her own room and stood at the window where she could feel the sun's warmth on her face. I followed her. I said, "Julia, I am not prepared to lose you."

Without looking at me, she answered, "One must lose himself to the body to gain the spirit."

I issued an order. "You are not to leave the house. Not with Desso, not with Margarita, not with anyone. Until you come to your senses."

Julia didn't answer or acknowledge my edict in any way. She kept her face to the sun. My eyes fell upon her bare feet against the floor, and I remembered her birth, holding her in my hands, each perfect finger and toe, counting them, admiring the perfection of her tiny body, not yet understanding that her eyes were unseeing. Now I was convinced that if only she had eyes to see she would understand the error of her ways. She was literally and figuratively trapped in darkness.

XLVIII

Valentine was arrested and delivered to my prison on the fourteenth day of December during the first year of the reign of Claudius II. The warrant of his arrest was signed by Balbinus Saccas, a minor magistrate and known protégé of Quintus Mimmius. The charge was Christian sedition, on the testimony of a certain Philip Nilus, who worked in the home of Quintus and claimed to know Valentine. It was apparent to me from the beginning that the charge was fraudulent. Everyone in Rome knew that Quintus's son had died, and many knew that Valentine was the boy's physician. No one doubted that Quintus was capable of scapegoating the doctor. For Valentine to have been a secret Christian, as claimed by Philip Nilus, bordered on the absurd; all who knew Valentine attested to his philosophical atheism. And then there was also the matter of his accuser, a boy of less than sixteen years of age, not legally old enough to provide unsupported evidence in a capital offense.

Of course, I remembered Valentine's kindness to Julia when he had given her the pony and his presence at Julia's birth. I went straightaway to his cell. He was held with half a dozen common criminals, pickpockets, vandals, swindlers, thieves.

I summoned him to the iron grill of the cell door. "Do you remember me?" I asked.

He approached and recognised me at once. He said, "You are the father of the blind girl, Julia. You are the administrator of this prison."

"I have not forgotten your gift to my daughter."

"And now I am you guest."

One of the knaves in the cell also recognised me. He told the others who it was at the door, and soon all six felons were hurling jibes at Valentine.

I said, "I want to question you, but we cannot talk here. I will have you transferred to a private cell."

I left him then to the abuse of his cell mates. It hurt me that a man of Valentine's education and stature should be debased in the company of rogues. I knew that by giving him special privilege I risked Quintus's ire, but I thought, too, of Julia and how once this man had rescued her from melancholy. Now she was again in need of a wisdom that I was not able to provide. Perhaps Valentine could tell me how to lead her away from the path of Christian martyrdom.

That evening I went again to the prison, to the cell where Valentine had been moved at my order. Not even Quintus could object that I was coddling my charge. The cell was barely large enough for the prisoner to stretch out prone on the mat of straw which was the only furnishing. There was a tiny window, a breath of air.

"There are no rats," I said, when the turnkey had admitted me to the cell.

"It is less spacious than what I am used to," said Valentine. He smiled.

"You are a Christian?"

He laughed. "I am a physician who made the mistake of losing a patient."

He was not the sort of person I generally harboured in my jail. He was immaculately groomed. His toga was of the finest linen, stitched with silken threads, his sandals fair and supple.

"I have a warrant," I said. "You have been accused by one Philip Nilus."

"I know no one of that name."

"According to my inquiries, he is a boy of sixteen years or so. The son of a tax collector. From Cyreniaca."

Valentine thought for a moment. "I met a boy, briefly, named Nilus. He was a friend of Quintus's son. He asked me if he might be my apprentice. He . . ."

Valentine became silent and turned from me to face the door. It was then, I believe, that he began to suspect what he would later confide to me: that Philip Nilus was his son by an early affair.

He said, "I am innocent of the charge that brought me here."

I answered, "It is not for me to judge. That is why we have magistrates."

"Magistrates, as you know, can be bought and sold."

"What happened to the boy?"

"The boy?"

"Maxi, Quintus's son."

"He willed himself to die. There was nothing wrong with him that my art could mend. He feared his father. He saw no future that he could endure. His murderer is Quintus."

"I'd watch my tongue, Valentine. You are in trouble enough already without accusing Quintus. How do you know that I will not report what you have said?"

Valentine searched my face. He said, quietly, "Because I believe you are an honourable man."

Was I? Was I an honourable man? My daughter accused me of conspiracy in murder. And now this man who once purchased a pony for my daughter out of his own pocket, perhaps saving her life, was remanded to my care while Quintus devised for him a suitable fate.

I asked, "How well do you remember my daughter?"

"Strong willed, unhappy, angry with her father. Not unlike Maxi. I remember a pretty girl, with fine black hair falling across her shoulders . . ."

"Now cropped like a boy's."

". . . about fourteen, fifteen years of age . . ."

"Now sixteen."

". . . serious, intelligent. And blind."

And *blind,* said Valentine. I cannot tell you why, but I was sorely tempted to tell this man everything. About Julia's new affliction—another kind of blindness, the blindness of superstition. But I did not yet know if I could trust him.

I asked, "You claim you are not a Christian, Valentine. What do you think of them? The Christians?"

"Is this an official interrogation?"

"Not at all. I have no authority to interrogate you. I am merely curious as to what a man such as yourself thinks of the Galilean sect."

"I know something of them. My sister was executed as a Christian. My childhood friend, Antonius, is a Christian."

"Your sister—martyred?"

"She went willingly to her death, by the account of my friend."

I thought of Julia, of her own willingness to lay down her life for the Galilean. This Christian appetite for death surpassed my understanding. "For a superstition?" I queried.

Valentine answered thoughtfully. "I would not use that term, if by it you mean a mere surrender of reason. There are certain philosophical qualities in Christianity. Moses and Christ were moral teachers. How do we distinguish Christians from those who call themselves Peripatetics, Stoics, Cynics, Sceptics? To dismiss them as superstitious is not enough. We must counter them on philosophical grounds."

"But their fanaticism does not admit to reason. It is pointless to engage in discussion."

"That's what Galenus . . ." He paused to see if I recognised his reference. "That's what the physician Galenus believed. The Christians and the Jews appeal to faith and the testimony of their founders, whereas true philosophers believe in reasoned argument and the primacy of the senses as evidence, he said. What is at issue is not the truth or falsity of a certain curriculum of beliefs, but the grounds upon which we hold these things to be true or false. It is pointless to engage in debate unless we first of all agree upon principles of philosophy."

Valentine had begun to leave me behind. I have no head for philosophy. But I know falsehood when I see it, and in the zealotry of Christians who had passed through my prison, I saw only mindless surrender to the hucksterism of their priests. At the same time, I grasped the core of what Valentine was saying: that Julia would not be dissuaded from her course by contrary argument. She must first of all be reunited with the substance of *things*—with those exhilarating moments of sensual pleasure that she experienced when she rode her pony wildly in the windy meadows beyond the

Pinciana Gate or on the strand at Ostia. I understood, too, that of all the people of my acquaintance, this young doctor who was now confined to a spartan cell was perhaps the only one who might turn Julia from her headlong course towards self-immolation.

XLIX

"Do you remember the physician who visited you when you were sick? Who sent you the Gallic pony?"

I was with Julia in the peristyle. She had a habit of sitting there every morning at the hour when the sunlight might fall upon her face. The birds were in song; cicadas, too. She prayed. To whom she prayed or how she prayed I did not know. Her dress and toilet were slovenly; she no longer allowed Margarita to dress her, brush her hair or clean beneath her fingernails with the silver blade, and Desso, too, she now considered to have betrayed her. But she was apparently happy—sublimely happy. Whatever she encountered in her darkness fulfilled her.

She did not acknowledge me, but I saw in her face that she considered my questions.

"He is in the Tiberian. My ward."

She turned, "What is his crime?"

"He is charged as a Christian."

This seized her attention. "A Christian?"

"Yes, that is the charge." I did not tell her that the charge was fraudulent.

"Valentine." She whispered the name. *In a short time you will no longer see me, and then a short time later you will see me again.*

"Would you like to see him?"

"Valentine."

Her hands went to her temples, then swept back along her close-cropped hair, combing the tresses with her fingers. I was aware that I was deceiving my daughter, but the alternative was more awful than I could bear.

She was silent a long time, thinking. Then she said, "A Christian is commanded to visit those who are in prison." Another pause. "How might I see him?"

"I can arrange a visit to his cell."

She rocked gently. She was examining my proposal.

At last she said, "*Blessed are they who suffer persecution in the cause of right, for theirs is the kingdom of heaven.*"

I knew then that she would visit Valentine. Meanwhile, I set about investigating Margarita's sojourns into the city.

L

And now my story reaches the moment it has sought from the beginning, when the arcs of two comets intersect in the sky. Looking back from the solitude of old age, I see that nothing could have been different, that Valentine and Julia were destined to meet and to love, and that the outcome of their affair would be tragic. I have never been a religious man, my offerings to the gods are perfunctory, but I know that things do not happen by chance. The stars in their courses are not chaotic. Ewes do not lamb in autumn. Fig trees do not bear plums. There is a rightness to the world, and when plague or war devastate our desired good order, we know that there is a purpose, too, in dreadful things. It is true that as a caring father I had endlessly besought the gods to let Julia see. I offered sacrifice. I consulted soothsayers and oracles. But as I did these things, I knew in my heart that Julia's blindness was ordained from the beginning and that my supplications and inquiries were part of script that had been written by the gods into the fabric of creation.

I had by this time spent several long sessions with Valentine in his cell. I had tested the quality of his mind and formed, I believe, a kind of friendship with him. He told me of his early travels, his years in Rome, his foolishness in becoming Quintus's private physician. He lamented the choices he had recently made and suffered terribly from a kind of hopeless resignation to his fate. He claimed to have ceded the very thing that might now give him a reason to live, the legacy of his teacher Theophrastus. I respected his honest self-examination, and it confirmed my intuition that he might be the one to rescue Julia from her illusions. I told Valentine about Julia's commerce with Christians and about her apparent fearlessness, even longing, in the face of martyrdom. She would come to him, I said, and I begged him to use his gifts of philosophy to bring her back to reason.

As I guessed, Julia soon asked to visit Valentine in his cell. I knew the risk. Quintus's agents were everywhere. I waited until night, when the prisoners were asleep and the wardens and turnkeys few, and appointed a watchman to Valentine's part of the prison whose loyalty I could count on. Our house was not far from the Tiberian Prison. I led Julia through the darkened streets and into that closet of human ruin through a private door to which only I had the key, then along a narrow corridor to Valentine's cell. I tapped on his door and waited until I heard him stir within. I had brought two small lamps, one to guide us through the gloom of the corridor, another to leave with Valentine and Julia in the cell. I removed the bolt that held the door shut and swung it open.

In the light of the lamp, Valentine's transformation was apparent. No longer was he the immaculate gentleman who had been remanded to my charge. His face was now rough with dark stubble, his toga stained with the grime of the cell—the residue of two hundred years of felonious enemies of empire. None of this Julia could see, although surely her nose was assaulted by the stench. She stood by the door, apprehensive and a little frightened. She had prepared herself for this visit, taking more care with her toilet than had recently been her habit, choosing her prettiest tunic and sandals, binding her hair with ribbons. Even these small gestures toward the recovery of her old self pleased me. As she stood framed in the darkness of the doorway, I saw that Valentine was smitten by her beauty. I saw my daughter through Valentine's eyes, and it was as if I was seeing her for the first time as a woman, not as a child. Her complexion was burnished by lamplight, the delicacy and blush of her features accentuated by the cold walls of the cell and heavy timbers of the door.

I made the prerequisite introductions, lit the extra lamp and left them standing awkwardly to either side of the tiny cell.

There was a interval of silence which Julia used to orient herself, assimilating the sounds and smells and tactile sensations of the cell.

Her tongue crept between her teeth to taste the air, thick with must and moisture. Her hands moved flat against the wall at her back, exploring the damp and mildew of the concrete. She listened for Valentine's breath, soft and steady.

"Why have you come?" asked Valentine. He spoke softly and with great gentleness. Of course, he knew from our previous conversation that Julia would make this visit, but he wanted to hear her own interpretation.

Her lips moved, but the words hesitated. Then she said, "I am a Christian."

"And you believe that I am a Christian, too?"

"My father told me that is why you are here."

"It is true, I am charged as a Christian. I believe it was my own son who swore to that effect."

"Your son?"

"Perhaps. A son who was conceived long ago in Africa when I was no older than you."

"Do you—have a wife?"

"I never married. The boy's mother is long dead."

A silence. Valentine had moved somewhat closer, and Julia reoriented herself to his person, shrinking slightly against the wall.

"Why did your son betray you?"

"I have no idea. Perhaps because I left his mother before he was born. I fled to Alexandria, then to Rome. I dismissed him abruptly some weeks ago when he sought to establish contact. He asked to be my apprentice and I turned him rudely away. I did not know then that he was my son. I am still not certain. Perhaps I am mistaken."

"You are lucky."

"Lucky?"

"Our teachers tell us that we should not deliberately seek martyrdom but that we should welcome it as the portal of heaven. I would gladly change places with you."

"Change places?"

"Yes."

"You are willing to die?"

"I am willing to give my life for my Saviour."

"Your life . . . your life is precious. To your father. To me."
Valentine found words came involuntarily to his tongue. "At this
moment I know of nothing more precious to me in all the world
than your presence here in this cell . . ."

"Christ promises . . ."

He would not deceive her. "Julia, I am not a Christian."

This struck her briefly dumb. She stammered, "My father . . ."

He moved closer and touched her bare arm with his fingertips.
She shrank from his touch, turning her head toward the door. She
knew exactly where the lamp had been placed on the floor from the
faint warmth that it cast.

"Julia, the charge against me is false. It is concocted by Quintus
Mimmius, the procurator of games, because I failed to prevent his
son from dying. I have committed no crime other than failing to
cure what cannot be cured."

She struggled to recapture her emotional bearings. His voice was
tender, consoling. He might have been one of the angels of her
visions. She said, almost whispering, "Perhaps God has planned this
for you, that you might come into his glory. There was a thief who
was crucified on our Saviour's right hand . . ."

At that moment, looking into Julia's unseeing eyes, Valentine saw
there the innocence that he had lost, the idealism that he had
foolishly squandered for affluence and social status. It was a
transforming realisation, irreversible. It took his breath away. It was
as if he had suddenly been knocked breathless by a heavy blow to
his chest. Even Julia detected that something had changed.

"Valentine?" she whispered. It was the first time she had spoken
his name.

He said, "Julia, tell me about your faith." He was not
condescending to her. He wanted to hear her speak, to understand
the grounds for her belief. Behind the murky philosophy of the
Galilean, the miracle stories, the otherworldly language, he thought
he saw in Julia's eyes something that he had not found in all of
Rome, something he had not felt in his own heart since he stepped
ashore at Ostia.

She began to speak, to tell him of the words of Jesus that she had
memorised and taken to heart, and the sound of her voice

whispering in the darkness was like a strigil scraping away a decade's worth of encrustations from his soul.

Her hands came away from the wall; she pressed her palms together at her lips. Behind her fingers, her lips moved, "Jesus said: *I am the light that is over all things. I am all. Split a piece of wood, and I am there. Pick up a stone, and you will find me there . . .*"

The words she spoke were not important. What was important was her voice. Though a whisper, it filled the cell like a spring mist rising from the Tiber marshes, like the glow of dawn on a summer's day.

"Jesus said: *Many are standing by the door, but those who are alone will enter the marriage chamber . . .*" The words and phrases tumbled out in no particular order. She could not focus her mind. She was frightened, set free from her moorings. After each phase she paused, hoping to hear his voice.

He listened, occasionally interjecting a question or comment, until the oil in the lamp was gone and the wick flickered out. Julia seemed not to take notice, but they were now in equal darkness. It was her voice now that filled his senses. He put out his hand and eased it towards her. He could not know that Julia detected his searching hand and moved ever so slightly towards him so that his fingertips at last touched her bare and shivering arm, but only momentarily, for he instantly withdrew his hand.

He said, "Do you know that I held you in my hands on the day you were born?"

She had no answer, so he continued. "Did your father tell you? I was there at your birth, as assistant to the physician Theophrastus in Alexandria. Your mother's labour was long and hard, but when you were born you were perfect. Your head was covered by the caul. I had never held a newborn babe. I held you in my hands . . ."

She interrupted, "Valentine, will you pray with me?"

"I am not a prayerful man," he said.

"Give me you hands."

He stretched out his hands and she unerringly took them into hers. She whispered, "Heavenly father, protect the soul of this man, who is your servant. Show him the way, the truth and the light, so that if his life is taken from us he will share with your Son Jesus

Christ everlasting life, as Jesus promised when he said, *It is my Father's will that whosoever sees the Son and believes in him will have eternal life.*" And so Julia prayed in this way, all the while holding Valentine's hands in her own thin white hands. He could not pray, but his eyes searched the darkness, and he felt glad to be prayed for. He exhilarated in her touch. He knew there would be no going back, that if somehow his life was spared, he would live in a way that would honour Julia's goodness.

I returned with the lamp. I stood at the open door and listened to the words of Julia's prayer. I examined Valentine, and what I saw in his aspect was not what I had hoped to see. His eyes were fixed on Julia's radiant face, on which now danced the light of my flame. What I saw in Valentine's eyes was not the determination of a philosopher to dissuade my daughter from superstition, but the countenance of a young man who was falling in love. The next night, and the next, too, I brought my daughter to Valentine's cell, with increasing misgivings. I am no fool; I saw what was happening. I saw the growing rapture with which Valentine questioned Julia, as much to hear the sound of her voice as to understand what she might have to say. And Julia, too, was falling in love with the man she hoped to bring to Christ. Each night she took more care with her dress and grooming; each day she mooned about, counting the hours until she might see him again. I heard only fragments of their whispered conversations, even when I lingered near the cell door. There were no physical intimacies between them, of that I am sure. They stood on opposite sides of the tiny cell. She prattled on with her Christian platitudes. She listened, too, as he told her about his life, his lapsed ideals, his hope for redemption. He did not specify what sort of redemption he had in mind, but her fertile mind invented some sort of eschatological bliss, Julia and Valentine in light-struck paradise, wearing the white robes of martyrs, resplendent in the blinding glory of the Galilean's love.

LI

Not much happens among the elite of Rome that is not soon common knowledge to others of the same rank throughout the city. Gossip flows from palace to palace, from mansion house to mansion house, from state apartment to state apartment, like the clear water of the emperor's aqueducts. It was not long therefore before Rufi was made aware of Valentine's arrest. He went at once to the office of Quintus Mimmius on the Via Labicana, where he had often been assigned as one of the procurator's bodyguards. He asked for an immediate interview with Quintus. After a long wait, he was ushered into the presence of the procurator of games.

The quarters of Quintus's sizable bureaucracy presented an unprepossessing public face; they might have been the buildings of any government agency—customs, taxation, quartermastering, trade. But inside, behind the drab concrete facade and the cheerless reception rooms, all was sandalwood and marble, with splendid mosaic floors and frescoed walls. Quintus's private suite was every bit as luxurious as his mansion on the Esquiline Hill and was entered through a door gilded with leaf of gold. The procurator was with his amanuensis as Rufi entered. Two walls of the office, to right and left, were frescoed with scenes from the arena and the theatre respectively. The wall opposite the door opened on to a colonnaded courtyard where fountains played in the winter sun.

Quintus looked up from his work with apparent irritation. "Captain Cosa? I do not recall seeing your name on today's rota."

Rufi was deferential. "Sir, I am here in an unofficial capacity, on behalf of my friend Valentine."

"Valentine?"

"He has been arrested. As a Christian. The charge . . ."

Quintus pursed his lips, then nodded deliberately. "Arrested? Too bad, he is a fine physician."

"Sir, I can aver to you that Valentine is not a Christian."

Quintus was abrupt. "Captain Cosa, why are you here? Whatever has happened to your friend has nothing to do with me. Surely, if Valentine has been arrested, it is by the proper authorities upon a legitimate warrant issued by a magistrate. Of course, since Valentine is—or was—my personal physician, I am naturally concerned. But we must respect the law, mustn't we? This is a city of laws, Captain Cosa, which—I might remind you—you are sworn to uphold. If you have evidence that would contradict the judgment of the magistrate, then perhaps you should go to the magistrate's office and swear out an affidavit."

Rufi stood before Quintus with military bearing, his brilliantly polished breastplate gleaming in the low winter light that entered from the courtyard. He cradled his helmet in his left arm; his right arm was stiff at his side. He said, "Sir, you are absolutely correct. Nevertheless, you are a person of influence and a friend of Valentine. I was hopeful that . . ."

Quintus cut him off. His tone was unctuous but firm. "Captain Cosa, you are a military man. These things are none of your business. I understand your concern for your friend, but I would advise you to stay well clear of Valentine. If it is true that he is a Christian, then we are all well rid of him. The life and security of the city is more important than our personal attachments. Now—you can see that I have much to do. You will recall that I have recently lost my son, unfortunately while under Valentine's care."

Quintus turned back to his amanuensis. The interview was over. Rufi acknowledged his dismissal with a snapped "Sir!" and backed out of the room. He knew, of course, that Quintus's protestations of innocence were a sham. He knew, too, that no number of affidavits avowing Valentine's innocence would deflect the official course of his friend's fate. He stood with his back against the wall outside of Quintus's office. Functionaries passed by and saluted him. They had seen him before; his presence here was not unexpected. But Rufi's thoughts were elsewhere. His options seemed few. Valentine had saved his life in the sea off Sicily. He would not now stand idly by as his friend was sacrificed to Quintus's vengeance. Perhaps he could arrange a rescue from the prison, spirit Valentine away, out of the city. But it was hard to imagine anywhere that Valentine might go where Quintus would not find him out. The man's influence was omnipresent; in every city of the empire there were men beholden to Quintus for their livelihood. And, of course, any rescue would cost Rufi his career, perhaps his life. He, too, would become a refugee. But honour required saving a life for a life. Once during a terrible storm Valentine had jumped without hesitation into a raging sea to save his servant. Now Rufi could do no less.

That night, at the midnight hour, Rufi appeared at the entrance of the Tiberian Prison. He was in uniform, with all the accouterments of his rank. At his knock, a small window slid open in the door. A watchman's face appeared. Rufi asserted his authority. He was admitted and began a negotiation. He was there at the behest of Quintus Mimmius, procurator of games. He wished to see a prisoner, one Valentine, a physician. It was imperative that no one know he was here, not any warder or turnkey, not even the administrator of the jail. He was prepared to offer a substantial bribe. Rufi showed the watchman a pouch of silver coins, one hundred sesterces, more money that the watchman might make in a year. He poured some of the coins into the watchman's hand; they glistened in the light of the feeble lamp. The watchman moved closer to the lamp and rubbed a coin between forefinger and thumb. It was important that Quintus obtain certain information from the prisoner. Rufi would not be long. No one would know.

The name of Quintus was enough to strike fear into the watchman's heart. Rufi's bearing, too, proclaimed authority. The quantity of money offered was irresistible. The watchmen asked Rufi to wait in the vestibule while he went to clear the way. A heavy key was turned in an iron door, and the watchman vanished into the murky interior of the cavernous structure, taking the only lamp with him. Rufi stood in darkness listening as the watchman's receding footsteps echoing forlornly off the metal door that barred entrance to—or egress from—the prison. Could the watchman be trusted? Might he even now be waking the warden of the prison? Rufi had no choice but to wait and see.

Presently the watchman returned, a second lamp was lit, and he beckoned for Rufi to follow. Their course took them along desolate corridors. From cells to either side of their passage came the pitiful sounds of the hopeless and the mad—the heaving breath of dumb sleep, the whimperings of terror, the babbled prayers of Christians— muffled by damp concrete and humid air. A door was opened, then another. They moved along a narrow passage, scarcely wide enough for their shoulders, and the sounds of the felonious night receded. A final door was unlocked. The watchman gestured with his hand for the pouch of coins. "When I return," said Rufi. The watchman was nervous and impatient. "I'll wait here," he said. "Tap when you are ready."

As the door closed behind him, Rufi took note of his surroundings. He was at the top of a short flight of stairs. At the bottom, a corridor extended for a dozen cubits to another door at the far end, which was open. Halfway along this corridor a door stood ajar and a faint light spilled out on to the floor of the passage. He moved cautiously along the corridor until he stood at the open door. The cell was small. There was a tiny window, but it admitted no light, only the night chill. Valentine sat at the left on a straw pallet, his back against the wall. His face had been transformed by a beard, tangled and black; his toga was gray in the smoky candlelight. Valentine saw Rufi at the same time that Rufi saw him. A girl stood against the opposite wall. She had been whispering, but she now fell silent. She turned towards the door, and the astonished Rufi nodded greeting. She turned back to Valentine, her face full of puzzlement.

"Rufi," whispered Valentine.

The girl brought her hands to her neck and pulled her woollen mantle tightly about her shoulders. She was pretty, immaculately groomed. A yellow ribbon bound her short hair. Her garments were not those of a prisoner.

"Rufi," Valentine whispered again. The girls eyes moved between the two friends, questioning.

Rufi entered the cell. He gestured toward the girl, inquiring silently.

Valentine said, "This is Julia. She is the daughter of the administrator—of the prison. She is . . ."

Julia interrupted, "Who is it, Valentine?"

Valentine was on his feet. He spoke first to Rufi. "She is blind." Then to Julia. "I have told you about Rufi. He was my servant when I came to Rome. He is now an officer in the urban cohort—and my friend."

Julia lapsed into dumb fear. She did not wish to share even one of her precious moments with Valentine, and she was frightened of what the soldier's sudden appearance in the dead of night might mean. When Rufi said, "I have come to effect your escape," her heart stopped. She did not know it yet, but after her several meetings with Valentine, her interest had ceased to be only that of a Christian aspiring to bring another soul to Christ. She had not—perhaps could not have—analysed her feelings, but Valentine's voice was present to her all the hours of the day, and from the moment she left him she counted the hours until her father brought her again through the dead of night to the private door of the prison. She did not yet even know what Valentine "looked" like; she had not allowed her fingers to trace his features. She knew only the texture of his hands, smooth and cool, with long thin fingers and glassy nails, his scent, his voice, but these were enough, and out of these qualities her practised imagination had contrived a person who had begun to intrude himself into her awareness in a way that confused and frightened her—a shortness of breath, a flush at her temples, a stridency of her body that she could feel to the extremity of every limb. She had taken this to be a manifestation of religious ardour—the spirit of the Galilean exciting her apostolic embassy.

Rufi said, "Quickly, Valentine. I have bribed the watchman. He is above at the door and will be easily dispatched. I have horses. A ship leaves Ostia for Africa at daybreak, and the ship's master is expecting you. He, too, has been bribed. We have just time enough to make it."

Valentine was bewildered. "Why are you doing this?"

"I could do no less. You saved my life once. I will stand by you now."

"And you?"

"I have contrived a reliable alibi. Quintus will suspect, but he will not be certain." He took Valentine by the sleeve. "*If* we make it. Hurry."

Valentine looked to Julia. "Julia . . .?"

Her face was a sea of anxiety.

Rufi asked, "Can she be trusted?"

"Yes."

"She has heard where you are going."

"She will not tell."

"Valentine, we must make certain of her silence." Rufi's hand was on the hilt of his short sword. But even as he made this gesture, he saw in Valentine's face that killing Julia was not an option, even if he could muster the will to do it.

Valentine whispered, with sudden determination, "I cannot go."

"Valentine, you are a dead man if you stay. I have risked my life to be here."

"I cannot."

"Why?" Even as Rufi asked the question, he knew the answer. The girl's hands were fisted at her chin. Her eyes moist with tears. Valentine gestured towards her.

"Rufi, I have found what I have been looking for all my life. I cannot leave it now."

Rufi was angry. "Nothing will matter if you are dead."

Valentine's gaze was fixed on Julia's face. Her eyes reached unseeing for his own.

Rufi said, "Then bring her with you."

This suggestion disconcerted Valentine. For an instant the possibility of a safe passage with Julia presented itself. He turned to her, but saw at once the fear and uncertainty on her face. Her hands shook. To leave her father without saying goodbye was unthinkable. It would take time to persuade her to go, more time than was available. She was not yet ready.

"I cannot." Valentine moved to embrace Rufi.

Rufi pushed him away, against the dismal wall. He drew his short sword and placed the tip at Julia's breast. He was red with rage. He said coldly, "Valentine, I would kill her to save you."

"If you kill her, you can be certain that I will not go with you."

Rufi lowered the blade. "You are mad. You are a fool." He sheathed his sword and turned to go. He hesitated at the door. He turned, looked to Valentine, then to Julia, then to Valentine again. He stepped forward to embrace his old friend and whispered in his ear, ". . . a fool." And he was gone.

They listened to Rufi's retreating footsteps on the flags of the corridor, then the stairs. A door opening. A whispered conversation. The door closing. A key turning in a rusty lock. Then a silence deeper than any they had known before, because now even their breaths were stilled. Their heartbeats, too, seemed muffled in their breasts. But for the faint flame of the flickering lamp, they might have been in their grave.

Julia was weeping. Valentine stepped to her and drew her to his breast. He stroked her hair.

When she spoke her voice was barely audible, "What did you mean when you said, 'I have found what I have been looking for all of my life'?"

He knew what she hoped his answer would be: that he took Christ as his Saviour; that he was prepared to die a holy martyrdom. He hardly knew how to tell her the truth: that it was *she* he had been seeking, that his heart was breaking for the love of her, that against everything he might have imagined, he was prepared to give up even his own life for whatever few moments he might spend with her.

He replied, "You came here to save me, and you have done so. Whatever happens, there can be no going back to my previous life." He remembered a story that she had told him. He whispered, "*My son who was dead has come to life; he was lost and is now found.*"

Valentine could not see, but Julia's eyes searched against his chest for the truth in what he said. She knew and did not know that what he said was the truth and not the truth. Her mind was too much awhirl to analyse her feelings, but she felt safe and secure in his arms, her cheek against his breast. Perhaps in some confused and hopeful part of herself, she imagined that his embrace was that of the Saviour she had so often fantasised.

She looked up to him. Tears welled in her eyes. He took her face in his hands and kissed her fully on the mouth. It was a brief kiss, but it was not the kiss that Christians exchanged at their meetings.

She was bewildered. Her body shook. She pushed him away and felt her way to the door.

Into her father's waiting arms.

LII

I had news for Julia. Not news she would want to hear, but news that she *must* hear. When morning came I went to her room. She had not slept. Her eyes were red, her pillow stained with tears. Throughout the dark morning hours she had been reimagining over and over the events in Valentine's cell, struggling to find their meaning. I could hardly bear to add more woe to her heavy store.

"Margarita has been arrested. And Cornelius."

She looked up with those darling, useless eyes, imploring me to let her be.

I did not spare her. "They were found together—in compromising circumstances. They are lovers."

Julia shrieked. She leaped from her bed and beat me with her fists. "You lie, you lie," she screamed.

"No, it's true. I have the information from a reliable source. Margarita and Cornelius have been arrested. They were discovered together. Cornelius denies that he is a Christian. Margarita is muddled and mad. She will not be coming home."

Julia pounded and pounded on my chest until I had to take her wrists in my hands. What I told her was true. What I did not tell her was that it was *my* agents who had followed Margarita, who broke in upon her tryst with the Christian priest, who arrested the lovers, made them dress, took them to a prison not my own, together with the various Christian documents—scriptures and letters from other congregations—that would indict them. Cornelius protested his innocence. He denied that the documents were his own; they were the girl's, he said. Margarita was too shattered to affirm or deny.

I was not proud of what I had done. But it was necessary. Julia must be made to see the Christian delusion for what it was— seditious, criminal, superstitious. Only then might she avoid her self-immolation. I led her by her wrists to her bed and made her sit.

"You lie," she wept. "You lie."

No, I did not lie, and I made Julia know that it was so.

I said, "We shall have to find you another companion."

LIII

Julia did not ask to see Valentine that night, nor the next. She kept to her room and wrestled with her demons, trying to balance the clarity of her previous visions with the reality of Margarita's and Cornelius's betrayal. *Salt is a useful thing, but if the salt loses its savour, how can it be seasoned again?* She "read" over and over again all of the words of Christ that she had committed to memory. *I am the light who has come into the world; whoever believes in me need not stay in darkness.* She searched and searched, too, for the sound of Christ's voice that she had heard speaking in her lucid dreams. *While you still have the light, believe in the light, and you will become sons and daughters of light.*

Valentine seldom passed out of her mind.

Desso came to see her. "Are you well?" the old woman asked in a voice that came from deep within moist lungs. Julia felt ashamed. For her coldness to Desso, and for Margarita's sin.

"What is the hour?"

"The sun is gone three hours," coughed Desso.

Julia took no more notice of her former minder, and Desso went away. Julia knew without being told that it was the third hour of the night; she only wanted her perception confirmed. She could gauge how long the sun had been gone by the coolness of the bedpost and the sheets. She went to the water bowl on her dressing table and splashed water on to the dry part of the bowl. She knew exactly how long it would take for the water to evaporate. When the bowl was dry, it would be midnight.

The house was asleep: Desso wheezed in her cot; her father's throat rumbled in his troubled rest. Julia wrapped her dark cloak about her shoulders. She knew where her father kept his keys—in a rosewood box in his private office; she went there and took them, careful not to let them chime against each other. Now would come her greatest challenge: her first venture from the house alone. It was seven hundred steps from the door of her house to the private door of the jail where her father had led her on four previous occasions. On the most recent of these journeys, she had counted her steps, memorised every turning, let her hands discern the texture of every wall. But still—to go into the streets, at the midnight hour! She tried not to let herself think of untoward consequences. She unbolted the door and slipped into the night, leaving the house unlocked behind her.

The stench of the night city hit her like a slap in the face. Without the protective company of her father, her senses were especially acute. She stood for a moment in the chill air, orienting herself to a thousand sensations, some overt (the rumble of the night-dirt carts on distant cobblestones), some subtle (the hissing stream of a man relieving himself on to the pavement from a second-storey window). The wind was landward, from the snow-covered Apennines, and she could detect the scent of pines as a sweet overlay on the rancid tastes of the city.

She followed a mental map she had made of a thousand remembered sensations, tastes, scents, sounds and tactile feelings. She moved deliberately, trailing her hand along the walls of buildings, letting her toe explore each step. She kept the river (with its sewerish smell) to her left, the piney landward scents to her right. At one point along her dark itinerary, she sensed the presence of someone following her at a distance, matching her steps, her lurches and pauses, but with a slight temporal displacement, so that when she paused and stilled her heaving heart the follower took just a step before pausing, too. She knew, because her father had told her often, that the city at night belongs to footpads, vagrants, gallows birds, rapists. A fear grew thick upon her until her senses became paralysed and her progress disoriented. Something fleshy and cold touched her bare calf and she stiffened. It was a dog, nosing and licking; she nudged it away. But now she was lost, she had dropped the thread of her memory. She flattened her back against the wall, spread her hands against the cold limestone. Limestone! Only one building along her way had a limestone facade—the porous texture, the blunted edges of corners and cornices where the stone had dissolved in the corrosive summer rains of the city. She moved again, counting, praying. A colicky infant crying. The gushing fragrances of a perfumer's shop: musk, ambergris, alcohol, rose and clove. She missed the private door of the prison, passed beyond it, became lost, retraced her steps. At last she found it, the flaking boards, the smell of dust and vermin. The keys! She would try them one by one in the lock, but to her surprise the first one fit, turned. The rasp of the sliding bolt seemed loud enough to wake the neighbourhood, but she knew the sound *as she perceived it* was amplified by her concentrated hearing. Her hand felt for the jamb as the door pivoted on its ancient hinges. Frigid air poured through the crack from the black interior. She grasped the thick wood and eased the door open. It would squeak, she knew, like an infant's cry, but before that happened she managed to slip through the gap. She nudged the door back into its jamb. Now she was safe. There would not be a watchman. Along the passage, a turning to the left, another door, also locked, then seven more steps to Valentine's cell. These she negotiated quickly, her heart racing.

At his cell door she whispered his name. "Valentine."

He had heard her footsteps, solitary. His face was at the peephole. The corridor was inky black. Where was the lamp? "Your father?" he asked.

"I am alone."

She slid the bolt. The door opened outward.

Julia had not planned what happened next. She fell into his arms and kissed him passionately. It was not what she had wanted. *The spirit gives life, the flesh has nothing to offer.* Yet it *was* what she wanted. It was what her prayers had been about, although she did not know it. *But if the salt loses its savour* . . . His arms were tight about her shoulders, his palm resting on the small of her back. When he moved his lips away from her mouth she followed him hungrily. She was burning in the touch of him. He pushed her away, gently. Her hands went to his face, exploring his eyes, nose, mouth, cheeks, sculpting a mental likeness. Her fingers brushed against his face as if she were painting his features.

"You are beautiful," she said.

"Julia . . ."

She kissed him again, devouring him, tasting the salt on his tongue, his teeth. Her angels murmured, *But if the salt, the salt, the salt . . .*

Again, he pushed her away. He whispered, "How did you get here?"

She was startled, drowning in love. His voice was like a surface voice to one submerged. Her fingers found his ears, his eyelids, his nose, his mouth. She pressed her lips on his again. The room was full of sound, clamourous, resonating, a ringing and a singing, voices, *the salt, the salt, the salt . . .*

"How did you get here?" He was insistent. "How did you get here?" Suddenly his voice crystallised out of the chorus of angelic sounds.

She answered, "I came alone. I have his keys."

"Julia, we can escape together. If we hurry. Will you come with me?" He did not stop to consider that if she came away with him it would place her life in mortal danger. *That* thought would come to him later, with its attendant regret. But now, at that moment, there was nothing between them but the urgency of love.

She nodded yes. "Yes, yes."

Quickly, he gathered up the letter he had recently received from Antonius and the reply that he had written (on a scrap of parchment that I had provided him). Then, hand in hand, they retraced Julia's steps. Closed the door of the cell and bolted it. Moved along the passageway. Two more doors, closed and locked behind them. Along the dark streets, more quickly now, with Valentine leading the way. At Julia's house he said, "We must replace the keys." At first she didn't understand, but then she grasped that Valentine was seeking to ensure that I would not be implicated in his escape. She slipped inside the house and returned the keys to the place from which she had taken them. As she placed them in the rosewood box, she sensed that someone was watching. She drank in every faint sensation but could not identify the presence. Perhaps she was mistaken. But no, it was Desso. The old woman stood at the doorway watching Julia return the keys to her father's cubicle, but Julia, in her urgency, never knew it.

There was no way they could bolt the door from inside the house. They closed it, left it unsecured, and ran through the night streets. They waited by the Pinciana Gate, and when the gate was opened at dawn they fled into the countryside.

LIV

Ides November
Alexandria

Valentine,

Astonishingly, I am in receipt of your letter, in which you recount your troubles with Quintus. Astonishingly, I say, because this city remains in turmoil. The Palmyrenes continue to trouble us. The Egyptians, too, disrupt the city's supplies. Roman administration is weak; our governor vacillates when he should take strong action, and he acts decisively when he should exert restraint. In the midst of chaos, I try to make a life. I practise my craft, although there is no one to buy my clocks and no possibility of exporting them. To scrape a living, I do whatever odd jobs come my way: the repair of jewellery or kitchenware, the making of props for the theatre on those few occasions when we experience enough stability for the governor to stage a show.

Two of my children, the girls, have died of poisoned water. At least that is what we are told—that the city's wells are polluted by our enemies. My wife, Justine, is devastated. During the girls' sickness, she made sacrifice to Isis, stormed the goddess's temple with her prayers. Nevertheless, the girls slipped away, first Felicitas, then Laetitia, in their mother's arms. But, praise be our Lord Jesus Christ, this tragedy had a happy issue: Justine converted to Christianity. She has abandoned her former veneration of Isis and now lives in the expectation of seeing her daughters again in heaven, for they had been baptised at my command. I cannot tell you,

Valentine, how pleased I was to see Justine take the waters of salvation. The thought that she might not share the reward promised by our Saviour was more than I could bear. Still Justine weeps. Her eyes are rimmed with shadows, her body thin and wan. Jesus promised that in the rapture every tear will be washed away. *Happy are you who weep now,* he said, *for you shall have joy.* Happy is Justine in her tears.

Our priest tells us that the end is near. The troubles that afflict our world—the diseases, the Palmyrene harassments, the poisoning of the wells—are the prelude foretold by John for the second coming of our Messiah. Paul compared the end time to a mother's birth pang; and surely now the world is pregnant with its own destruction. The seven bowls of God's wrath have been emptied over the earth, and we await a new heaven and a new earth. He will wipe away the tears from our eyes and lead us into paradise. And so we struggle, we suffer these tribulations, knowing that the morrow will bring the new Jerusalem. *Suffer the little children to come unto me, for they shall know eternal life.*

As for the bequest you make to me, the chest of money—take care lest you lay up a treasure on earth and lose your immortal soul. Valentine, he has a place for you, too, at his right side. Your sister is there now, garbed in white. She waits for you with milk and honey.

Antonius

LV

Rome

Dear Antonius,

You letter has reached me here in the Tiberian Prison in Rome. It was delivered to me by the warden of the prison, who—before the events I will now recount—had shown me this and other kindnesses, not least of which was allowing visits of his daughter Julia. Julia! This is my second attempt at a response to you. The first letter, which I began several days ago, is lost. I now begin another. It will certainly be my last. I am condemned to die.

You will laugh, Antonius, but I am accused of following the Galilean. Your old Epicurean friend is jailed as a Christian! Of course, the charge is false. I am betrayed by my employer Quintus, for the reasons I told you about in my previous letter (yes, the boy, Maxi, died, and I am held responsible). I believe that my son Philip was instrumental in my betrayal, by providing false information to a magistrate. Of this I have only circumstantial evidence and perhaps only myself to blame.

So much has happened. It seems as if most of my life—and certainly the better part of it—has unfolded during the past few days. It began when Julia came to my cell with her father. He hoped that I might dissuade her from her Christian faith, which he thought might lead her to an untoward fate—the very fate that wasted the life of my sister, dear Helena. His fears were not unwarranted, given the present climate of suspicion and xenophobia that afflicts this wretched city. Rome, it sometimes seems, is cess pit to the empire. Even the emperor stays away, avoiding the stench and putrefaction. Our prefect, Gallienus, is a good man, but weak. The real power lies with men such as Quintus, of vaulting ambition and obscene tastes. Yet somehow Romans continue to believe that they are exemplars of culture and refinement, when in fact their sole export to the world is a harrowing cruelty and unprincipled hedonism. Antonius, as you will know from my previous letters, I was up to my neck in this poisonous morass.

Then Julia came into my life with her exhilarating innocence and Christian empathy. As we talked in my cell throughout four successive nights, it was not Valentine who dissuaded Julia from apostasy—as her father hoped—but rather Julia who converted Valentine. I began to understand what it was about the teachings of the Galilean that attracted my sister Helena and my friend Antonius. I had dismissed your Jesus as an impostor and magician— for which the eastern provinces are famous. Julia made me see that his teaching was of tolerance and charity, not unlike the ideals of my old friend and teacher Theophrastus. However, I cannot accept that your Galilean carpenter was divine or that he rose from the dead or performed miracles. All of this leads back into the quagmire which is Rome, with its deification of the emperor and proliferating gods. But when Jesus says—or rather when Julia says—*Enter by the narrow gate, since the road to perdition is wide and spacious,* I hear something that I once knew to be true but had forgotten.

I did not attempt to divert Julia from Christianity, even from those parts of it which I held to be superstitious. Rather, I listened, as she tried to convince me of the correctness of her faith, and I watched—Antonius, she is blind, she has lived in darkness since the day of her birth, and I was *there,* I was there as Theophrastus's protégé sixteen years ago in Alexandria when Julia was delivered from her mother's womb into a lightless world. At that time her father was posted to the White City, and Theophrastus was called to assist at the birth. We did not know then that the child was born blind. Theophrastus held the bloody little thing in his hands, examined her for imperfections and saw none. He passed her to me. I held her briefly, then passed her to the midwife, and Julia disappeared from my life. Now, after all these years, that unseeing child has helped me see the light. And more. As we talked together in my cell—lit only by the light of a single tiny lamp—*I fell in love,* something I have never felt before, a pure and utter certainty that this innocent young woman was the fulfilment of my life. I was like a child again, experiencing the same urgency I felt with Olivia, but with a full and mature understanding that loving Julia would make me responsible for ever for her happiness, and she for mine. To touch her eyelids with my fingertips, to feel her own sweet hands exploring my face, my neck, my breast, was a more thrilling experience than I have felt with any other person; not even Nibi moved me so thoroughly to the core of my being. Antonius, do I effuse? Do I sound like a schoolboy? I do not apologise. She is gone now, taken away from me, perhaps condemned to her own cruel and terrible fate, but for those hours—days—we had together I cannot be anything but happy.

She provided my escape from jail. She came to me in the night with her father's keys and together we fled the city. It was a rash and impetuous thing to do. If I had been less under the sway of love, less smitten by the desire to attach my life to hers, I would not have risked her life in so uncaring a way. All I can say in justification is that at the time *anything seemed possible.* In some unarticulated way, I imagined that we might find a safe haven, Africa perhaps, or some more remote province—Luisitania, Britannia—beyond Quintus's reach. It was a foolish hope. His reach is everywhere. His reach is as long as it needs be to satisfy his depraved desires.

We left the city at dawn, on foot. I had no clear route in mind; we briefly followed the course of the Virgo aqueduct eastward from the city walls, then turned south through open country, moving parallel to the Via Appia. Julia's sandals were not made for rough country, nor mine, but she was surprisingly sure-footed. I held her hand, but sometimes it seemed as if she might have been guiding me, so agile was her step. By midmorning we had travelled one hundred stadia. We had nothing to eat. The fields were uncarpeted floors of winter earth, the orchards bare. Only when we stopped to rest by an icy stream did we wonder upon the audacity of our flight. Julia, surely, was thinking of her father: his carelessness would be discovered. I could sense the worry welling up behind her sightless eyes, but she did not speak of it. Her close-cropped hair was plastered to her brow with sweat, her feet and ankles crisscrossed with the thin red stripes of winter briars. I said, "Julia, we can go back." She answered, urgently, "No!" She touched my face, trying to discern my true feelings. Parsed my voice. "Where are we going?" she asked. "Far," I said, not knowing what else to say. And then I said, "Julia, I will cherish you always." It was a foolhardy promise, given the precariousness of our situation, and I could not tell if my declaration gave her courage or merely augmented her fear. "We cannot stay here," I said; "we must keep moving." And it was true: we needed to put as many stadia as possible between ourselves and Rome. But our progress cross-country was slowed by ravines and tangled leafless vines, and by the uncertainty of our course, so at last there was nothing to do but leave the desolate countryside and risk the road. Even then, when we had achieved the Via Appia, the going was slow, our sandals flapping against the stones, the cobbles uneven, the verges in disrepair. We were often forced from the pavement by traffic. It was a bright day for the month of Janus, surprisingly warm, and carters were taking advantage of the clement weather to transport their cargoes to and from the city. Any one of these people might have noticed and wondered at the mismatched travellers—one well-groomed and neatly dressed, the other bearded and unkempt—who made their way south with suspicious haste.

There was no question of staying at an inn. We had no money. The day was growing long. Julia was hungry and exhausted. She did not complain. At certain moments I could see that she was sick with worry; at other times it was as if she were on a country outing, so ebullient were her spirits. There was never an instant, Antonius, that my eyes did not esteem her: the way she leaned her head into our journey as if hurrying to be wherever it was that we were going, the white perfection of her neck and shoulders, her taut, athletic body, her scratched and tortured feet. My love for her grew each moment we were together and with it my desolation that I had placed her in such mortal danger. Much to my shame, I knew that I would not give her up, not as long as there was the slightest chance of finding safety and happiness with her.

The sun dangled in the west, exciting the Sabine Hills with rosy winter light. The warmth of the day would not survive the setting sun. It was imperative that we find a sheltered place to stay. We left the road and moved again across the countryside—sparsely settled land, a patchwork of farm and forest. We gave the few inhabited cottages wide circuit. At last, where our path debouched into open fields and orchards, we found a villa shuttered against the season. Not far away, a rougher hut with signs of human habitation, the caretaker's house perhaps. The villa presented a stern outer wall to the world; the windows and doors were boarded up. But the open door of a hay shed offered refuge. We grasped it eagerly.

There was no lack of food. Two nanny goats tethered near by surrendered milk. Goose eggs, too, from the shed, we took and ate, sucking the raw liquid from punctured shells. Where a bit of yellow yolk ran down Julia's chin, I wiped it up with my finger and returned it to her mouth. As the sun set, we heard someone approaching, or rather Julia was the first to hear. She stilled my voice with her fingertip and bid me listen. We crept into the corner of the shed and crouched low behind the heaped hay.

The door opened, the two nanny goats were shooed inside, the door closed and secured. The goats now shared our refuge. They bleated against the slatted door. When we were certain that our human visitor had departed, Julia went to the goats. They were the first animals she had touched since moving to Rome from the countryside, other than Mel her pony. She took them into her arms, snuggled their heads to her breast, sank her fingers deep into their woolly pelts. In the security of her embrace, they stopped bleating. They pressed their moist noses against her cheek. And as I watched, I could not help but remember what Julia had called the Galilean— the good shepherd. *I will lay down my life for my sheep*, she had quoted her Christ. I went to her. I knelt before her and removed her sandals. I kissed each scratch on her feet. I do not hesitate to tell you this, Antonius. Each scratch seem precious, an emblem of our flight, a promise of our future together. The goats nuzzled her neck. She said, "*He will put you in his angels' charge, and they will support you on their hands, so that you will not hurt you foot against a stone.*" We spread the hay to make a bed and covered ourselves with Julia's cloak. As she had cradled the goats in her arms, now she found shelter in my embrace. There was none of the passion of that moment in my prison cell when our bodies lurched into urgent union. Instead—a tenderness, a certainty of loyalty. And sleep. Exhausted, Julia fell into dreamless oblivion.

I slept but little that night, as you might well imagine. In darkness, the devils came out to play—doubt, worry and hesitation. I wondered if Julia, who spent all her life in darkness, was likewise afflicted by nocturnal disquiet. She showed no sign of restlessness. Holding her in my arms, her cheek against my chest, I wished those sweet hours of darkness might be extended for ever. But I knew that the coming of day was inevitable and with it the resumption of our hopeless flight. I had no idea where we might find haven. Julia's Christians might help us, hide us, feed us, smuggle us on our way. But how would we find them? How would they recognise us? Perhaps at Brindisi. Perhaps if we could achieve the port at Brindisi we might take passage to the east, where Christian communities were more numerous and open. But Brindisi was two thousand stadia away, two week's march through an unknown and perhaps inhospitable region, with Quintus's spies everywhere. Any rational analysis of our situation would deem it hopeless, and in the darkest hours before the dawn indeed it seemed so. With every sleepless breath I swung from hope to despair, from gratitude for Julia's love to anguish for the responsibility that love imposes. The night seemed endless, and my rest was so troubled that I doubted I would have sufficient energy on the morrow to continue on our way.

Julia woke with first light, a goat nuzzling her arm. I woke to see her gazing into my eyes, and it was a moment before I remembered that she could not see. Did she know that I was awake. Of course.

She said, "Did you sleep well?"

"Well enough," I lied.

And now her hands found my face, and her mouth covered my face with kisses. Then she stood. Her cloak fell away. And her tunic. And before I could grasp what she was doing, she stood before me naked, the goats at her side. Vertical sheets of dusty morning light entered through the slats of the door. The goats, one gray, one black, brushed Julia's calves with their woolly flanks. The air in the shed was musty and still, suffused with a cool tenebrous light. I stood. I removed my toga and undergarment. Julia held out her hands, palms open toward me. I reached out and locked my fingers with hers. And so we stood for a long time in a kind of trance, shivering naked in the cold. Jupiter might have rent the ground with thunderbolts; we would not have noticed, so completely were our senses taken up with the amberic attraction that united our bodies through our outstretched arms.

I mention this, Antonius, I share these intimacies because only then will you understand what happened next. Had we been more attentive to the world beyond the enraptured envelopes of our skin, we might have heard the caretaker approaching. Not even Julia, with her heightened sense of hearing, detected his presence until the door swung open and his bulky silhouette was framed in a brilliant rectangle of light. Julia froze. What she sensed I do not know: a sudden intensification of the cold? An exhalation of dust as sunlight fell on bedded straw? The coarse breath of the caretaker? I faced him, but could not see his shadowed face. Did he see my face in the dusky light? Our nakedness, yes, most certainly. Julia did not turn; she stood stock still. Her lips framed the three most perfect words one human can speak to another: "I love you." The man at the door sucked dusty air through his nostrils. And closed the door. We heard him bolting and bracing our sole means of egress.

If I had moved quickly, thrown myself at him as he stood in the rectangle of yellow light, I might have overpowered him and secured our escape. But I was hardly able to gather my thoughts, so completely was I under Julia's spell. But now the trance was shattered. We untangled our fingers and snatched up our clothes. I wrapped myself roughly in my toga, disregarding the undergarment. Julia slipped into her tunic and wrapped her cloak about her shoulders. We briefly kissed in the shadowy light, then I threw myself at the door. Again and again I heaved my shoulder against it, to no avail. I looked for something to use as a battering ram, but found nothing. I began examining the walls and roof of the shed, searching for some weakness. It was firm and strong. But wait! In the back wall, almost buried by hay—a small rectangular opening to the outside, a place for geese to enter and exit the shed. Too small to admit my body, but perhaps Julia . . .

"Julia, there is a hole. You might slip through."

"Show me."

I guided her to the hole. She examined it with her hands.

"It is too small for me, but this is your chance to escape."

"Try," she implored.

I knew it was impossible, but to please her I lay on the floor and tried unsuccessfully to force my body through the hole.

"Now you," I said.

She did not move.

"Julia, go, please. Find your way back to Rome."

She put her fingers to my lips and guided me to the place were we had slept. We sat there in the dusty hay, her head against my chest, my arms enclosing her, and waited for our inevitable fate. I attempted to speak, to apologise, to give her the courage I did not have. She put her finger to my lips.

Antonius, it was almost a relief when the soldiers arrived, a patrol from the Via Appia summoned by the caretaker. We knew that even if we somehow had managed to extract ourselves from the shed, our freedom could not be long sustained. Julia was at peace. She dozed as we waited. She had resigned herself to martyrdom, dreamed of it even, of her certain transport to paradise. Now, as she dozed, she dreamed of light. She wore a gold ring on her left hand, a simple band of gleaming metal. She knew the taste and touch of it. The colour? "Like evening sunlight on breaking waves," I had answered during one of the evenings we conversed together in my cell. She dreamed now of a golden city, lambent in unending evening sun. Our bodies, too, she dreamed aureate. She had been prepared to give herself to me. How she reconciled her proffered gift with her idealisation of Christian virginity she did not say, but in her dream we inhabited paradise together, our bodies chastely one.

And so, Antonius, my dearest and oldest friend, you know it all. I have shared with you what will certainly be the most precious moments of my life. It is shattering to realise that the trajectory of a life could find the summit of its arc in so narrow a cusp. Days, only days. Hours, really. Julia and Valentine. Oh yes, on two previous occasions our trajectories had even more briefly intersected: once at Julia's birth and again in Rome as she crossed the threshold into womanhood. But our nights conversing together in my cell and the thirty hours of our flight opened like a night-blooming flower— yellow-throated, virginal, white. All of the marbled mass of Rome cannot crush that blossom.

I am returned to the Tiberian Prison, awaiting whatever fate pleases Quintus. My cell is smaller than previously, windowless and verminous. Julia's father has not visited; he has his own troubles. Where Julia has been taken I do not know.

Dear friend, take care. You will not hear from me again. I wish you long life, happiness and whatever paradise your carpenter Messiah promised. For Julia's sake, too, I hope your Christian heaven waits. As for myself, I expect no life beyond the grave. I am grateful for the fullness of the life I have led, for what small good I have done, and especially for Julia, for having glimpsed what paradise might be *here on earth* if only we could learn to live as your Galilean prescribed. I close my eyes. I see two goats against a sheet of morning light. I see Julia's slender body—her breasts, her belly, the cottony swelling of her sex. And, Antonius, I am glad. I am glad that the consummation of our love was interrupted. Glad for Julia that she will go virginal to her bridegroom, glad for Valentine that he knew a love so pure and sweet.

I do not date this letter. I have lost track of time.

Devotedly,
Valentine

LVI

It was I who sent Valentine the papyrus, pen and ink with which he wrote Antonius. And I undertook to see that his final letter was placed aboard a ship to Alexandria. I worried that the letter might be intercepted and used as evidence against him; only later, much later, when Antonius sent all of Valentine's letters to Julia, did I know that this last communication from the Tiberian Prison reached its destination. I did not visit Valentine in his new cell. Personal contact between us now was far too dangerous. My position as servant of the state had been compromised by his escape and by the complicity of my daughter. Word came from the prefect of security that I was to be transferred to Paraetonium, a town far to the west of Alexandria on the road to nowhere, at a tenth of the salary I commanded in Rome. I had no doubt that my exile was the work of Quintus Mimmius, whose hand controlled the strings of the imperial security services. He would have considered Valentine's escape my personal lapse, as I suppose it was. That I lost my daughter, too, meant nothing to him: a father's tears in a sea of sadness. The orders for my transfer were to take effect in three weeks' time. Quintus wanted me in Rome until the matter of Valentine and Julia was settled. He had a part for me to play yet.

When Valentine was returned to my prison, I made no concession to his comfort. I placed him in the lowest dungeon, in a cell I had previously taken out of service as inhumane. A finger's breadth of fetid water stood on the floor, rats had gnawed access through the timber door, cockroaches scurried on the dripping walls. Quintus, who surely knew of the conditions of Valentine's confinement, could not fault my earnestness to please. But was it only to satisfy my superior that I treated Valentine so harshly? Or was there also an element of vengeance on my part, anger at Valentine for leading Julia astray, perhaps even a need to scapegoat my own failings as a father? After all, it was I who brought them together in the vain hope that Valentine's steady philosophical character might deflect Julia from her cultish path.

Where was Julia? She had been apprehended with Valentine in their flight by two soldiers of the Appian garrison, after discovery by a peasant farmer. The soldiers questioned Valentine, ascertained his identity and that of Julia, then dispatched the lovers to Rome. Valentine was returned to my custody. Julia was placed elsewhere; I was not told where. God knows I tried to determine her whereabouts. I sent messages of enquiry to all of my fellow jailers, to the prefecture of security, to every influential person of my acquaintance. I received no responses. It was as if Julia had vanished from the face of the earth. Old friends ignored my interrogations. Officials who owed me favours turned deaf ears. At last I begged an audience with Quintus himself, pleading my long service as imperial jailer, which included—although I did not say so in my importuning—occasional implications in his illegal and nefarious schemes. It was not gratitude, I am sure, that caused him to grant me an audience, but rather a perverse desire to see me further humiliated.

I was not summoned to his offices on the Via Labicana but to his palace on the Esquiline Hill. I wore my finest toga and carried the insignia of my office. I was met by a slave and escorted to an atrium where I was kept waiting for an hour and where, had I chosen to do so, I had ample time to admire the columns of Phrygian marble, the tortoise-shell inlays, the bronze statues. Another hour. Until at last I was led to what must surely have been the grandest room of the house, with a broad porch overlooking the city, where Quintus sat on the sort of throne usually reserved for divinity, his wife Lycisca reclining on a nearby chair inlaid with ivory and gold.

I stood rather awkwardly for their inspection. The slave who had guided me into their presence backed subserviently out of the room.

"So," said Quintus.

"Sir . . ." I began, stammering.

"Sir?"

"Quintus Mimmius. Your excellency . . ."

"Ah."

My lips were dry. My tongue rolled like a fat plum in my mouth.

"You have met my wife, Lycisca." A statement, not a question.

I bowed deeply to Lycisca. I did not let my eyes wander in her direction.

Quintus said, "You have lost a daughter?"

"Sir . . . your excellency . . . she has been arrested. With Valentine."

"And?" He led his finger along the scar on his shoulder. He pretended impatience.

"Sir, I thought that perhaps in memory of past service you might help me discover where Julia . . . my daughter . . . is being detained. That I might visit her." Suddenly the floodgates of my emotions opened. My eyes filled with tears. "She is only a girl. She acted impetuously. She was under the sway of Valentine. She . . ."

Quintus cut me off by raising his hand. He looked to Lycisca. "Is it possible, Lycisca? Is it possible that Valentine has such power over women?"

"She is a mere girl, sir," I implored. "A virgin."

"A virgin? Are you sure, Julius Marius Favus? As I understand it, she was often alone with Valentine in his Tiberian cell while he was ostensibly in your care. They were apprehended together, were they not, after a night alone?" He unrolled a report, glanced at it. "Apparently, the rustic who discovered them found them naked. Are you quite sure she is a virgin?"

Quintus possessed information that was unknown to me. And he knew things I thought to be secret. I stammered and shifted in my place.

Quintus continued, "But as a matter of fact, Julius Marius Favus, your daughter is intact. She has been examined by a doctor." He looked up from the report, his asymmetric face oddly benevolent.

"A doctor?"

He read from the report, "Your daughter is blind and—yes—a virgin."

"Sir . . ."

"And . . ." He glanced again at the document. ". . . she has admitted that she is a Christian. She insists upon it, actually. She has been charged on that count, too."

"Too?"

He rolled the report, laid it on the table at his side, patted it gently. "Abetting an escape. Refusing to sacrifice to the emperor's gods. As you know, both offences are capital crimes."

"Sir, she is young, blind . . ." I glanced at Lycisca; her face was inscrutable.

Quintus leaned forward in his chair, opened his hands. "Julius Marius Favus, there is nothing for us to say to one another. Your daughter's fate is in the hands of the courts. I have other business. As you know, the emperor's birthday is in a few weeks time, at the festival of Lupercalia. We will celebrate this auspicious occasion with special games. Perhaps in honour of the emperor we can devise entertainments that the people of Rome have not seen before. What do you think, Julius Marius Favus? What entertainments might titillate the plebes, make them understand that the most excellent Claudius and his Roman administrators have the people's best interest at heart? You can understand the pressures I am under. Perhaps your daughter and her Valentine can help us in this important undertaking."

He dismissed me with a wave. A slave appeared as from nowhere to escort my departure. Flustered, crushed with anxiety, I bowed to Quintus. To his wife. And again to Quintus. I had been humiliated. I knew no more of Julia's whereabouts than when I arrived, except that my daughter had been examined by an agent of Quintus. I staggered down the Esquiline Hill in a kind of trance. Somewhere in this teeming city Julia languished. Her life forfeit. Her dignity violated. And try as I might, I could think of no remedy.

LVII

Eventually I did discover where Julia was taken. It was not through the intervention of friends or colleagues that this intelligence came to me; friendship or collegiality apparently mean nothing within the bureaucracy of Rome. Rather, it was by bribing a junior guard that I elicited the information I required (every officer in the security services seemed to have heard the story of Quintus's physician and blind Julia, one more of the notorious anecdotes that constituted the public reputation of the procurator of games). She was in the dungeons of the Flavian Amphitheatre, somewhere in the rat's maze of tunnels and chambers that spread out from the arena under the white marble of the city. She had been placed in a cell with other Christians, held in readiness for the extravagant games that Quintus planned to mark the emperor's birthday.

Cornelius was there and Margarita. Julia's former maidservant shunned her and sought to have the other incarcerated Christians shun her, too. She accused Julia of betrayal, spat upon her, snatched away her food. Margarita bore enmity, too, for Cornelius, for his weakness and betrayal. Whenever a watchman or warder visited the cell, the erstwhile priest protested his innocence, denied Christ, pledged sacrifice to the gods. If he had been an ordinary convert to the Galilean faith, he might have been given a hearing, allowed to offer libations, possibly set free. But a bishop! A leader of the seditious rabble. His protestations were in vain. This must be said: among the Christians in that place there were many who ministered to Julia, shared with her their few morsels of food, embraced her with affection. They prayed together with her and recited aloud whatever passages from their holy books they had committed to memory.

All in that dismal cage knew their fate. And yes, that is what it was: a cage. No different in plan or purpose from the many other cages in that subterranean warren that held wild animals—lions, panthers, aurochs, bears, bulls—gathered from every part of the empire for the entertainment of the people of Rome. With one difference. The animal cages were cleaner than those which held Christians. The animals were better fed and occasionally brought up into the open air for exercise or training. Among the pampered beasts confined at the Flavian were the two tigers, gifts of an Indian potentate, sleek and muscular, glistening in their golden pelts striped with black, trained (at Quintus's orders) to viciously attack any animal or man. Beasts, Christians, gladiators: the catacombs of the Flavian Amphitheatre were astir in anticipation of the big day. Agents of the procurator issued orders. Slaves arranged iron grills and hoists, redirected corridors, installed trap doors, all beneath the sandy floor of the arena. The thousands of spectators who would fill the tiers, applauding the absent emperor under the watchful eye of the city prefect, would be unaware of the hundreds of men who laboured underground to make the entertainments possible. All of this Quintus organised with a genius for detail.

I was refused permission to visit Julia. It broke my heart that my child might die without our reconciliation. I was crushed by the needlessness of her fate. She had survived her mother's death at birth through the skill of an Alexandrian doctor whose name I had forgotten until Valentine reminded me. She had survived half a dozen plagues and the many dangers and vicissitudes that might bring harm to a blind girl who is active in the world. There could be no doubt that the gods of our household kept watch over my darling daughter. But I am not so naive as to believe that those idols of clay and bronze removed obstacles from her path, deflected accidental blows or dissipated the miasmas of disease. Rather, the idols stood in their alcoves as representatives of empire, the rule of natural and civil law, sanitation, clean water, the subduing of wildness—all of those attributes of a well-ordered society that keep misfortune at bay. Like the fasces of the magistrates, the household gods convey continuity, stability, inclusion. Their worship is the life-breath of the empire, the thing that binds us to Caesar and Augustus, to Tiberius and Nero. It was only when Julia removed the statues from her room, in her Christian trance, that her troubles began. The false god of the East entered our lives, with his promise of freedom from death. What does a Christian care about balance, order, rule or law? For a Christian, life on earth is a mere prelude to eternal life, the vestibule of heaven. Why bother building roads, bridges, aqueducts, prisons or city walls when a city with streets of gold awaits the martyr? Julia could have had everything; blinded by the promises of the Galilean charlatan, she chose death. It made no sense.

In her crowded cell, she sat alone and in silence. She had much to think about: the message of Christ, which she had taken irrevocably to heart; the hypocrisy of Margarita and Cornelius; and most especially, her love for Valentine, the ache of desire which warmed her from within. All of this she considered, wondering. And then, on the third day before the emperor's birthday games, she was taken from the company of her fellow Christians, removed to a chamber above the ground, a room of relative luxury, with a south-facing window, a cot, a chamber pot, a bowl and pitcher of clean water on a scrubbed plank table, and as much food and drink as she desired. They asked her, "What else do you want?" She said, "To join my Maker in paradise." They replied, "Not yet." She asked, "Then bring someone who will read to me the gospels of Christ."

This was easy enough to do. Many copies of the Christian scriptures and letters from Christian bishops had been confiscated; they cluttered the archives of the magistrates. Most of these writings were in Greek. A Greek slave girl was found to read them. She sat beside Julia on the cot and read the words of Christ: *No one lights a lamp and hides it under a bushel, but places it upon the lamp-stand so that it lights the room. The lamp of your body is the eye. When your eye is sound, your whole body is filled with light, but when it is diseased your body will be in darkness. See to it then that the light inside you is not darkness. If your body is filled with light, with no trace of darkness, it will be light entirely, as when the lamp shines on you with its rays.*

LVIII

The Flavian Amphitheatre had stood between the Esquiline and Palatine Hills for two hundred years. At the time of the birthday games for Claudius II, it seemed as if it had been standing for as long as the hills themselves. Its construction was begun by Vespasian, completed by Titus. Those were the glory days when Rome was still radiant in the sun of Augustus, when emperors worthy of divinity resided in the city, cared for the common weal, embellished the city with structures worthy of a people who laid claim to the sea that stretched from the Pillars of Hercules to Galilee, Mare Nostrum, "our sea". The Flavian Amphitheatre, the Circus Maximus, the Forum of Trajan, the Stadium of Domitian, the Baths of Nero, the Temple of Jupiter Capitolinus: who today could imagine building such ornaments? In these diminished times our public monuments have fallen into disrepair. The Theatre of Marcellus tumbles down and is filled with weeds and vines. The temples have lost their shine. The frescoes in the baths crumble from the walls, the books in our libraries moulder. Even the Circus Maximus and Flavian Amphitheatre are in need of repair. Oh yes, at the time of Claudius II there was still new construction going on in Rome—grand palaces for the rich on the Esquiline and Palatine hills, gaudy monuments to lucre in a city where two-thirds of the people were fed at public expense. And where were our emperors then, as the wealthy grew fat on imperial taxes? Who had seen them? Our princeps were not even Romans, but Arabs, Germans, Gauls. Coarse army men. Upstarts for whom Latin was a foreign tongue. Of Claudius Gothicus's dozen immediate predecessors, nine had been murdered; such was the awe with which we held divinity.

Even in its valley, the Flavian Amphitheatre dominates the city— a mountain of travertine stone, quarried near Tibur and brought to Rome, it is said, by a road especially constructed for that purpose. An oval, four hundred paces in circumference, four stories high. Fifty thousand people fit comfortably inside the great tiered bowl to watch the entertainments which emperors and their agents devise to distract the people from their misfortunes. Anyone with a smattering of literature will remember Juvenal's tirade, *Now that no one buys our votes, the public has lost its care for democracy; the people that once bestowed commands, consulships, legions and all else now meddles no more with politics and long eagerly for just two things— bread and circuses.* It is no different now than in Juvenal's time. I have grown old; Rome has grown older. It is said that our new emperor, Constantine, will suspend the games. No longer will criminals condemned for capital crimes be given to the beasts; nor will the arena hear the clash and clang of gladiators's swords. We'll wait and see. For the moment the games continue, the beasts roar, the gladiators vie, as they have for three hundred years. And the amphitheatre falls ever more grimly into disrepair.

My career has been dedicated to the games. My first job as a young man was as a clerk in the cavernous offices on the Via Labicana where the predecessors of Quintus plied their deadly commerce. I was posted to Alexandria, where I acted as a procurer of beasts and men for trans-shipment to Rome. Tiring of the provinces and depressed by my wife's death in Egypt, I left the imperial service for a post at the gladiatorial school in the Alban Hills. Then, as jailer in Rome, my duties still were mostly occupied with satisfying the demands of the arena. Now, retired, I remain in Rome. The window of my tiny apartment looks out on the Circus Maximus. On racing days the roar of the crowd fills my rooms. When the wind is right I catch the smell of horse flesh and dung.

Although my career was almost exclusively concerned with the games, I was never an enthusiastic spectator. I attended the arena only when professional responsibilities compelled me to go. It was not that I had moral reservations about what happened there; it seemed to me to make little difference whether an execution for a capital crime was carried out at the city gate by a public executioner or on the arena floor by a lion. Some gladiators freely chose to fight; others, condemned to die in any case, at least had a chance to win their freedom by skill at arms. The games had been around, it seemed, as long as Rome itself, and few were willing to challenge tradition. The emperor Domitian tried to replace the gladiatorial bouts with games in the Greek style: foot races, boxing, javelin casting, that sort of thing. He built the Circus Agonalis for this purpose and initiated prizes. In the Odeum he honoured poetry and music. It is said the poet Martial sang the praises of prizewinners. But the people of Rome were not easily diverted from blood sports. The Greek games withered, the clash and gore of the arena revived. By the time of Quintus and Claudius II the carnage was taken for granted; it was as much a part of the city as the water that flowed into the public cisterns through aqueducts from the distant hills. But, of course, when it was Julia's turn to die in the arena, my acquiescence in the games was tested. Then I saw the games for what they are: a monstrosity beyond any human control, a gaping maw of empire hungry for guilty and innocent alike, insatiable, indiscriminate, demanding to be fed. Starve the monster, deny its feasts of human flesh, and it would run amok, shaking down the walls of the Flavian Amphitheatre, shattering the foundations of Rome itself. The founders of our city were suckled by wolves; the blood of wolves runs in our veins.

Quintus made certain I knew that Julia would be part of the birthday games. A *special* part, said my informant. Now—my dilemma. Should I go to the arena to see my darling die? Could I bear to watch? No! But then again, what if my presence might in some way divert the course of fate, perhaps invoke the sympathy of the crowd. What if my voice—"Let her go, let her go"—one of thousands, might be the one that made the difference between thumbs up and thumbs down? Even the slightest chance that I might save Julia seemed to demand my presence. But in the end I could not force myself to attend. I stayed in my office at the Tiberian Prison and shuttered the windows so that the crowd's voice—rolling like thunder across the city—would not offend my ears. In the last hour of the sleepless night before that terrible dawn, agents from Quintus arrived at my office with a warrant for Valentine's release into their care. I acquiesced without a word; this was the humiliation for which Quintus had delayed my exile. I signed the appropriate document and discharged my prisoner. I did not watch as Valentine was taken away, so deep was my shame. Then, within the hour, Cosa Egyptus, Valentine's friend whom he called Rufi, came in full military regalia, with two armed personal slaves, demanding Valentine's release. He had but one purpose: to save his friend from death in the arena. Too late. Rufi was prepared, it seemed, to spirit Valentine away, against his will if necessary. I reminded Cosa of his sworn oath to serve the emperor and uphold the laws of Rome. "It is not a soldier's job," I said, "to bear the scales of justice. Civilisation requires that law take precedence over personal loyalties. If every soldier acts independently, then we might as well fold our hands and wait passively for the barbarians." He left, dejected and distressed, to attend the games. And I knew that my speech to Cosa had no other purpose than to salve my own battered conscience. The words turned to vinegar in my mouth even as I spoke them.

Later, I would hear accounts of that infamous day on a hundred tongues.

LIX

On the eve of Lupercalia, Lycisca met and seduced the son of Valentine. She went into the kitchen after the evening meal to upbraid a slave girl for scorching a broth. The offending girl and another kitchen maid were scrubbing up the plates and goblets. The boy Philip was also there, sulking in a corner, watching the girls, who giggled at his attention. His dark curls spilled down across his blazing eyes, and, briefly, Lycisca thought she was seeing Valentine.

"Who are you?" she asked. She was attired in a gown of soft Egyptian cotton, richly embroidered. A fire blazed in the cooking hearth.

His response was slow. "I am Philip. Your husband employed me. I tend the fires."

She pointed a long finger at him. "You. You gave evidence against Valentine? Why?"

The boy cast down his eyes, guiltily.

"Surely you did not perjure yourself for a job as a kitchen boy?"

The boy's mouth worked but did not speak. He was troubled and attracted by Lycisca's interrogation. He sensed the possibility of an alliance with Lycisca but did not know how to win her to his side. He needn't have wondered. She had already decided who he was and how she would engage him.

"You are Valentine's son?"

He nodded affirmation, wondering how it was she knew.

"Come to my chamber," she said, and abruptly left the kitchen. The boy looked to the two girls. They put their chins against their chests and giggled.

They knew, those girls, the games that were played in that household. And Philip knew, too, when he appeared at Lycisca's door that he was entering upon unfamiliar ground.

For a woman who loved luxury, Lycisca's bedchamber was surprisingly spare. A sandalwood bed and chair. A bronze lampstand with seven flames. She sat on the edge of her bed—a mattress of rich wool shorn from the Leuconian flocks of the Meuse Valley and bolsters stuffed with swan's down.

The boy stepped through the door but immediately slipped to the side and stood with his back against the wall. He noticed ashes on his tunic and brushed them away.

She said, "You know that your father will die tomorrow in the arena?"

He did not respond.

"*Why?* Why did you betray him?"

The boy struggled to find order in his thoughts. "He abandoned me . . . he abandoned my mother."

"Don't be foolish. He was no older than you when he went away. He was frightened."

"If he had not gone away, my mother would not have died."

"How did she die?"

"Of plague."

"How could he have saved her?"

"He was a physician."

"But he would not have been a physician if he had stayed."

There was no logic to his hatred. He said, "I asked to be his apprentice. He sent me away."

She knew nothing of this. "When?"

"Weeks ago, when I came to Rome."

"Did he know you were his son?"

"*You* knew."

She smiled. "I know many things that Valentine doesn't know. Your father is naive."

He pressed his shoulders against the cool marble. He almost whispered, "Can you save him?"

"Save him?"

"From the arena."

She smiled again, a smile of exasperation and pity, and combed her long fingers through her hair. "I *could* have saved him. I could have made your father a rich and happy man. He chose not to be my ally."

The boy slumped on to his haunches, his back still pressed against the wall. "How will he die?"

She ignored his question. "Valentine is an attractive but foolish man. You are like him. The same hair, same eyes. He must have looked very much like you when he was your age."

He asked again, "How will he die?"

She moved her hand to her shoulder and undid a jewelled clasp. Her gown fell from her shoulder, exposing her breast.

His mind was like a tangled ball of wool. He struggled to find a sensible thread of thought. Once more he stammered the question that had lodged itself like an anodyne to reason, "How will he die?"

LX

As the sun rose over the hills to the east of the city, the streets near the Flavian Amphitheatre were already alive with activity. In a hundred stalls shaded with brightly coloured awnings, merchants hawked their wares. Food and drink. Programmes for the day's events, each copied by hand. Souvenirs. Knickknacks. Statuettes of gods and gladiators. Bookmakers standing on benches took bets on the individual gladiatorial combats, the odds posted on tablets affixed to posts behind them. For those who could afford a programme, pairs of combatants were listed by name and by owner or school, with a summary of previous wins or loses in the arena. Many of those who would fight that day were known to the crowd; a few were as famous as the city prefect. Two unspecified events on the afternoon programme were listed as special surprises for the audience. From every quarter of Rome people streamed into the amphitheatre through one of the seventy-six gates, climbed the stairs to their designated tiers, took their seats in the golden light of a Februarius dawn.

A blare of trumpets, more trumpets than this crowd had ever heard before, announced the opening of the games. Quintus was outdoing himself. He wanted word of these birthday celebrations to reach the ears of the emperor, who was fighting the traitorous Juthungi on the Danube borders; when Claudius came to Rome, Quintus intended to be among his favoured courtiers. From the entrance gate at one end of the long axis of the arena came twelve lictors bearing the fasces of imperial government. They marched with sober dignity, their shouldered bundles of axes and rods a solemn reminder that even in his absence the emperor bore in his heart and mind the care of Rome. Next came soldiers of the urban cohort, their breastplates and helmets shining, some bearing the standards of their legions, others—drummers—beating a martial tattoo; their presence also asserted the emperor's authority, for their well-paid loyalty was to him alone. Then followed priests with censers and sacrificial animals, and statues of the gods borne on rich litters by uniformed slaves.

Now, a change of mood from official to festive: musicians, dancers, tumblers, ostriches and an elephant, the first of these magnificent beasts that had been seen in Rome for a generation. The prancing pachyderm was magnificently attired with cloths of embroidered silk and silver ornaments and guided by a single naked boy who rode astride the animal's neck. The spectacle of the elephant brought the crowd to its feet; how, they wondered, had Quintus conspired to bring such an animal into the city without anyone knowing of its presence? And finally, at the end of the parade, preceded and followed by a dozen flautists, came two-wheeled cages, one of silver, one of gold, drawn by dark-skinned Nubian slaves. Each cage held an animal that no living person had seen in the arenas or circuses of Rome—an Indian tiger, sleek and muscular, prowling its barred enclosure with apparent fury, snatching at the air through the bars with razor-taloned paws.

The marchers and musicians took up their places in the fresh white sand of the arena. From a portal to the left of the emperor's throne, Quintus entered with his retinue and took his seat of honour. Among his escort was Lycisca, dazzling in a blue silk gown embroidered with Persian gold, her hair braided with roses in a style no one had seen before, with four female slaves almost as beautiful as their mistress, and at her side the boy, Philip Nilus. Quintus was content to let his wife evoke gasps of admiration from the crowd; he and his lictors and lieutenants wore togas of sober hues, so as not to upstage the man who would serve as editor of the games. Another fanfare of trumpets. From an archway to the right of the emperor's throne came the retinue of the city prefect—lictors, family members, courtiers, hangers-on—and then the prefect himself, Gallienus Narcissus Syrus, his gleaming toga trimmed with purple.

His benevolent smile and shock of grandfatherly white hair had long ago won him the hearts of Romans. Gallienus stood beaming, thin and wiry in the midst of his more corpulent attendants—a conduit of the emperor's grace. He waited until the hubbub settled down. Then, with a nod to Quintus, Gallienus indicated that the games should begin.

I will not describe all of the events of that memorable day, for only the last "entertainment" on the programme is a necessary part of my story. The morning was occupied with the usual animal excitements—panthers and bulls against bestiarii, murderers and incendiaries dropped into cages with lions or bears, that sort of thing. What was extraordinary was the number and variety of animals that Quintus had assembled and the imaginative pairings of beasts against men that his inventive mind had devised. Before the sun had reached the meridian, a hundred animals and sixty men had soaked the sand with their blood. As the last amusement before the midday break, the elephant was given to the naked boy to slay. The slave child, no more than twelve years of age—condemned for some petty theft—was armed only with a spear. With this he poked and prodded the confused and ponderous beast with no more effect than to finally provoke the animal to a fury. By all accounts the boy put up a brave fight, annoying the animal with numerous wounds, even darting between its legs to jab at the elephant's belly with his spear. With each drawing of blood the crowd roared its approval. But the boy dashed beneath the beast once too often; the enraged animal knocked him down with its powerful trunk and crushed him with its foot. Other slaves with spears moved in to finish off the beast.

It was at the midday intermission that I expected Julia would be killed with her fellow Christians. These grim spectacles occupy the hour when many of the spectators have left the arena for their midday meal. Quintus and the city prefect were absent; row upon row of seats, especially in the lower tiers, were empty. But many of the plebs stayed in their benches and munched on bread that they had brought from home, either because they could not afford to buy from the vendors or because they did not wish to miss any part of the day's entertainments. Forty men and women were herded into the arena—common criminals, Christians and perhaps a few who had committed no other crime than offending some person of influence. Trap doors sprang open around the oval perimeter of blooded sand, and a dozen African lions bounded into the arena, starved for food and trained to kill. Some of those who were confined there accepted their fate with eyes closed and heads buried under their hands. Others ran from the lions but found no place to hide. If they tried to climb the iron railing that fenced the arena, they were driven back by slaves with spears. The Christians knelt and prayed. Most offered themselves unresisting to the lions, including, to her credit, Margarita, although I heard it said that Cornelius bawled like an infant as the beasts approached and began their bloody business.

Valentine and Julia were not to be seen.

Now the mauled bodies were dragged away and fresh sand was spread and raked. The prefect and his retinue returned. Lycisca, too, with her slaves, and Quintus's companions and bodyguards. But Quintus was absent as the afternoon events commenced; he was in the bowels of the amphitheatre, personally arranging his surprise finales. Each of the gladiatorial schools, including my former establishment in the Alban Hills, had sent their champions: samnites, hoplomachi, Thracians, retiarii, secutori, essedarii. The amphitheatre rang with the clash of arms, the rumble of chariots, screams of threat or pain. No one present could remember such a surfeit of activity, such a valorous and vain spilling of blood. Meanwhile, hidden from the ken of the crowd was the bustle of activity in the subterranean tunnels and chambers of the amphitheatre. Gladiators were prepared for combat, their bodies oiled, their weapons stropped and polished. Two by two or in opposing teams they were sent up the ramps into the dust and roar. Singly or in gory clusters their lifeless bodies were dragged from the sand and wheeled below on bloody carts. The bravest and most skilled of the combatants left the arena through the Gate of Life, to have their wounds treated by the score of surgeons that Quintus employed beneath the stands. Those few who won the laurel crown and freedom-bestowing rudis strutted with pride in the presence of those who were yet to fight.

Quintus sought out Valentine in his barred cell in the echoing basements.

"Well, physician, you honour Rome with your presence," said Quintus, his voice thick with derision. His lictor stood behind him.

Valentine came to stand at the bars, his face only inches from Quintus's lopsided smile. He said only one word: "Julia?"

Quintus laughed. "Seducer of children, Valentine? Was not your lust for Lycisca enough to satisfy you?"

"Julia is not a child. Where is she?"

"You will meet her soon enough."

"Why do you hate me so? I did my best to save your son. He willed himself to die because he could not bear the brunt of your love, which was not love at all but self-aggrandisement."

Quintus moved his face closer to the bars; his sour breath made Valentine back away. He sneered, "I do not hate you, Valentine. I do my duty, which is to entertain the people of Rome. You made the mistake of committing a capital offense, and so you gained the right to be part of our show."

"You know very well that I am not a Christian. I am here because you begged or bought the concocted testimony of my unhappy son. . ."

"Your son?" Quintus was momentarily perplexed.

"I have a son named Philip. He would be about the age of the boy who betrayed me."

Quintus laughed. "Ah, you see, Valentine, the gods have a way of balancing the scales. The boy is here, in my entourage, as a reward, so to speak, for performing his civic duty. He will watch you die."

"Where is Julia?" Valentine's whispered entreaty was all but drowned out in the cacophony of the show above.

The twisted side of Quintus's mouth lifted in an almost smile. He turned to leave, pushing his lictor before him, then paused to address final words to Valentine. "Within the hour, physician, you will have a chance to see—your Julia . . ." He spit her name off his tongue. ". . . choose between her Valentine and her Galilean god."

As he left the dark corridor, Quintus snapped his fingers at slaves who came to prepare Valentine for his role in the drama that Quintus had devised for the lovers. But before the procurator of games presented this, his most extraordinary offering to the crowd, he had one more score to settle—one more diversion to delight the people of Rome.

LXI

Flamma Africanus—tall, black, powerfully built, with eyes that flashed like summer lightning, and glistening skull—was Rome's favourite. A champion of forty-seven contests. The slave of Quintus, but with the freedom of the city and access to the atriums of the rich. A man of great personal wealth; he had won many bowls filled with coins of silver and gold and had amply shared in the fruit of Quintus's wagering. Six times he had won the rudis, the wooden baton that released him from the obligation to fight in the arena, but still he fought, out of confidence and pleasure—the thrill of basking in the adulation of fifty thousand cheering Romans. Women of status and privilege vied for his attention; Lycisca had wooed him to her bed. He lived in expectation of manumission, but Quintus had long delayed, and now, unknown to Flamma, his master knew of the affair with Lycisca. It was not the dalliance itself that rankled Quintus so, but the pregnancy. That the seed of this black champion from beyond the African wastes had taken root in Lycisca's womb, when his own seed had failed to give him the legitimate son he so earnestly desired, was more than Quintus could bear. There would be no manumission for Flamma now.

The programmed contests of the afternoon were finished. Already, spectators in the western tiers were in shadow. The sand was raked and freshened. Now came the moment everyone had waited for all day with keen anticipation—the surprises promised by the procurator. Not a person had left his seat. The crowd was hushed, eyes fixed on the gate opposite the emperor's empty throne. The great Flamma entered the arena. He was recognised at once, and fifty thousand Romans sprang to their feet and cheered. He was naked, except for a white loincloth, and unarmed. This was unusual; the crowd was used to seeing Flamma gloriously armed. But two slaves followed with Flamma's familiar equipment: short sword, heavy shield, helmet decorated with silver fishes, leather strapping for his fighting arm and sandals: all the accoutrements of the mirmillo, or fish man. Where then was the retiarius with his net and trident? Flamma discreetly looked behind him to see who might be following. He knew something was amiss. In all of his previous combats he had armoured himself below and entered the arena with his opponent. But now, as the roar of the crowd washed over him, he kept his head erect and, with dignified self-assuredness, marched to the foot of the prefect's box. Gallienus Narcissus Syrus rose to greet him. The snow-maned master of the city fanned the air with his palms and the amphitheatre hushed. He said, "Flamma Africanus. You have fought in this arena many times well and bravely. Quintus Mimmius has informed me that upon your victory today you will be manumitted from his service. To that gift of freedom I will personally add ten thousand sesterces." Those spectators within hearing applauded, and the prefect's words were soon transmitted throughout the amphitheatre. The crowd roared its approval. Flamma preened. But who would he fight? As he turned to accept the acclamation of the crowd, he looked vainly for his foe. The arena was empty except for the two slaves bearing his kit. Flamma walked to the sand below Quintus's box and bowed deeply to his master. Briefly his eyes met Lycisca's, and in that instant he guessed that Quintus knew of their affair. If so, his death warrant was signed. He turned to see the two slaves disappearing through the far gate with his gear. The gate slammed shut.

He was alone in all of that empty space, nearly naked and unarmed, with no apparent adversary. He stood taller, straighter, as honour required, and waited in the awful silence. The crowd waited, too, breathless, expectant. The moment was sustained by Quintus until the suspense in that huge amphitheatre was almost unbearable. The shadows of the awnings touched the mid-arena sand. A hush. An unnatural stillness. Then—two claps of sound! Billowing plumes of smoke gushed from the bare floor of the arena. A blare of trumpets and drumroll. The smoke cleared to reveal two cages, one silver, one gold, which had risen from the earthen floor of the arena as if by magic, and in each cage an Indian tiger. As the crowd watched gaped-jawed, the doors of the cages dropped open and the tigers emerged, creeping tentatively on their bellies across the sand. Each beast wore a collar of jewels and feathers. Flamma turned to Quintus and held out his open hands as if to ask, *Where is my weapon?* Quintus, jaw in hand, did not respond. Gallienus also looked to Quintus, the same question on his face: *Where is Flamma's weapon?* It dawned on every one of the fifty thousand spectators at the same moment: there would be no weapon. Flamma would face the two magnificent beasts barehanded.

I will not recount the terrible scenes that followed except to say that Flamma fought with extraordinary courage. The outcome was foreordained, as Quintus well knew. Each of the tigers weighed more than twice that of the man they faced, and they were armed with teeth and claws. Furthermore, they had been trained to kill. For a quarter of an hour Flamma held his own with blows and kicks, all the while being torn and bloodied by the tigers's teeth and claws. The crowd never left its feet, and finally, as it was clear that Flamma had not the strength to fend off the animals much longer, a few voices shouted "Let him go! Let him go!" and the chorus was taken up by others. Gallienus Narcissus Syrus looked to Quintus for his cue, but the procurator of games remained impassive. Flamma was too preoccupied with survival to hear the chant of the crowd. He understood that he had but one chance for life. Summoning his remaining strength, he stumbled for one of the cages that still sat at the centre of the arena on their elevating platforms. When the crowd observed this act of retreat, the chant turned ugly. "Now he's got it!" Flamma crawled inside the cage and attempted to raise up the door. It would not budge. One of the tigers clamped his jaw to Flamma's foot and dragged him from the cage. It was over.

LXII

Shadows lengthened, but still the spectators in the Flavian Amphitheatre kept their seats. They were emotionally exhausted by Flamma's battle with the cats. They chatted restlessly and shifted on their benches as slaves with spears, dogs and nets drove the tigers back into their cages. Flamma's shredded body was placed on a litter and carried below. A glum sense of guilt settled over the audience, as if they understood their complicity in an unfair fight. Their favourite champion was dead, the tigers unscathed. As they negotiated their remorse, fresh sand was spread and raked for the last event of the day.

In his box on the podium, Gallienus Narcissus Syrus was conflicted. He wished to express his distaste for the spectacle he had just witnessed, perhaps by leaving the amphitheatre with his entourage. But he was afraid of offending Quintus, who sat immobile and expressionless not far away on the opposite side of the emperor's throne. For this Gallienus was ashamed; after all, he was prefect of Rome and Quintus served at his pleasure. But Quintus's power was such that a public slight was risky. Removing Quintus from office might be riskier yet; many officers in the urban cohort were said to be on the procurator's secret payroll. So Gallienus bit his lip and tried to rationalise Flamma's murder. He knew that Flamma and Lycisca had been lovers; all of Rome were in on that dirty secret. Quintus therefore had a legitimate grudge against the gladiator. And for all of their ex post facto unease, the crowd in the amphitheatre had been thrilled and entertained by an exhibition such as they had never seen before. And the tigers! It would have been inopportune if these glorious gifts to the emperor had been harmed.

Now it was time for Quintus's greater surprise. Rumours and speculations swept the crowd: what final amusement would the procurator offer? They waited for the fanfare of trumpets, the drumroll. And waited. What they heard instead was flutes. At first, faint and distant. Then, through the Gate of Life, came a parade of young musicians, boys and girls, dressed as shepherds in rustic tunics, barefooted, garlands in their hair. Their piping was lyrical, countryesque, a melody of birdsong and tinkling water. Many in the crowd recognised traditional tunes they had learned as children in rural villages. Behind the flautists came more youngsters with garlands in their hair and baskets of flower petals on their arms; they scattered petals across the sand—roses, poppies, blossoms of jasmine and orange—even in this winter season Quintus had access to these things. Then followed Julia, my Julia, led with ribbons by two children—two acolytes of Eros with tiny bows and quivers. She wore a leather tunic, spirals of gold on her upper arms, silver sandals. Behind her came one last acolyte, bearing a sword. Quintus made no public announcement; he had planted the message that now swept across the serried tiers like a sudden wind: she is a Christian. She is blind!

The retinue of youths who led Julia into the arena circled the oval sand and departed, their piping lingering like a whiff of scent on the air. Only Julia, with her ribbon-bearing acolytes and sword bearer, remained. She was led to the foot of the prefect's box. When she understood that she had reached her destination, she opened her hands and let the ribbons drop. Her senses were alive and sharp. She had never before been in this amphitheatre or any amphitheatre, never attended the games, but she had heard many descriptions of the games from her friends. Now from clues of scent and sound and tactile sensation, she constructed an image in her mind, orienting herself in the colossal bowl. She knew she was standing nearer to one wall than the others. The air was still and pungent with the mingled scents of blood and blossoms. The sound of the assembled populace of Rome was a cascading murmur, like water flowing into a valley by a thousand tiny waterfalls and rivulets.

Gallienus Narcissus Syrus rose from his seat and walked to the railing of his box. Julia stood erect before him . He gestured for silence by patting the air with his hands, and the crowd obeyed; the spectators strained to hear his words.

Gallienus knew the identity of the blind girl, and he knew why she was here. He asked, "Julia, do you know why you have been brought to the arena?"

She answered in a strong voice and fearlessly, "I believe in Our Lord, Jesus Christ, the Son of the one living God, who came to earth to redeem us from our sins and lead us into paradise."

"You understand that to refuse libations to the emperor's gods is a capital offence?"

Julia said, "He has written: *I am the lord, your God, who brought you out of the land of Egypt, out of the house of slavery. You shall have no gods except me.*"

Gallienus did not now look to Quintus; he would save this girl if it was in his power to do so. He said, "Julia, as prefect of the city and representative of the emperor, I implore you to renounce this foolishness and offer libations to the gods who have protected this city for a thousand years, and who now have the power, through my intercession, to protect you."

Julia swayed gently on her feet, her eyes searching the exterior darkness. She answered, loud enough for the prefect and all near him to hear, "When you crucified Christ, our Saviour said to the man who was crucified with him, *This day you will be with me in paradise.* Open your heart to the redeemer and you, too, can have eternal life."

Gallienus tried one last time. "I have been told that you are the daughter of one of the emperor's faithful servants, the jailer Julius Marius Favus. Think of your father, Julia, how you will break his heart if you needlessly sacrifice your life."

She was resolute. "I have but one Father, who resides in heaven. Who sent his only Son . . ."

The prefect slumped back into his chair, frustrated, frightened, as Julia prattled on, mouthing the platitudes of the eastern magician. He had no idea what Quintus had in store for this beautiful, unsighted girl, but after the ugly episode with Flamma he knew it would not be pretty. Quintus's sense of drama was too keen for that. Gallienus watched wearily as the procurator of games gestured to Julia's acolytes.

The ribbon bearers retreated, backing away across the arena floor to where a circular veil had been placed on the sand by the slaves who had dressed the arena after Flamma's futile fight. The child who held the sword on the flats of his hands came forward and proffered the gleaming blade to Julia. She sensed the boy's presence. She extended her hands and explored the weapon. She recognised the short, flat blade of a hoplomachus; she had often handled such weapons at her father's gladiatorial school. She lifted it, felt its heavy bulk in her hand, held it high. Then she placed it on the sand and said, "The Messiah said, *It is the spirit that gives life, the flesh has nothing to offer.* The words of Jesus, the Son of God, are spirit. They give eternal life."

Julia backed away a few steps and knelt in prayer.

Quintus gestured again. The ribbon bearers lifted the circular veil, which was suspended on a ring supported by thin y-shaped rods. The drapery made a circular enclosure, higher than a man. Now came the thunderous fanfare and drumroll that the audience had been expecting. The din echoed back and forth in the tiered arena. Then the sound stopped abruptly and the children dropped the veil. There, in the middle of the arena, as if by magic, was Valentine, naked but for a loincloth, bound to a pole.

The crowd applauded; they were used to such tricks. At Quintus's side, Lycisca slouched back in her chair, her hands interlaced at her mouth, her cheeks flushed, her eyes narrowed. Beside her, the boy Philip felt a cold anger and filial loyalty vying for his emotions.

Julia was alert, her prayer interrupted. She sensed a transformation of the audience's mood. The sword bearer came and took her by the hand, lifted her from her knees and led her to Valentine. When she was standing before him, she knew at once that it was he. His name formed soundlessly on her lips: *Valentine.*

He did not speak. Her hands explored his torso and face. He was bound, gagged. Her fingers caressed his eyes, his temples, his ears, then down along his neck and shoulders. She turned toward the prefect, her hand on Valentine's breast, her face a mask of anguish.

And what was Valentine thinking, lashed to the stake and exposed to the multitude? Wanting to speak Julia's name, to touch her cheek, to embrace her. To carry her away to some place where their love might flourish in peace and rectitude. So simple: *Why had he not seen it?* In the library of Alexandria there were tens of thousands of volumes, and he had learned more from this blind girl in a matter of hours than he had learned from months in the library. *Consider the lilies of the field* . . . But Galenus had had it, too. And Lucretius. How had he forgotten? Only now when all was lost did he understand how little really mattered. Julia. And *the boy.* The boy standing there in the procurator's box. The boy who had asked to be his apprentice, whom he had sent away. His son. Had he lost that, too?

The three children—the ribbon and sword bearers—had meanwhile exited the arena. Julia and Valentine were alone at the focus of fifty thousand gaping pairs of eyes. But something else was happening, subtly, unheralded. Through the gate at the end of the arena a wolf pack entered—twenty massive gray wolves from the Apennines. They moved slowly, warily, fanning out across the arena floor. It took a moment for the audience to assimilate what they saw, to ingest this new sensation. Never before in the history of the Roman games had wolves been used in the arena.

Gallienus Narcissus Syrus was on his feet, glaring at Quintus, and all the audience followed. A voice rang out: "Sacrilege!" Others took up the chant: "Sacrilege! Sacrilege!" Wolves are sacred to the people of Rome. A wolf had suckled Romulus and Remus, founders of the city, in a cave at the foot of the Palatine Hill. And this day of the emperor's birthday games, Lupercalia, was the feast that celebrated that event.

"Sacrilege! Sacrilege!"

Twenty slaves with spears entered the arena through gates in the railing to keep the wolves at bay. Quintus rose from his seat and stepped to the front of his box. He gestured for silence. The audience hooted and stamped their feet; the amphitheatre echoed their indignation. He waited, erect, with a forceful dominance, and slowly the uproar subsided. When all was silent, he spoke, loud and clear.

"Romans. The continued prosperity of our noble city requires the best efforts of all of us. Our emperor, the most excellent Claudius, is even now fighting the barbarians on the Danube to preserve our precedence above all the nations of the earth. Here at home we are faced with another threat, perhaps more dangerous than the barbarian hordes. Christian subversives seek to profane the gods of Rome, to defile their images, tear down their temples. They refuse to recognise the authority of the emperor and instead give fealty to an eastern sorcerer, whom they exalt above all the gods of empire, and above the emperor himself."

Not everyone in that vast structure could hear his words, but the gist of what he said soon swept the crowd.

As Quintus spoke, Rufi entered at the entryway behind him and took a place along the back wall of the procurator's box. He was uniformed, though unarmed.

With the briefest of glances at the city prefect, Quintus continued, "It is the sacred duty of Romans to defend our traditions and our gods against these upstarts who are resolved to wreck the glorious work of centuries. What you see before you is an emblem of our resolve. The girl—the blind girl—and her paramour are Christians. You have heard her defy the emperor, refuse libations. The man, Valentine, has been convicted of sedition. What can be more appropriate at this time of crisis than to call upon the sacred animal of our city to purify our spirit, to rid us of the corrosive force that will destroy us from within." He paused for dramatic effect. "And see, the Luperci are here to bless our enterprise."

At that moment, the priests of Lupercalia entered the arena near the base of the podium, clothed in the bloody goatskins of that morning's sacrifices and bearing censers. They chanted prayers and waved in the air the strips of blood-soaked hide, the februa, from which the month of Lupercalia takes its name. Gallienus slumped in his chair, defeated. He guessed rightly that the priests had been bribed by Quintus, but he sensed, too, that the mood of the crowd had turned. Novelty had quashed indignation, lucre had subverted true religious feeling.

Quintus stood with his hands pressed flat against the broad marble railing of the box. He waited, as the smoke of incense added its fragrance to the scents of blood and blossoms. As the priests paraded with their gory strips of animal flesh, the last dissident voices quieted. When Quintus sensed a unanimity of purpose, he gestured to assistants. The Luperci marched back into the bowels of the amphitheatre from whence they came, chanting and waving their censers. The slaves who had kept the wolves at bay retired to their stations behind the iron railing. Julia and Valentine were again alone in the dusty oval.

Now the wolves began to circle closer. Julia smelled their scent, which she recognised from childhood. *Wolves. One. Two. Three. Many wolves.* She grasped the danger, not only to herself, which she was ready to accept with Christian resignation, but also to Valentine. She understood why Valentine was there: *to ensure that she fought.* The luminous angels of her dreams beckoned both Valentine and herself to paradise, but his presence in the arena stirred her to the depths of her being in a way she did not fully understand. It was not a spiritual love she felt, but a physical tenderness that overwhelmed her reason. Quintus had judged her correctly. She would not let Valentine die while she had breath in her. She touched a finger to Valentine's gagged mouth—and ran to the place where she had placed the sword in the sand.

As she bolted, a wolf leapt after her. She fell to her knees, frantically searching for the sword with her hands. The animal snapped at her foot, tearing her flesh and taking a sandal. It backed away, wringing the silver sandal in its teeth. Another wolf approached. Julia's hand touched the sword. She grasped it and whirled on to her back just as the wolf leapt toward her. The blade plunged into the animal's neck and it fell dead. She jumped to her feet and ran with the sword to where Valentine was bound to the post. The wolves circled warily.

The silent awe of the crowd had vanished. They were on their feet and shouting, encouraging Julia. "Strike! Slay!" Julia reached out for Valentine, found him with her hand. She was disoriented, her hearing flooded by a roar like a mighty ocean in storm. Her nose searched out every scent; she removed her remaining sandal so that she might better feel the earth beneath her feet; her tongue tasted the air. But the sound of the crowd was deafening, incapacitating.

The more the audience cheered, the less able she was to ascertain the actions of the wolves. Gallienus Narcissus Syrus was the first to understand her plight. He sprang to the front of his box and flagged his arms, signalling for silence. The crowd understood. And then something happened that had never before been witnessed in the Flavian Amphitheatre, or any other amphitheatre of the empire. An awful and deadly silence descended over that place. It was as if even the breezes abated as fifty thousand breaths and heartbeats stilled. In the last sunlight of that Februarius afternoon, a deathlike hush embraced the arena and, it seemed, the entire city.

See. Gallienus, the city's prefect, still standing, arms extended, old doubts rekindled, troubled for his people, gloomily assessing the fate of Rome. Quintus, the procurator of games, his face a mask, his eyes crookedly fixed on the girl with the sword—he has set in motion the machinery of vengeance; the gods will determine the outcome. His wife, Lycisca, feeling again the desire for Valentine that had so often troubled her sleep after his visits to the Esquiline palace, but worried, too, by a converse desire to see his body torn and bloodied. The boy Philip, Valentine's son, now in the service of Quintus, impassive—an unarticulated anger, long harboured, has devoured his filial compassion. And loyal Rufi, stricken by his inability to find a way to release Valentine from his plight, resigned to the death of his former master, determined for honour's sake to watch.

No one in that audience understood what followed next, except those among my friends or associates who knew of Julia's upbringing at the gladiatorial school in the Alban Hills; she had been schooled in the use of the sword by the best gladiatorial trainers of the empire. For the vast majority of that great crowd, Julia's deftness seemed a miracle, as if angels guided her actions. More than a few wondered if what they witnessed was the intervention of her Christian god. Julia stood a few paces in front of Valentine, the sword clenched in her two hands. The wolves, singly or in pairs, dashed forward from the pack to snap at her legs or leap full on to her body. One by one she dispatched them, darting, twisting, meeting them with her weapon, until a dozen animals lay dead or wounded in the sand. The wolves showed no interest in captive Valentine, who struggled ineffectually against his bonds; it was the spirited girl who excited their fury. The spectators watched in unnatural silence, on their feet, awestruck, admiring her skill, thrilled at the girl's success in this ostensibly unequal battle.

Suddenly, three wolves attacked at once. Julia whirled and struck, catching one animal aside the head, slashing the belly of another. But the third beast leapt past her swinging blade and clamped its jaw on to her right arm. She shook her arm to throw it off and with the sword in her left hand jabbed at the wolf, but still it clung. Now she dropped to the her knees so that the wolf's body squirmed against the ground. She hacked and hacked until she had severed the animal's head from its body. She leapt back to her feet, alert, turning, listening, feeling, tasting, smelling, the sword outstretched in her left hand, her right arm hanging useless now, the wolf's gory head still attached. The crowd could contain themselves no longer. With one voice the cry went up: "Let her go! Let her go!" Thunderous, unceasing. The amphitheatre was a sea of waving handkerchiefs. The prefect, too, was on his feet, thrusting his thumbs in the air. He did not look to Quintus for guidance; whatever happened now, he would risk the procurator's wrath. Twenty slaves with spears dashed into the arena from their places behind the iron railing and drove the remaining wolves away from Julia. Then two slaves pried the wolf's jaws from her bloody arm.

Gallienus Narcissus Syrus beckoned and Julia was led before him. He gestured for silence, then said, "Julia, daughter of Julius Favus, you have astonished us today with your bravery and skill, which seem preternatural. The people of Rome have indicated their wish that you go free. I heartily concur and grant you liberty. Go and let the doctors see to your wounds. Then later you must visit me. News of your exploit will surely reach the emperor's ears."

Julia said, "Sir, I beg you to allow me to substitute my life for Valentine's."

The prefect marvelled at Julia's resolve. He looked to Quintus, now slumped passively in his chair. The procurator of games moved his head almost imperceptibly from side to side. Gallienus understood the gesture. Julia's request was being denied. He turned back to the girl. "Brave Julia, it is not in my power to . . ."

The crowd shouted, "Let him go! Let him go!"

The prefect looked again to Quintus. The gesture was the same. Nevertheless, Gallienus turned to Julia and said, "I give him to you. You are both free to leave the arena. We wish you happiness."

The crowd roared its approval. Valentine was cut from his bindings. Julia went to where her lover stood among the carcasses of wolves. She stood beside him as the people of Rome exhausted themselves with adulation.

LXIII

The procurator of games had no intention of allowing his scheme to be frustrated by the city prefect. Even as Gallienus spoke, Quintus had left his box. As Valentine and Julia were led into the sublevels of the amphitheatre, they were met by guards under an officer of the urban cohort and led into Quintus's presence. He had commandeered an almost empty room. No one was there but the children who had led Julia into the arena, still dressed in their rustic garb, waiting to be told what to do next. The procurator's wrath was barely contained.

Of Julia he said, "Take her to the doctors," and she was whisked away.

Quintus approached Valentine and whispered in his face. "You asked me once why I hate you so. I told you that I didn't hate you, that I was only upholding the law. But I lied, Valentine. I do hate you. I hate you with every fibre of my being."

"Why?"

Quintus smiled the lopsided smile that Valentine knew so well. "I don't *know* why. Isn't that strange? I've hated you since that first day I laid eyes on you in the baths. There was something about your look that caused in me a particular revulsion. I invited you into my house and into my service, and I hated you every moment." He ran a finger like a dagger's blade down along Valentine's naked chest. "No reason, Valentine. Some things happen for no reason at all."

Then, to an officer, "Take him in a covered cart to the usual place outside the Flaminian Gate and do what should have been done before."

The officer protested, "Sir, the prefect . . ."

Quintus snarled, "Centurion, do not to bite the hand that feeds you. I will deal with the prefect."

LXIV

In the gathering darkness of Lupercalia eve, a closed cart drawn by two horses rumbled through the streets of Rome towards the Flaminian Gate, escorted by a mounted officer and six mounted soldiers of the urban cohort. The last spectators making their way home from the arena leapt from the path of the flying column. Vendors yanked their wares aside. Ragamuffins scrambled. Meanwhile, Rufi was in the bowels of the amphitheatre trying to ascertain Valentine's fate. Slaves and attendants merely shrugged. But at last a child, one of Julia's ribbon bearers, spoke up and said, "They took him to the Flaminian Gate."

Rufi hadn't a moment to lose. He ran through the subterranean tunnels that led to the amphitheatre's stables, used the authority of his uniform to commandeer two saddled horses, and galloped into the streets. He reached the Flaminian Gate as it was closing for the night. He ordered it opened. "By what authority?" asked the gatekeeper. "By the authority of my sword," shouted Rufi, and drew his weapon. Wearily, the gatekeeper ordered the gate opened. As it swung back on its heavy hinges, seven soldiers of the urban cohort and an empty cart, its curtains flying, thundered back into the city.

Rufi knew then that he was too late. There was no point in wasting time ascertaining Valentine's death. He would return later. Now he must find Julia and assure her safety. That was the least he could do for his friend. Leading the extra horse, he galloped back through the emptying streets to the Flavian Amphitheatre. In the lamplit chambers beneath the arena floor, slaves and their supervisors were completing the business of the day—placing animals in wheeled carts for return to their keeping places, cleaning and storing weapons and armour, swabbing blood and gore from the surgery floor. "Julia? Julia? The blind girl?" She had been tended by the physicians, someone said. She could not have left the arena alone. "Who did she leave with? The blind girl. Julia. Yes, the daughter of Julius Favus." Perhaps it was with Quintus's lictor, someone said. Of course. Of course. Quintus would no more honour the prefect's wishes regarding Julia than he had honoured the promise of freedom for Valentine.

Rufi's next stop was the palace on the Esquiline Hill. He pounded on the door until a servant answered, brushed the minion aside, swept through endless empty rooms to the astonishment of servants and slaves who competed their chores by lamplight. Through the peristyle into a room that glowed with the light of a hundred lamps. Lycisca reclined on a couch. A slave child gilded her toenails. She startled at Rufi's abrupt entry.

"Captain Cosa, by what right do you enter my private rooms?"

Rufi drew himself to attention. "Forgive me, madam, I have an urgent message for your husband."

She adjusted her gown on her shoulder. "You won't find him here. He never comes home after the games. Surely, he is in the arms of one of his mistresses, or whoring with his friends."

"Madam, forgive me for asking . . ."

She interrupted him, "Is it really necessary to enter my house armed?"

Rufi touched his sword. "No, madam. I did not stop to think. I am looking for Julia, the girl who fought in the arena."

Lycisca threw back her head and laughed. "But of course. Presumably everyone in Rome is looking for lovely Julia. But you are at a disadvantage, Captain Cosa. My husband will have snatched her up. So silly of me not to have thought of it . . ."

"Where?"

"Let it go, centurion. You have a brilliant career in front of you; don't throw it away for a child."

"Where?"

She languorously extended her leg toward the slave child who knelt with the paint pot. "You know well enough not to evoke my husband's ire. Leave the girl to Quintus."

"Madam, the girl was given her liberty by the prefect . . ."

She laughed. "If my husband wanted the prefect's daughter, he would not hesitate to take her."

Rufi knew this was true. Valentine had been executed against the prefect's express command. He bowed and backed away towards the door.

She asked after him, "Valentine? Where is Valentine?"

He answered, "Madam, Valentine is dead. He has been executed by your husband."

Without further explanation or intelligence, Rufi departed. Lycisca sat up on the edge of the couch. She took the paint pot from the child and hurled it across the room. Rufi heard the clatter as he crossed the peristyle. As he passed through the entrance hall, he impulsively picked up a scroll from a table and tucked it in his belt. Where next? Quintus could be at any one of a dozen places around the city—at the apartment of one of his mistresses or at one of the brothels frequented by himself and his wealthy friends. But if Julia was with him, then he was most probably on his own ground. Rufi rode to the Via Labicana.

At the gate he flashed the scroll and was admitted; Cosa Egyptus was well known at the offices of the procurator of games. But before he could be admitted to Quintus's private apartments, he would need to marshal yet more bluster. He flourished the scroll, which he claimed to be from the prefect, but refused to show it to any but Quintus himself. "He left express orders not to be disturbed," enjoined an aide. Rufi stressed the urgency of his message. "I cannot leave," he said, "until I have placed this message in Quintus's hand." At last, disarmed of his sword, he was asked to wait while an adjutant went to seek Quintus's pleasure.

Then Rufi was led through the drab corridors of the bureaucracy to the more luxurious rooms of Quintus's offices, and at last to the golden door that opened on to the inner chamber. Rufi had been here before. The frescoed walls with scenes from theatre and arena. The colonnaded courtyard, now closed off with heavy drapes of damask silk. The sound of the fountain playing beyond, squandering the city's precious water in the winter night.

Quintus said, "Captain Cosa, you have the irritating habit of interrupting my repose."

Rufi stood at attention. He was at a loss of what to say. Quintus was dining with the legatus legionis of the urban cohort, Senator-General Marcus Graecus, well-known to Rufi. Julia was not present.

"You have a message, centurion?"

"Sir."

Quintus saw that Rufi was taken aback. He guessed the centurion's purpose. He said bluntly, "I take it, Captain Cosa, that you *don't* bear a message from the prefect. I take it that you are once again here on behalf of your friend, the Christian, Valentine."

"Sir . . ."

Quintus looked to General Marcus and smiled, but with an undercurrent of cynicism and disdain. He said, "Cosa, how many time must I tell you that I have nothing to do with Valentine. Wasn't he reprieved by the editor? Surely he is out celebrating his freedom."

"Sir, Valentine has been executed." He resisted adding . . . *as you well know.*

Quintus showed no surprise. He spread his hands as if to say, *What is that to me?*

Rufi was uncertain of his next move. He placed the phony document into his belt. He said, "The girl . . .?"

Quintus ignored his question. He was silent a long time before he spoke, in a tone that had changed from supercilious to ingratiating. He said, "Captain Cosa, you may be just the person we were waiting for. Perhaps your arrival here is providential." With a sweep of his hand, he invited Rufi to the dining couches. He pushed a flagon of wine across the table towards him.

Rufi protested.

Quintus said, "Is it the girl you are interested in? Marcus Graecus and I together have a proposition for you. Perhaps you will listen if I bring in the girl."

He snapped his fingers to the adjutant who had escorted Rufi and now stood waiting by the door. Rufi approached the table and sat. In a few moments, the adjutant returned with Julia. She was still dressed in the short leather tunic of the arena, now stained with blood. Barefooted, her silver sandals gone. Her right arm was bound with clean white cloth and held to her body by a sling. She was dishevelled, frightened, wary.

Quintus dismissed the adjutant. He got up from his seat and approached Julia. He touched her shoulder with his knuckle. She shrank from his touch.

He spoke into her ear, "Well, girl, you certainly impressed us all today. Who would have guessed your skill with the sword?" He took her by the elbow. She pulled her arm away. He said, "No need to be frightened. No one is going to hurt you. We are here to honour you. We invite you to join us at table. General Marcus Graecus is here, the legatus legionis, and Captain Cosa, who is a friend of your Valentine."

At Valentine's name, Julia became less wary. She let Quintus guide her to the table. Exploring the seat with her left hand, she sat, next to Rufi, who said, gently, to reassure her, "It's me, Rufi, Valentine's friend." She turned toward him and formed a question on her lips: *Valentine?* He did not answer, but she sensed an answer in the change of his breath. She knew then that Valentine was dead.

Quintus pushed food toward her—poultry, lamb, cheese, fruit, bread—a cup, a knife. She had not eaten in twenty-four hours. She explored the dishes and ate ravenously.

Quintus turned to Rufi. "Now that you know the girl is safe, perhaps we can discuss the matter of Gallienus Narcissus Syrus."

"The prefect?"

"Yes, the prefect. Who, as it turns out, has been robbing the public treasury. Enriching himself at the expense of the people of Rome."

Rufi knew this to be a lie. He asked, "By what evidence?"

"Evidence? We'll leave the legal matters to General Marcus. He has decided that our loyalty to the emperor requires that Gallienus be removed. We—*he,* General Marcus, can use your services, Cosa. You are an ambitious man. Your soldiers adore you. They will follow you without question. If you help us in this endeavour, you will rise high, a generalship, perhaps. Who knows, even the rank of senator?"

"Why doesn't General Marcus do his own dirty work?"

"Cosa! Rufi. We are not talking about 'dirty work'. We are talking about an action to restore the honour of Rome—returning dignity to the office of prefect. General Marcus has another, more important agenda, for which he will need the support of senators. What is required now is for someone to execute the quick arrest and execution of Gallienus. The legions will then follow us: Marcus will see to that. The emperor will thank us. And you, Captain Cosa, will cover yourself with glory."

Rufi stood up. He had not eaten or drunk from the table. He considered his next move, how he might save Julia. He knew that if he rebuked the procurator's proposition he would not be allowed to leave those premises alive. He was either a willing collaborator—in the coup against Gallienus—or dead. General Marcus was drunk. He was separated from Quintus by the table. Rufi considered that he might grab Julia and bolt for the door. But how quickly could a blind girl move? There were a dozen of Quintus's and Marcus's adjutants between the inner apartment and the street. He was unarmed.

Quintus rose, somewhat unsteadily. He came to where Julia was sitting. She tensed. He asked Rufi, "How much do you make, Cosa? One thousand denari? Two thousand? What *does* a centurion make?"

"Enough."

"Join us, Cosa, and I will give you an outright gift of ten years pay." He placed his hands on Julia's shoulders. "Is it the girl you are interested in? Join us and I will give her to you." He moved his hand to her neck and up under her chin, lifting her face. He said, "She wanted to be a virgin martyr. Not a martyr, poor thing; Gallienus spared her that. And you, Cosa, can relieve her of her vir . . ."

As Rufi watched, Quintus's eyes suddenly gaped wide. The words stopped in his throat. At first he thought that Quintus was having some sort of attack, an epileptic fit perhaps. Then the procurator stepped backwards, and Rufi saw the knife that Julia had plunged into his breast, thrusting the blade with her wounded arm up under her left arm without ever turning around.

Marcus saw, too. He rose clumsily. Rufi leapt across the table and clapped his hand over the general's mouth before he could call out. Together, Rufi and Marcus fell hard on to the table. Julia scrambled across the table, searching with her hand for another knife. Beakers, salvers clattered to the floor. She heard Quintus drop to his knees.

She heard him struggle to speak though a foam of blood. She heard Rufi and Marcus thrashing on the table, tumbling on to the floor. She found a knife. She crawled to where Rufi and Marcus fought, her wounded arm now out of its sling. She raised the knife with her left hand, but had no idea where to strike. With her right hand, in terrible pain, she sought to distinguish between the entwined figures. A hand grabbed her left wrist, pulled the knife down. She felt a resisting force as the blade penetrated flesh, slowly, then fiercely, deep. The battlers separated, one stood, one lay still. She waited, terrified, her eyes searching, wishing herself to see.

LXV

All of her life Julia would remember Rufi speaking her name. "Julia." Three syllables like a blaze of light in darkness. She was still in the spell of her violent action. She had struck without thinking. *God is the light, there is no darkness in him at all. He is known by the name, the Word of God, his cloak is soaked in blood. Out of his mouth came a sword, to smite the pagans. To smite the unholy one. Satan. The Prince of Darkness. The Prince of Darkness is struck down. The beast once was and now is not.* He took her hand. He said, "It's not over yet. We have to get away." They stepped to where Quintus had slumped to his knees, as if saying his prayers, not yet dead. His dropped lid and curled lip made his face a horrible mask. He looked to Rufi, struggled to speak, reached with his two hands to pull the knife from his chest. Rufi stepped behind him, pushed him forward to the floor with his foot. The tip of the blade penetrated the back of Quintus's white tunic, expelling before it an ooze of crimson blood.

Mustering all of his authority, Rufi led Julia from the apartment. To the first adjutant he met he said, "Quintus asks for a tablet and stylus," so abruptly and with such apparent urgency that the adjutant unhesitantly obeyed, went off to find the required utensils. At the entrance to the procuratorial chambers, Rufi pushed the rolled scroll, still in his belt, into the hands of the armed night watchman. By the time the watchman realised that the words on the papyrus bore no reference to the events before him, Rufi and Julia were in the street. A cry of discovery echoed through the corridors.

"I will guide your horse," said Rufi when they had mounted. He had not collected his sword.

She pulled the reins from his hands. "You go, I will follow," she said.

She sat erect on the intimidating steed, the reins clutched in her left hand, her right arm held to her chest, her bare legs locked tightly on the animal's flanks. Rufi was sceptical. He walked his horse through the dark Via Labicana, leading Julia's. "Faster," she said. A clamour erupted into the street behind them. He began the gallop and saw her keep to his animal's tail.

Like Valentine before him, Rufi had no fixed plan of escape. The gates of the city would be closed, and even if he were to convince a watchman to open, the delay might be intolerable. By dawn every gate and bridge would be guarded. He rode toward the Tiber in the north-west precinct of the city, past the Temple of the Sun of Aurelius, the Mausoleum of Augustus, the Altar of the Augustan Peace. He led her to a place where the city wall along the riverbank was in disrepair, a tumbled gap where children came to play and swim in the malodourous stream before it received the overwhelming ordure of the city. From here their mounts could swim the short distance upstream beyond the land wall, to a landing beyond the Flaminian Gate and near to the place of Valentine's execution. The river gleamed in the light of a rising quarter moon, sliding with its ancient inevitability toward the sea.

"We are at the river," he said.

He considered if he should let Julia mount behind him on his own steed for the swim. Could his animal fight the current with the two of them on its back? As he pondered his predicament, she nudged her mount down the bank. She smelled the river, tasted its acrid burden, heard it lick the cobblestones of the paved embankment. Rufi shook his head in astonishment and followed.

"Follow me," he said, and pulled his mount's reins to direct it against the sluggish current that swept past their bare thighs. The animals struggled, but soon they were beyond the wall and on to the bank. From here it was only a short distance to the Flaminian Gate.

Valentine was still bound to the post of execution, but slumped forward so that his forelock touched the ground. His body pierced with arrows. Carrion crows paced on the dismal ground; the body was not yet cold and already the birds had gathered for their feast.

Near by, shadowed forms huddled by sputtering campfires, paupers who lived outside the gate in lean-to shanties thrown up against the city wall—vagabonds, ragpickers, the scrofulous and diseased. Already, Valentine had been relieved of his loincloth and whatever other garments he had been wearing.

Rufi dismounted and helped Julia dismount, too.

"Where are we?" she asked.

He answered, "We are outside the Flaminian Gate, at the place of execution."

Then she knew. "Valentine." The word was like a prayer on her tongue.

He took her hand and led her forward. He scattered the crows before them; they fluttered up like black flames. When Rufi and Julia reached the stake, Rufi bent to his knee and spoke to Valentine, "I'm sorry, friend. I should have been quicker."

Julia's hands reached out for her lover. She found his head and caressed the familiar features. She explored his body and found the arrows—one, two, three thin shafts. She dropped to her knees and held Valentine against her breast.

The shadowed figures came forward, gathered round. Rufi untied the knot that held Valentine to the stake and let him fall into Julia's arms. The arrow points, too, had been broken off by scavengers; even those tiny tips of iron had value. She gently withdrew the shafts from his flesh. Rufi observed the shattered grief on Julia's face. He had no way of entering her blindness, no way of walking with her through her despair. She did not weep. For a long time she held Valentine to her, her fingers stopping the holes where the arrow shafts had been. He thought he heard her whisper, "Wake up from your sleep and Christ will shine on you."

A woman came forward, pocked face framed in tangled hair. She asked Julia, "You are a Christian?"

Julia's eyes searched the darkness. She nodded yes.

The woman nodded toward Valentine. "Is he a Christian?"

Julia hesitated. Rufi spoke, "Yes."

A few others had gathered behind the woman, other Christians. The woman said, "We will bury him. There is a Christian cemetery . . ." She gestured toward the hills.

Reluctantly, and only with Rufi's urging, did Julia surrender Valentine into the arms of the ragged few who now came forward. One of the Christians removed his threadbare cloak and with it they wrapped Valentine's body. Another gave her cloak to Julia, who was shivering with wet cold in the night air.

"Thank you," said Rufi. His hand instinctively searched for his purse, that he might reward these people for their kindnesses. "We must go," he said. "We are pursued."

A crow shrieked overhead. Rufi looked up to see the lanterns of ten thousand stars. He remembered the voyage from Alexandria, the nights of calm seas and starry skies when it seemed as if he and Valentine had all the world and all of time before them. The physician and his young servant had talked about the proper way to live a life. Neither of them had quite lived up to their aspirations, but Valentine at least had found with Julia a way home to honour.

Within an hour they were in the hills to the north-east of the city, where at last they paused in their headlong flight. Rufi turned his mount so that he faced Rome. The city sprawled in the distance, riding its seven hills, anchoring an empire. A scattering of lights echoed the stars.

"It is beautiful," he said.

Julia lay on her horse's neck, stroking its sweaty flesh. She looked toward him quizzically.

"Rome. From this distance, at night, the city is beautiful."

She said, "Can I see you?"

He was puzzled.

"Can I see who it is who has saved me?"

She tugged at her horse's reins to bring her mount alongside Rufi's. With her hand she reached up to explore his face. He leaned into her palm.

LXVI

Rufi and Julia had no need to run. Word of Valentine's illegal execution quickly reached the ears of Gallienus, prefect of Rome. Angered by Quintus's usurpation of authority and emboldened and shamed by Julia's courage in the arena, Gallienus sent contingents of the XXIV Legion Roma to the Esquiline Hill and the Via Labicana to arrest the procurator of games. The soldiers arrived at the procuratorial offices just after Rufi's and Julia's flight, to find the place in an uproar and Quintus dead. The document which Rufi had unthinkingly snatched up at Quintus's house turned out to incriminate Marcus Graecus. The quarters of the general were searched and more damning documents were found, standing orders for a long-planned coup. Marcus's ambition included the imperial throne itself.

So, in fact, when Rufi and Julia were arrested and returned to Rome after three days of freedom, it was not to imprisonment or trial, but to the gratitude of the prefect, who had been spared the difficulty of dealing with the two most dangerous men in Rome by Rufi's ostensibly treasonous action; with Quintus and Marcus dead, their web of conspiracy collapsed. However, it would not do to retain an officer of the urban cohort who had been disloyal to a superior, even in the service of an honourable cause. Rufi was pensioned from the army and given a farm from Gallienus's personal landholdings south of Rome. Julia went with him. They live there still, in the company of their children and grandchildren.

Of Philip, Valentine's son, no more was heard.

I have lived longer than any man has a right to live. With the death of Quintus, the orders for my banishment were revoked, and I continued to serve at the Prison of Tiberius until my retirement. When Constantius Caesar died in Britannica, thirty-six years after the marriage of Rufi and Julia, his son Constantine proclaimed himself emperor, and almost immediately restored to Christians the right to own property. Only then did Rufi openly admit his conversion to Julia's faith. And now, with the Edict of Toleration, in the 338th year since the ascension to the throne of the divine Augustus, all of Julia's family worship as Christians publicly and together. For myself, it is too late to teach an old dog new tricks. I lament the waning of the ancient gods. I like their quiet domesticity, their human forms. I have no head for abstractions, for endless debates about attributes of the Father and his relationship to his Son, the exegesis of scriptures, theological hairsplitting. Nor have I any use for the temporal power of the Christian bishops, who seem intent upon establishing a parallel empire. Two empires cannot be sustained; I fear for Rome. I have heard it said that in the eastern provinces the shoe of persecution is now on the other foot. Temples of the Roman gods are desecrated by Christians, statues smashed. Prophets and oracles of the ancient divinities are tortured and made to recant. Eventually, I suppose, those of us who adhere to the gods of the Caesars will be fed to lions in the arena. This city of the divine Augustus and Marcus Aurelius appears destined to yield primacy of place to an upstart empire in the east.

And so it seems to me important that Valentine should be remembered, as one of the last philosophers in the old tradition before the world turned topsy-turvy, an admirer of Epicurus, Galenus and Lucretius, men who had their feet on solid ground, who struggled to live honourably as mere men in a god-struck world, who had no truck with epiphanies, visions, superstitions. As the reader will see in the letter that follows, already the Christians have taken up Valentine as one of their own, even as they appropriate the shrines of Apollo and Diana and fit them out as temples of Christ. Julia endorses my endeavour to put Valentine's story on papyrus, that it might be honestly told. She credits Valentine with her life, with saving her from the fanaticism of Cornelius and Margarita, for leading her to love and, of course, to

Rufi. Now, as a woman of fifty-seven years, her faith has matured into a kindly solicitude for her family, friends and neighbours. In her enduring darkness, she prays. She looks forward to the heavenly Jerusalem when all shall be revealed to sight. With her fellow Christians, she anticipates the end of time and the second coming of Christ.

And, in a way, the world is indeed coming to an end—my own poor life and the life of the city that I served are drawing to a close. But I am not distraught. My darling daughter lives, my grandchildren and great-grandchildren are clustered about her. The world goes on. New cities will rise on the dust of Rome, as Rome replaced Athens, as Athens replaced Troy. There will be strife and discord, but happiness, too, and occasional beauty. Other children will be born blind, and other children will find love. The sun will warm another young girl's face, a gentle rain will fall into her outstretched palms. Julia believes that the world is guided by a divine plan that will lead all men and women, even vanquished Valentine, to Christ. *That*, of course, is the last thing Valentine would want; he had no use for an afterlife; he sought only to live virtuously in this world, following the example of his master Theophrastus, doing what he could to alleviate the suffering of his fellow men.

So how, then, will Valentine be remembered? That will depend, I suppose, upon the disposition of this manuscript, which I send as a messenger of truth into the world. Other stories of his life and death are in circulation, stories which bend and subvert the truth. Truth is a fragile thing, difficult to sustain intact, perhaps impossible to know at all—as the following letter makes clear, the last from Antonius, Valentine's childhood friend, whose correspondence has been so important a part of this narrative:

To Julia, daughter of Julius Favus, jailer, Rome
Domina,

I am Antonius of Alexandria. I greet you. I send you Christian blessings.

We have heard tell in letters and homilies of a certain Valentine, martyr, who was executed in Rome during the reign of Claudius II.

Imprisoned for his holy faith, he was asked by his jailer, a certain Julius Favus, to share the gift of God's grace with his blind daughter, Julia. And this he did, bringing the girl to Christ. Refusing to deny their faith, Valentine and Julia were sentenced to the arena, where they were asked to offer libations to the pagan gods. They refused, and so wolves were set upon them. Because of her blindness, Julia was given a sword with which to defend herself, and with it she attempted to fend off the beasts. Valentine, who was bound, invoked God's intercession. Julia's eyes were miraculously opened, through the agency of the love which knows no bounds. "I see, I see," she is said to have exclaimed before the assembled throng. She then dispersed the wolves and so impressed the editor of the games that he released her from her fate. But Valentine spoke to the editor from the arena floor and said, "Now you are blind, but in the light of faith you shall see God face to face." Angered, the editor sent archers into the arena, and Valentine died in the grace and favour of his holy Saviour.

Such is the story. I cannot help but feel that this Valentine, martyr, is the same as he who was my childhood friend in Cyrenaica many years ago and with whom I have corresponded over the years. He was a physician, trained in Alexandria by the famous Theophrastus, and he went to Rome during the time of Valerian. When last I heard from him, at about the time the martyr Valentine died in the arena, he was resisting the grace of faith, stubbornly adhering to the teachings of pagan philosophers who did not know Christ. I write to you, hoping to find you alive and well, and asking you to confirm or deny that the sainted martyr was in fact my friend.

It would give me great happiness to know that my Valentine was blessed by our glorious Redeemer with that most perfect of gifts, holy martyrdom. We are told by our bishops that a martyr's rewards exceed those of all other Christians, effacing all sins and speeding the martyr's soul, pure and spotless, to heaven. No intervals of cooling and refreshment, no minor corrections or disciplines in the bosom of Abraham. The martyr has vanquished Satan, who stood behind him in the arena, and won the everlasting prize, blessedness in the heavenly Father's eternal love. How glad I would be to know that my Valentine has joined Marion, Perpetua, Polycarp and all the other saints who shared the fate of Jesus himself. His glorious death will mark the day of his martyrdom into all eternity.

Antonius Cyrenaicus
clockmaker
Alexandria

BOOKS BY CHET RAYMO

ALSO PUBLISHED BY

BRANDON

In the Falcon's Claw

A Novel of the Year 1000

Based on real events, places and people, *In the Falcon's Claw* is a resonant tale of love, friendship, religion and betrayal. In 998, two years before what many believe will be the year of the Apocalypse, the abbot of the abandoned island monastery of Skellig Michael is called to account for heresy. His accuser is his best friend, once a charismatic fellow monk who introduced him to literature and geometry, and to the pleasures of the flesh . . .

"A novel of never-ending pleasure . . . superbly innovative. It is a work of rare and irreverent intelligence." *Le Figaro Littéraire*

"There are many strands in this fine novel – love, religion, the stars and the nature of time, church politics, Latin and Irish verse – and they are skilfully put together in a vigorous language that invokes a fresh, unexplored Europe of 1,000 years ago." *Sunday Tribune*

"A metaphysical thriller comparable to Umberto Eco's *In the Name of the Rose*, but more poetic, more moving and more sensual." *Lire*

ISBN 0 86322 204 8; 222 pages; paperback

CLIMBING BRANDON

Science and Faith on Ireland's Holy Mountain

"Philosopher and scientist Raymo uses his own decades-long knowledge of the mountain as a springboard for meditations on the juncture of science and spirituality. Raymo . . . shows how science, far from being in conflict with spirit, can inspire and illuminate the mystical mind. Not only for those interested in Ireland, this fine, short book should appeal to readers interested in earth spirituality as well." *Booklist*

"Fascinating reading . . . Celtic polytheism, Christian monotheism, and scientific rationalism, all tied neatly together into an Irish arabesque." *Kirkus Reviews*

"Vividly descriptive prose . . . an uplifting contemplation of Irish animistic traditions and the power of landscape in the land of 'saints and scholars'." *Publishers Weekly*

ISBN 0 86322 331 1; 208 pages; illustrated hardback

HONEY FROM STONE

"An entrancing meditation on stones and stars and mossy ruins . . . Raymo revels in the mysteries explored by science." *San Francisco Chronicle*

"Precisely lyrical, deeply prayerful despite metaphysical skepticism, this is the work of one who, besides being a science professor, is a true poet." *Publishers Weekly*

"*Honey from Stone* is . . . a travel book about the world of ideas. Raymo uses the natural setting of Dingle as a place in which he asks you to explore with him through his own private universe . . . *Honey from Stone* is a beautiful book that is well worth reading." *Irish Echo*

ISBN 0 86322 232 3; 160 pages; illustrated paperback